LOCUST
SUMMER

First published 2021 by
FREMANTLE PRESS

Reprinted 2022.

Fremantle Press Inc. trading as Fremantle Press
PO Box 158, North Fremantle, Western Australia, 6159
fremantlepress.com.au

Cover images by Wikimedia Commons, *The Loose
Smuts of Barley and Wheat*, 1909; Alamy, *Summer wheat,
Triticum aestivum 1, winter wheat, T. hybernum 2, and
English wheat, T. turgidum 3*. Handcoloured copperplate
engraving of a botanical illustration from G.T. Wilhelm's
'Unterhaltungen aus der Naturgeschichte', *Encyclopedia
of Natural History*, Augsburg, 1811.
Designed by Nada Backovic, nadabackovic.com

 A catalogue record for this
book is available from the
National Library of Australia

NATIONAL
LIBRARY
OF AUSTRALIA

ISBN 9781925816365 (paperback)
ISBN 9781925816372 (ebook)

 |

GOVERNMENT OF
WESTERN AUSTRALIA

Fremantle Press is supported by the Western Australian State
Government through the Department of Cultural Industries,
Tourism and Sport.

Fremantle Press respectfully acknowledges the Whadjuk
people of the Noongar nation as the Traditional Owners and
Custodians of the land where we work in Walyalup.

David Allan-Petale

LOCUST SUMMER

 FREMANTLE PRESS

David Allan-Petale is a writer living between the bush and sea north of Perth, Western Australia. He worked for many years as a journalist in regional WA with the ABC and internationally with BBC World. Written while travelling the globe over five years, *Locust Summer* was shortlisted for the Australian / Vogel's Literary Award, a Western Australian Premier's Book Award, and selected for a fellowship at Varuna, the National Writers' House. The final drafts were crafted during an eighteen-month lap of Australia in a caravan, ranging from the red dirt of Wingellina to the tip of Cape York Peninsula. He's now back home restoring a yacht in the driveway, while his wife and daughters keep him busy planning their next adventures.

For Parma, who best educated me.

1

Perth, 1986

The drunk lay moaning on the pavement beneath the neon sleaze of the nightclub's entrance. Both his eyes wore bruises. His forehead was gashed. 'No-one who'll be missed,' Detective Lovestone said, winking at me while he approached a security guard who had skinned knuckles.

'Talk to me and tell me what you know,' the sly copper said to the man. 'Or I'll just make it up, and say you told me.' I scribbled in my notepad – *oldest trick in the book*. While the meathead mulled it over, Lovestone turned in a slow circle, smiling at all the revellers that had gathered around the crime scene. Two medics lifted the moaning victim and took him to an ambulance. As they pushed him through the crowd, I saw my brother on the stretcher, the wounds on the drunk's face echoing Albert's autopsy photos.

Uniformed officers closed in on the bouncer. 'Bring this idiot to the watch house,' Lovestone ordered. 'Leave his hands as they are.'

Bloody as this was, none of it would make it to print. It would be too routine for Holt, my editor, who wanted me to 'get some real marrow for the afternoon edition', and this was just weeknight typical. He would say, 'Deal in facts. Only facts. Use short sentences. Direct language shorn of sentiment. Anything else is literature. And that has no place in a newspaper.'

Lovestone's bulk weighed down the suspension of the black

Ford as he lowered himself inside. 'Boozy bullshit I can handle,' he said, settling in the seat. 'When I started it was blokes doing the six o'clock swill on a Friday and hitting their wives. Now it's ten o'clock drugs on a Thursday.'

Some coppers go quiet when a vulture like me observes them. Not Lovestone – he enjoyed playing the part. 'The bouncers stomped on that bloke's head when he was down. He'll be lucky to spell his name.'

The image of the drunk's bloodied face came again, holding the humour of my brother's eyes. He'd been dead for two years. Still I saw him walking down the street, sitting down next to me in a pub, reflected in the gore my profession sometimes elevated to the front page. Lovestone lowered his sunshield and looked at me in the mirror.

'You okay, son?'

I swallowed hard and held my hands to stop them shaking. 'Just tired.'

Lovestone snorted and nudged his partner awake – Sergeant Wilson, whom I suspected had had a few drinks before, and during, the shift. 'Come on, mate, our ace reporter here needs some more action.'

Wilson dropped the column shift into drive and the plain-panelled Ford rumbled through Northbridge, both detectives wearing dark leather jackets to conceal their pistols and badges. Traffic lights glowed horror-movie red and a few wide-eyed lads pointed at the car, shout-singing a version of 'Camptown Races' – 'What's the colour of a two-cent piece? Copper, copper.' – pleased to have made out a plainclothes ride. Lovestone wound down his window and gave them the finger as the lights changed green.

'I'll have to move away when I retire,' he said as the Ford crossed the Horseshoe Bridge into the city proper. 'This is no place for nostalgia.'

Up St Georges Terrace the workday streets were deserted, the only movement from office buildings where cleaners were pulling the night shift. Scaffolds and cranes and skip bins stood guard at a dozen worksites where towers of glass and steel were going up, replacing squat limestone classics designated unfit for heritage. A few remained: Newspaper House, the Treasury, and the old guardhouse of the pensioner barracks. Wilson gunned the engine and threaded the Ford up the hill, past the dark embrace of Kings Park, leading us to Subiaco where the car radio was broadcasting another bashing, this time a melee near the football oval. Plenty of marrow, but nothing for the afternoon edition.

Their shift ended at midnight, and when we got back in the Ford to head for HQ, Wilson drove us along Mounts Bay Road, threading its riverside curves twenty k's above the speed limit. We stopped under the lee of the CBD's buildings where there was a clean, fluorescent place serving hot drinks and hot dogs. Lovestone ordered three of them, coffee for Wilson and me and a tea for himself, everything served in polystyrene that squeaked as we ate.

'What I wouldn't give for a murder,' Lovestone said, and tapped the notepad I'd placed on our table. 'That's off the record.'

'No such thing,' I said, remembering one of Holt's dictums: 'Your taxes pay their wages. Everything's fair game.'

Lovestone frowned, concentrated on his hot dog, and devoured it in three efficient bites. Like me, he had the appetite of a man who worked through his lunchbreaks. He belched into his hand and said, 'How did you get the police round, son?' Light tone, listening eyes, while Wilson glowered at me over his coffee. Good cop, bad cop, never off the clock.

'Been with the paper a few years. Had an interest –'

'Yeah, that's not good enough. Where you from?'

How easy it would be to be able to say Joondalup. Warwick. Greenwood. Some bland Perth suburb up the freeway they could roll their eyes at and tell a drug story from. 'Wheatbelt,' I said, keeping it vague. 'Up the Mid West.'

'Wheat and sheep?' Lovestone said, stirring sugar into his tea.

I nodded. 'Tough line of work that.' I nodded again. 'You going back for harvest? Got cousins in Bruce Rock. Time of year for it.'

I should have been able to say 'when I can', but Lovestone's eyes waited in ambush for lies, to pull the whole story from me. Before I could answer, Wilson cleared his throat, lit a cigarette and said, 'Grew up on a farm meself. Couldn't get out of there fast enough.' He stared right at me, as if seeking recognition. Silence at the table grew. He broke it by looking past me, out the reflecting windows to the Swan River where navigation lights burned their night-time warnings.

'Don't let him fool you,' Lovestone said. 'It was a hobby farm. His father was police commissioner.'

'Fuck off,' Wilson said, and stood to leave, exhaling a cloud of impatience at Lovestone's reclined pose. 'Your turn to pay.'

Lovestone grinned at me. 'They give you expenses?'

I reached for my wallet. 'I haven't got a story yet.'

Wilson muttered, walked out to the Ford. Lovestone knocked back the dregs of his tea and rapped the mug on the table, inhaling slowly, gathering a lesson for the initiate. 'Can never please you journos. When it's too bloody, you look away. When it's not bloody enough, you complain.' He leaned in, holding his stare. 'You're the one who picked a weeknight. And you didn't answer my question. You going back for harvest?'

'No,' I said, unable to bullshit. 'I'm too busy.'

'Shit excuse,' Lovestone said, and signalled the girl at the till to ring up the bill. 'You're alright, mate. Come out with us again next week. We might have better luck.'

The detectives were good enough to drop me at my flat in Scarborough. Lovestone whistled at the coastal digs, said, 'Not bad for a hack,' shook my hand hard, and then flicked a cigarette butt as the Ford guzzled away down the road.

Two floors up, my place opened empty and sparse, cluttered with packing boxes and drifts of books with cracked spines. I took a beer from the fridge and stared at a photo stuck by a magnet between a power bill and a real estate calendar marked with X's till the blank October 31st. There was Mum and Dad in the middle, Albert at the old man's right hand, me at her left, smiling in the home paddock. A dull ache sat like tetanus in my neck. So I took a swig from the bottle and slumped onto the couch where I reclined in another memory – my brother's funeral, the last time I'd been home.

Right in the middle of the wake at the pub, a lightning storm blinked mutely on the horizon, sending rolls of thunder through the corrugated roof to cut the power: a quick thrill, a magic trick, electricity cutting electricity. Everyone drank in the dark till Dad tapped me on the shoulder and led me out under the cloud-steeped sky to where his ute was parked.

'Back her in,' he ordered, his hands and voice shaking. 'You remember how to do this?'

I cranked the door and slammed myself inside the old Toyota: a cracked windshield, a tape deck stuck on 6PR talk and sinus-bending dust on every surface. The engine turned over and breathed through a smear of insects covering the radiator grill. Steering reverse, left became right, and the big metal tray swung over to Dad's waving arms, back and back and back till he held up a slow surrender.

'Go get a lead from the kitchen,' he rasped, and hauled himself up onto the tray where a generator was bolted to the floor.

Running to the back room, I found the old publican working by candlelight, scraping ice from the sides of the deep freeze. 'Garnish for cocktails,' he said, face cut with shadows. 'And the beer if it comes to it.'

'Dad's got a better idea,' I told him, and we rummaged around for an extension line in the odds and sods next to the sink. He found a greasy orange coil and plugged it into a wall socket. I hurried back outside, the long line unravelling from my hand as the generator yawned and teased and protested.

'Start, you bastard,' Dad said as he gave it a kick. The machine coughed, turned over, and roared into rumbling life.

'All set,' I said to Dad and passed up the female end of the line. He plugged the generator's power pack and the pub's lights fired up again – cold sweat back to the beer taps.

'Good to see city hands work,' Dad said, patting me on the back as we walked around to the veranda, his careful cadence measured with the plosive tick of the generator. When we came through the door, the crowd inside cheered.

Mum stood alone at the bar, staring at me with hard eyes as if to say 'should have been you'.

2

The phone chimed and I woke in my work clothes on the couch. The digital clock on the oven glowed five am. A month before summer, just before sunrise, faithful to the timetable. I picked up the receiver, and after some chalky pleasantries, Mum's voice carried clear.

'Harvest,' she said, and got straight to it. 'Can you come?'

I breathed slowly, tiredly, buying time. Imagined her in the kitchen at the homestead, watching the sun over the paddocks. Maybe she had a coffee on the go, one for Dad as well, the old man slipping his workboots on at the veranda where the dogs were worshipping at his side.

'There's a lot on,' I said. Mum cleared her throat, held her silence, making me wait for a response. Something was up. Usually she let me off the hook easy after I refused, saying they'd handle it without me before changing the subject to the weather, the price of grain, who was cheating on who in town. The call was a courtesy, prodding the ashes of my farming connection.

'I'm selling,' she said, and I sat up straight, groggily awake, sharpening to her words. 'Your father's in no shape to lead this one.'

'Dad wants to sell?'

Mum fired back quick. 'He can't make that decision anymore.'

Perhaps we were all pretending the day would never come when Dad couldn't keep going. Time was up the moment the power cut out at Albert's wake. On the land the earth spins steady, the moon rises, and all crops grow: wheat, sheep, dementia.

'You said he's getting treatment.'

'Not enough for him to carry on out here.'

'How long does he have?'

She exhaled slowly. 'I've got a deal that will get him the care he needs.'

Mum had a workforce for the fields. Contracts for shipments. Buyers lined up for the grain. Why did I need to come? If she was serious about selling, then movers could pack the house. She already took care of Dad and refused all help.

'Rowan, will you come?'

The sea breathed through the living room curtains. Rising light was bringing the promise of another hot day; hotter inland where desert winds trapped eddies of heat over the paddocks of wheat ready for threshing.

'I'll see what I can do,' I said, and Mum breathed relief. A smash like a cymbal rang through the phone. She was forever dropping plates and cracking glasses. At least that would be one less item to pack from the generations of crockery her kitchen cupboards held.

'We'll get it done quickly,' she said, and rang off.

I left the phone off the hook.

Awake far too early. There was no coffee in the cupboard and nothing on the TV. So with nothing else to do till I was due at work, I walked from my flat down the hill to the ocean where choppy waves surged through the shallows. The muffled tang of salt was in the air and early commuters revving along the coastal highway. I wished I could sink my hands into officework instead of thinking of all the calluses a harvest would inflict.

I bought an espresso and the new day's edition from a café and rifled through the pages, looking for my by-line, scanning for stories I'd missed or been elbowed away from. The beach held a few early-morning walkers, keen joggers and beachcombers searching along the tideline. Out at sea a few container ships rode at anchor in Gage Roads, while the shimmering mirage of Rottnest Island refracted under high clouds. Views for a postcard. But my mind twisted north, driving up the long roads past the Swan Valley junction to the saltbush country of Jurien Bay and then the ghostly stretches of trees made hunchbacks by the trade winds. Up to the wheat-growing country where the farm waited with what used to be my Dad, a light bulb without a spark.

I went down to the shallows and shucked off my thongs at the water's edge, then my shirt and shorts till I was wading in my jocks to where the waves broke in gouts of white flame. Diving beneath the turbulence, I groped through green darkness and emerged where the swell gathered in wide ridges. I floated on my back, feeling the hot sky above and the cold depths below.

Without a story from the field to tell to the new day's editorial meeting, I pitched a feature on the just-appointed police commissioner and his love of Rugby Union – a game that was mostly alien to Western Australia. I thought it could illustrate his outsider status as a splice from New South Wales. Holt chuckled and said to dig up any charges the commissioner may have had for rough police work so we could say 'Scrum Bag' in the headline.

I wasn't able to stand it up. And when the instant sunset of the five pm deadline was half an hour away, Holt strafed my desk with haughty commands. 'Brockman. Office. Now.'

Waving through the smoke of the cigarette he'd just flicked onto the carpet, I followed past the subs desk and the beat reporters to the only office with a door, which he slammed shut. The bashing of typing keys and panicked chatter was muted.

'Sit,' he said, and I took a battered chair while he perched on the edge of his desk, a bare metal slab more like a factory workbench; he had it hoisted into the building through a window when he was made editor. The joke was that he played chess with the lives of his reporters on its drumming surface, shifting us around with the knowing randomness of a despot.

'No yarn on our top cop then?' He lit up a cigarette, offered me one, which I refused. He puffed thoughtfully, looking down his nose at me from his hip-high altar. 'You didn't hustle hard enough.'

I answered the only ways he accepted – quickly and frankly. 'Just couldn't stand it up. He's a good man.'

'No such thing. He's just never been caught.' Holt smiled. 'Or he's never made a decent enemy. Which means he's boring and unimaginative.' He punctuated the air with the tip of his cigarette. 'Breaks no rules. Loves the limitations. Works within the law. That's because he loves Rugby Union. If he was a League man I'd be interested. Fast, flowing, improvising. And over quickly so you can go to church, play a match and then get to the pub on a Sunday. It's the workers' game.' He ran a hand through the last of his hair, pleased with the homily. 'Your man's a cake eater. What we'd call a clubbable man. And this city needs a different kind of man.' He stubbed the cigarette out in a standing ashtray. 'Write the hit piece anyway.'

Full stop. Capital letter. Get out.

Perhaps I took a second too long. Or maybe it was because I refused the cigarette – unusual for a man facing what could have been a firing squad. Nothing got past Holt.

'Distraction kills intention,' he said. 'You've something else pressing to attend to.'

'I don't want to bother you with it,' I said, and his response was to spread his hands wide, as if to say 'I'm all ears'.

Harvest. Dad sick. Mum selling. Bare facts arranged in the house style.

'How long has the farm been in your family?' he said, lighting another cigarette, offering me one again, which I took.

'Three generations. Story goes that the land was staked out by John Septimus Roe. He was the explorer –'

Holt held up a hand. 'You're no farmer then? Not keen to inherit a money-making machine?'

'No. I'm a journalist.'

He bellowed. 'To succeed as a newspaperman you need a grasp of language, vague work ethic and rat-like cunning. In fact, you can dispense with the others and keep the cunning. Do you want to go?'

'No. But it's my duty.'

'Said like a first-born son.'

I shook my head. 'I'm the second.'

He looked me up and down, as if reading me all at once. 'What happened to your brother?'

'He's dead,' I said, and looked to the door.

Holt didn't press the issue, just said, 'When my mother died I took the morning off for the funeral then came back to work.' He sucked hard on the cigarette, stubbed it out on the ashtray neatly next to his last one. 'You're only as good as your last story. You don't want to miss out on anything here.'

So that was a no. Before I could get up to leave, Holt clapped his hands together and drummed them on the desk. 'Write me something while you're there. Keep your hand in back here and knock out some prose for the weekend editions. How long will you need away?'

In my mind I ran through the key events of a harvest routine: Prep. Strip. Terminus. 'Three weeks,' was the final tally.

'Take it as annual leave,' Holt said, standing to usher me out. 'Go tomorrow and write what you will. Remember that our soft-handed city readers love tales of the hard bush.'

I opened the door and let the newsroom's chaos back into his office. As I stepped out, he threw a dagger. 'Empty-handed from a ride-along with the cops. No dirt on the commissioner. That could be two strikes. Leave a telephone number we can reach you at. I want real marrow, whenever that will be.'

3

My car was a charmless Holden without air conditioning that became a heat sink for even the slimmest chink of sun. The radio was busted. So I wound down all the windows and decided to relish the heat, become a reptile crawling up the Great Northern Highway at 110 k's an hour, the blond land and black road smeared together by the bow waves of passing road trains.

When the fuel gauge showed a quarter, I stopped at a road-house to fill up, about halfway between our farm – Brockman's Place – and the coast south of Perth where our family would head every summer after harvest to wash away the work of the year. Those summers were long gone. Eaten away by the locusts. As the tank filled I watched the cars driving south disappear over a low ridge. Not many went north.

I looked out over the forecourt and imagined Mum's station wagon pulling up to the pump next to me, the back loaded up with all the family's bags and an esky of food, then fishing rods and gidgees cinched to the roof rack with ratchet straps. There was Dad stretching his arms wide, twenty years younger, no sickness or age stooping him. While Mum cleaned dead bugs off the windshield with a squeegee, Albert popped the tank open and squeezed leaded petrol expertly inside. And there I was, sitting in the back seat, reading a book. Dad knocked on the window. 'You want some hot chips, mate?' I shook my head no, and he strolled into the shop to pay, play-fighting with Alby while Mum laughed, admiring her boys.

The pump clicked full. A road train slammed past and my ears popped as though I were a diver equalising before the long blue plunge.

'Headin' to Septimus,' I said to the bloke sitting behind the till, making the clip of my accent leaner and hungrier. 'For the harvest,' I explained when he exchanged a blank look for the money.

'Bumper crops this year,' he said, fossicking for change. He stood from his chair and leaned on the counter where bags of lollies were plumped for sale. 'I can't get a new shipment of fuel till next week. Farmers are taking it as soon as I can get it. Makes it hard to do business.'

'That's too bad, mate,' I drawled, using him as practice.

'From the city are you?'

'Septimus,' I claimed, perhaps a bit too quickly. 'We're selling up.'

'That's too bad, mate,' he said, drawling the phrase back at me. He picked up a magazine and thumbed it open. 'The land's not for everyone.'

The air was warm with the smell of something close to baking bread. On both sides of the road, hectare after hectare of ripeness passed by, the wake of my car shivering the stalks closest to the edges.

There. A hundred metres ahead. A single kangaroo, standing up straight, transfixed by my oncoming bonnet. 'Hit it,' Dad's voice yelled in my ear. 'Dead centre. Foot on the gas. Don't stop.'

I hit the brakes hard till they locked. The tyres screeched. The car fishtailed as I wrestled dead weight to the road shoulder. Orange dust swirled around, settled on the windscreen. The roo bounded off into the crops. 'Always hit them,' Dad said, continuing the lesson I couldn't seem to follow. 'You can fix a bonnet easier than you can fix this.' I felt his hand press my shoulder, electric touch. 'Never trust the road.'

I sat there for a long while with the engine ticking over. A delayed surge of fear pulsed through my veins, gyred in my stomach, then trickled out again. I fought the urge to turn the car around and drive away. To climb down the ladder of the long black road all the way back to Scarborough where riptides churned the surf and the phone was still off the hook.

'Come on, mate,' I said to myself. 'Get about it.'

The last long miles bumped along an arrow-straight road, heading direct for a place where meridians of sun, soil and water converged in a great estuary of farmland. Septimus. Same name for town and district.

I slowed the car to sixty for the run across the main and only street. It was all as I'd left it: farmers' wives stocking up their supplies, workers blown in from across the country buying sausage rolls at the bakery and smoking in the street. Servo. Bottle-o. Takeaways and council office. I slunk low in my seat, and pressed the pace up fast when the speed sign changed back to eighty.

Finally my car's tyres chewed the rocks of the homestead track and the noise of the world slammed shut behind. I killed the engine and got out stiffly, a sweat patch on my back cooling in the afternoon gusts. No dogs barked. No TV or radio chattered. A load of washing waved on the line like signal flags.

In my head I had conjured a scene where I'd slip into the kitchen and say something nonchalant like 'need a hand?' and the dining room would fill with food and we'd sit laughing with Dad at the head of the table challenging me to pull the wishbone from a roast chook while Mum poured herself a white wine. Instead, every door was locked. The garden was overgrown with weeds. There was a metal handrail bolted to the front veranda steps. Something you see for the elderly. Or the sick.

I trudged around the perimeter of the garden and the house, peering in through windows spattered with water stains from retic that ran on a timer. The lawn was spiky with overgrowth. Inside there were packing boxes in each of the rooms with lids bloomed to accept whatever Mum would decide to keep. She would save the photo albums and the heirlooms and the best of the books and records and picture frames. The rest would probably just go to St Vinnies. Or into a skip bin. Maybe whoever bought the place would bulldoze the house and raze the garden.

Like an idiot I didn't even think to bring a book or newspaper to pass the time. So I sat on the front veranda and lit up a cigarette, ashing into the pot plant that used to hold the spare key. After a while, Albert sat beside me, his face unblemished and whole. He said, 'G'day, Rowan,' in his effortless way, and cadged a smoke with a sure tilt of his eyes. 'Mr City come to teach us how to grow wheat.'

'Some of us have to do the thinking,' I said, and we laughed.

'Good to have you back, mate. Not been the same around here.'

'How so?'

'There's no-one to make me look good.'

I laughed, knowing it was kind of true, but he shook his head to dismiss that. 'Nah, whatever, Ro. This is just shitkicking. You can do it with your eyes shut.'

I was half asleep when slits of light came through the driveway pines and Mum's station wagon came roaring up to the top of the slope. Squinting in the sudden brightness, I could see Dad slumped asleep in the front seat as she parked at the foot of the veranda steps. I waved as she got out, and approached cautiously.

'Rowan, why didn't you call?' Her face was a scowl. 'How long have you been waiting?'

I played a straight bat. Asked, 'How's Dad?' as quickly as I could.

She put her hands on her hips. 'The usual. Check-up in Geraldton. He's steady. More or less.'

He looked shaky to me when I opened the car door and tried to wake him. We both took an arm and marched him up to the house where she unlocked the door and we plopped him on the living room couch. With the lights switched on, the house became mess, dust and cobwebs.

'When did you last clean up?'

Mum ignored that, bustled past me to the kitchen where she set a pot of water to boil, talking a stream at me to smother the strangeness of homecoming. 'You've caught me short. So I'll do us a pasta. Something easy. You can clip some herbs from the garden. The basil is rioting in the heat.' She handed me a pair of scissors and went down the hall to the library. 'Any requests?' She put on a record, Bach's *The Well-Tempered Clavier*. 'Puts him out like a light,' she said as she walked back to the kitchen, jerking her thumb toward my dad, who was snoring in time with music I had heard too many times.

'It's like something from a TV ad.'

Mum clicked her tongue. 'I like it. Now, I need a handful of basil. Two if you can manage.' As I went out the back door, she said, 'There's gardening gloves if you need them.'

Outside, I flexed my office hands to feel their lack of real work. 'Where are the dogs?' I called through the screen door, which hung askance on squeaky hinges. The pack usually ran in from the fields for their dinner with the timing of a radio news bulletin. Mum wiped her hands on a tea towel and frowned through the mesh.

'AB died on Sunday. I sent Lillee and Bradman over to the Chambers' place while we sort things.'

I nodded, unsure of what to say other than, 'AB was old.'

'As the hills,' she said. 'The others will be happy enough with the Chambers.'

She flicked the towel over her shoulder like it was a rifle and marched back to the kitchen where she picked up the phone and dialled. When I came back with the basil, I said the line I'd practised on the drive up from Perth.

'Need a hand?'

She shook her head. It was all under control. The vegies were chopped, the meat browning in the pan.

'Why don't you pour some wine? There's a red in the cupboard.'

'You don't want white?'

She laughed. 'I haven't drunk white in years. You know I can't stand it.'

I found a dusty shiraz of fresh vintage and levered the cork out to let it breathe while I unpacked my bags. My old room had already been stripped bare. But with a deft touch, Mum had made the bed with a perfect three-inch fold and laid out a set of work clothes with ruler-straight creases ironed into the legs and sleeves. If I wore that ensemble in the fields, the boys would never let me forget it. I shoved them in a drawer when she called, 'Dinner's ready.'

Dad sat at the head of the kitchen table. It was set for three with salt and pepper and a shallow dish of grated cheese on a placemat in the middle. He kept clearing his throat as if to say something, looking at me and nodding, focusing his eyes strong and clear. He didn't say a word. Just ate his food and kept quiet.

The normal Dad was so talkative at the table he'd always end up reheating his plate in the microwave. This version wolfed the food Mum served to him, chewing and swallowing, twirling his fork in the spaghetti's junctions to repeat the process again.

'How was the drive up?' Mum said.

'Boring. My radio's busted.'

She hummed. 'Must have been tough.'

Dad cleared his throat again, looked at me and frowned.

'How are you going, Dad?'

He clattered his cutlery. Looked over his shoulder to the living room, then slid his chair back so he could get to the couch and sit in front of the unlit television.

'I'll get him to bed now I think,' Mum said, and took her plate to the sink. I got up to help with Dad, but she dismissed the move. 'You've got an early start.' She shuffled off with Dad and shut the bedroom door.

I went to do the dishes, saying, 'Good to have you back,' to my reflection in the kitchen window.

4

A hand with the thumb and forefinger missing mashed the light switch by my bedroom door.

'Righto boy,' a voice barked.

Boots thumped off down the hall. The world outside the window was deeply black, summoning the working hour. I dressed quickly with little fires of resentment puffing through my eyes.

'Cuppa?' Sterlo asked as I skidded on my work socks into the kitchen. 'No shit,' I felt like saying as he shovelled two spoonfuls of International Roast into two metal mugs, squirted them with milk and curdled it all together with the whistling kettle.

Mum had left a pair of workboots on the deck and I slipped them on with a set of sock protectors, which made my feet look like the fetlocks of a horse. It was better than picking up scratches from grass burrs, but I still felt ridiculous in the get-up, especially with the pleats still striping the shorts and shirt.

We got into the cab of Sterlo's Datsun ute, and I cradled our mugs carefully while he drove down to the main road. As the sun's light loomed in the east I began to orient myself, knowing we were heading to the top paddock of the land within Brockman's Place's boundaries – high ground where we could look over all the other paddocks. When Sterlo pulled up, I passed him a coffee and we looked through the windshield together at a great carpet of crops stretching out blue as a bruise in the rising light.

'Simple plan,' Sterlo said, blowing steam from the mug. 'We

start at the top and work our way down. We've been doing it bottom to top all these years. We'll change it up this harvest.'

'Why not stick with what we know?' I asked.

He breathed slowly. 'Best this time if we get closer to your mum rather than further away. Don't you think?'

Anger swelled in my stomach. I let it drain away.

Sterlo was a fixture of Brockman's Place. He'd lived in town in a bachelor's quarters since his divorce and had no soil of his own, working ours for as long as I could remember. There's probably a bloke like him on every farm in the world. A professional pain in the arse.

'You going back after?' he asked.

I wound down my window and tipped the coffee from my mug. 'Once we're packed up. I've got three weeks off. So I can see it through.'

He pulled a cigarette pack from the dash and lit one. The sun broke clear of the landline and rose fast as a loose balloon.

'Well, mate. Let's get on with it then.'

Our ten paddocks were neatly set out in a five-by-five grid cleaved by tracks that allowed access for vehicles. My dad liked to quip that the highway was the spine, the paddocks the ribs, and the tracks the veins. Sterlo guided the ute along each of them as we checked the fences and looked for anything out of place in the uniform heights of ripe wheat, like we were inspecting a vast parade of troops.

The homestead may have been a mess, but the land was in perfect order. There were no weeds lining the edges of the wheat. No breakages in the fences dividing the paddocks. No big rocks in the furrows holding their mohawks of ripe wheat. Sterlo even stubbed out his fag ends in the dashboard ashtray instead of chucking them out the window.

'How's your dad then?' Sterlo asked, taking us back onto the main road for home. 'Haven't seen him much lately.'

'He's fine. We had dinner. He didn't say much. He fed himself okay. Then we put him to bed.'

'Sounds like he's doing better then.'

Sterlo braked and slid the ute onto the rusted pebbles of the road shoulder, threw it in reverse and took us back to the turn-off for the last paddock's access way. There was a water bore just up the way, and its glassy reflection bounced in the morning sun. 'Found 'em,' he said, and drove toward an apron of grey slop leading down to the pool. Three white shrubs stood at the water's edge. Sheep. Concreted to their bellies in sun-baked mud.

'Those poor bloody animals,' he said. He lit another cigarette and smoked it quickly. From our vantage point I could see the sheep were beyond help – their eyes and noses streamed with mucus, their tails all blown with flies. They'd break their legs struggling if we tried to dig them out.

'Thought Mum sold off all the sheep,' I said, trying to place them.

'She did. Look again.' The animals had wild coats of wool twined with sticks and dirt. 'They're roamers. Probably from another property. Or maybe we missed a few in the count. No matter. I'll have to shoot them later.'

He frowned, shut his eyes, then switched on a CB radio. 'Justine, you got anything to eat, over?'

Mum replied, her voice squashed with white noise. 'Morning, Sterlo. Sausages and eggs. Plenty to go around, over.'

He looked at me and grinned. 'You're not a damn vegetarian now as well?'

'Is this all we're going to do then?' I said, changing the subject. 'We take a drive out for half an hour and then we head back.'

'Hardest part of the day is waking up. You need to get in the habit.' He clapped me on the back. 'Always need a good breakfast.'

At the table Sterlo and Mum chatted airily about the weather and the crops and the usual way of things. Dad sat at the other end next to me, struggling to dissect scrambled eggs with a knife and fork.

'Pass the salt,' Sterlo asked me, and before I could reach it Dad paddled the cellar with his knife and slid it over.

'Go easy with it, mate,' he said. 'It'll harden your arteries.' We all laughed, taken aback by this sudden surfacing.

'How are you, mate?' Sterlo smiled. 'You having a win?'

'All the time, Sterlo. All the time.' Dad winked at me. 'Albert's home for the harvest. Love, did you see Alby's back with us?'

Mum reached and squeezed his hand. 'Of course.' She nodded to me, stilling my urge to correct him. 'Now eat your eggs before they get cold.'

He sighed as his eyes wandered glassily. 'I'm not hungry. Why have you given me this? I never asked for it.'

Sterlo cleared his throat and excused himself from the table, taking Dad's food away. He returned for Mum's empty plate and took it to the sink where he ran the tap.

'Cup of tea?' he asked, and put the kettle on without waiting for an answer.

Mum got up and sat next to me, whispering while Dad looked out the window. 'Don't correct him. It will only confuse him. And then he'll get distressed. Just play along and try to steer him in the right direction.'

I swallowed hard. 'Why doesn't he remember me?'

Mum shook her head. 'Love, he doesn't remember me sometimes. It's not personal. Just go along with it.'

Perhaps the worst job on a farm is mending fences. And though our morning tour hadn't revealed a busted wire or a loose picket, Sterlo set me to work pinching in a new section of livestock fencing near one of the gates linking our paddocks to the neighbouring Chambers' property.

'See how those office hands stand up,' he said, handing me a pair of pliers and a hammer. 'I'll roll it out, you fix it to the posts.'

By lunch my fingers ached with arthritic tension, and by knock-off at five they could barely make the fists I wanted to shake at the whole blasted place. As if reading my mood, Sterlo drove me to the front bar of the Terminus at dusk, right as the light tumbled behind the grain silos. That engine of twelve vertical cylinders cast shadows that jailed the only licensed premises for fifty kilometres. It was the kind of place where the publican would make you a cocktail as long as it was a rum and coke. When I ordered two pints of beer, he slid them spilling across the bar in glasses clouded with dishwasher streaks.

'How long you in town for, mate?'

'Just as long as harvest takes,' I said, swapping money for booze. 'Sterlo will be whipping me, so it won't take long.'

The man leaned over the bar, addressing me, ignoring Sterlo. 'You give my regards to your mum. Haven't seen her around much.' He went to chat to some old regulars, blokes who looked like they'd been oxywelded to the chairs.

'Good to have you back,' Sterlo said. 'Even if it's for a short time.'

He held up his pint. We clinked glasses and I returned the serve.

'It's a pleasure to be here, Sterlo. I wouldn't miss it for the world.'

We laughed, both of us in on the bullshit. Then skolled the beers and ordered two more, drinking them slowly, listening to the chatter of the bar as it filled up with itinerant workers and the same old Cold Chisel tunes on the stereo.

'It's been a while since you've been on the tools.' Sterlo lit a cigarette and sent a cloud into the ceiling fan. 'Reckon you'll remember what to do?'

'Like riding a bike,' I said.

Sterlo leaned in. 'Look. You don't have to be with us all day. Your mum needs help packing the house. Taking care of your dad. You'd be better off there.'

'I'll work,' I said. 'She asked me to help with the harvest. That's what I'm going to do.'

'You can't avoid it,' Sterlo said, his voice barely audible above the pub's chatter. 'I didn't know he was so bad. He knew me.

And then he didn't.'

'At least he got your name right.'

I drained my beer and called for two more. I looked around the pub, remembering the last time I'd been there was for Albert's wake.

'Look, mate. I'll tell you straight.' Sterlo leaned in, dropping words in my ear. 'It's going to be a bumper crop this year. She hasn't signed anything. Why can't the farm stay in the family, and you get someone to run it?'

I shrugged. 'She wants out. It's up to her.'

'And you don't care? How many generations of Brockmans?'

I flicked up three fingers. 'I'm not my brother. He was the heir. I'm the spare.' I squeezed my hand into a fist and rested it on the counter.

Sterlo refused the next beer when the publican offered it. 'Give it to this bloke.' He stood and patted me on the shoulder. 'Just ask her to consider keeping it. I can keep on running it like I do now. She gets the income all the same.'

'Why don't you ask her yourself?'

He thought for a moment, and then grinned. 'Because I asked you to.'

I sat back and looked at Sterlo a second too long, and blinked before he did. I shook his left hand while his right mangled his ute keys and jangled them out the door. He left me with, 'Righto boy, early start tomorrow.'

5

Five drinks in I called Mum from the bar's payphone and told her I'd be back late. She sounded relieved.

'Remember you've an early start.'

I rang off and ordered another beer, and while the publican pulled it, the noise in the bar trebled as though someone had jacked up the volume.

'Rowan bloody Brockman, how are you, mate?' Hands gripped my shoulders and I was surrounded by all the local aristocrats: Peter Courteling, Ryan Slater, Walter de Groot, Michael Hoth, sons and heirs of the big-name properties, a mob of sharply pressed work shirts and store-fresh jeans.

'When did you get in?' Courteling asked, and we went through the motions of 'I'm back for the harvest and yes Dad's going well thanks for your concern and yeah it's a shame but that's life and the crops will be bumper and let's hope the weather holds'.

With pleasantries out the way, Hoth dropped that he was having a party the next night. The circle closed, all of them grinning. 'Back paddock of our place. Bring whatever you want. Bless the harvest and all of that, eh?'

I flicked a pair of notes on the bar, made it my shout, and five glasses got whipped under the taps and doled out. Just like old times. Courteling held up his glass like a musketeer, putting a hand on my back.

'To Albert,' he said. 'Who would have been here. And Rowan, who came anyway.' We clinked and drank and ordered more. Before I could remember to order some food the drinking took over and the room swooned around, shouting talk and barking laughter mixed through with four-on-the-floor tracks from the shitty speakers caged to the ceiling. One sharp word insisted above the others.

'Alison, Alison, Alison,' I found myself saying, grabbing her arm as she struggled through the crowd past our group. Alison Chambers. Her nose corrugated in that maddening way when she saw me, and I was eighteen again, taking off her bra, lying on a blanket in a copse of trees at the dry creek. She hugged me tight, asked how I was, and listened as I answered with my career.

'I'm on the cop beat for the newspaper. Worked my way to it. You wouldn't believe some of the stories. There was a drug raid I went on where the uniforms had to knock a dog out with a night stick.'

'It's very noble what your mum's doing,' she said, cutting me off. 'She's brave. I hope you know that. I can't imagine ever doing it. But it's great you're back supporting her.' I said thanks, and she dug me in the ribs. 'I read your articles sometimes.' Pride swelled till she said, 'They come in handy whenever I stoke the fire at home.'

'Maybe I could interview you while I'm here. I could make a great subject out of you.'

'Nothing to tell really. I moved out of home and went to uni, just like you. Only I moved out bush again. Down south to Walpole.' She changed tack. 'Your dogs are at our place, you know? AB and Lillee –'

'Lillee and Bradman. AB died the other week.'

'Sorry. You can come visit them if you like.'

'Maybe I will. We could have a cup of tea.'

She cupped my chin with her hands. 'You're still an arsehole, and I'm still mad at you. So don't come over for tea.' She pushed her way back through the crowd and chatted to some of the boys, glancing over with smiling eyes as I stood at the bar, unsure of what to do next.

Hoth sidled up, clinking his glass to mine. 'Old habits, mate. Hard to shake.'

'Some are easier than others,' I said, and held up my hand to order another round. The bar man was too busy to notice, so I fed a few lines to Hoth. 'What are you up to these days?'

He pinched his sunburned nose and shrugged. 'Did a few years as a deckie on the cray boats. Went on some mines up north. Good pay. Fucking boring.'

My turn to shrug. 'I get shit pay and all the excitement. Want to swap?'

Hoth smacked me on the back. 'Such a smart-arse, Brockman. Make sure you come tomorrow night. It's gonna be a big one. Bring your own booze, but.'

With him gone, Alison came back over, checking her watch in the chinks of light flickering through all the bodies. 'Look, I'm going home, I just came for a late one with the girls. Want a lift?' She waved to a coven of friends cackling in a booth, fending off the eager approaches of harvest workers trying it on. The voices of Sterlo and Mum took an ear each and said, 'Remember you have an early start.'

I said my goodbyes, clasped handshakes where I could and waved to the barman, who rang the bell for last orders as if to peal me out the door.

'I can't stand that bogan dump,' Alison said as we crossed the gravel to her car. 'You know the women's toilet has a urinal? We're just an afterthought.' She got in a boxy hatchback and slid a hand to the passenger side to unlock it. 'We have to meet there though. I guess it's a tradition. The only place for miles. Unless you drive to the Railway Hotel. But that place is even more of a dump.'

She kept up her tirade, changing gears and turning corners with a blathering of complaints till we reached the main road. I grabbed the handhold and relaxed, just glad to be in a car instead of walking home – there was only one taxi and its flag fall at that time of night was extortionate.

When we reached the turn-off for Brockman's Place she straddled the car across the gateway.

'You're looking good,' she said. 'Better than last time I saw you.'

She had worn colour to Albert's wake instead of black – a dark-blue dress with a Liberty scarf of purple paisley.

'How long are you in town for?' I asked.

'Just till the harvest is done. I'd like to stay longer but I've got things to do down south.' She paused a moment. 'I'm surprised to see you here.'

'Mum asked me to come. It's the last one for us.'

'Yeah, I know. Everybody knows. I'm still surprised you came. But I'm glad you did.'

I wanted to lean over the handbrake and kiss her – run my hands through her hair and push the seat down and put her under a spell. Instead I said, 'Thanks for the lift,' and got out, a tingling sheet of pressure shedding from my body.

The car got in gear to drive off. Then she wound down her window. 'See you at Hoth's?'

'Maybe,' I said.

She blew me a kiss.

The hatchback veered to the property next door, high beams moving down the road like lanterns falling in a well.

Stumbling up the veranda steps, I gripped Dad's handrail and used it to vault up the final indent. Mum had left a plate of cold leftovers on the kitchen table – a few wedges of curried egg sandwich, sausage rolls and a dollop of tomato sauce encased with a dry skin. They all got wolfed down in a gorge of faded concentration, sitting at the table under two strips of fluorescent light. In the shower I ran the hot water till the tank emptied and cold water made the homestead disappear, the harvest recede, taking me back to the waves at Scarborough where I dived under the breakers with Alison, both of us naked, hand in hand, into the black water.

6

I slept with one foot planted on the floor to stop the spinning in my head. I dreamed of night skies over a desert dotted with the lights of 24/7 mine sites – the view Albert loved to take from a hill above Kalgoorlie, the red-dirt town he'd made a home for two years. He'd pretend those landlocked constellations were the running lights of passenger liners floating on a black sea.

Once awake, I couldn't shake the feeling that my brother was just next door, in his old bedroom, fast asleep with his expertly rumpled clothes laid out ready for a working day he'd have relished. The clock radio beside my bed flicked to five. It was not long before Sterlo would arrive to holler through my door. Maybe he'd be impressed I had gotten up without his prodding. More likely he'd just tell me to get my arse into gear.

I crept through the house, careful not to creak the floorboards or bash a shin into a packing box. Light spilled from under the library door and when I opened it Mum chimed 'hello' as casually as if it were midmorning. She was reclined on a couch by the room's bay window, a blanket over her knees and a book balanced in the cleft. She wore reading glasses at the end of her nose – a new addition.

'Don't fret about the noise. Your father could sleep through an earthquake these days.'

I ran my fingers over the spines of books at chest height, searching for a title amongst the hundreds that lined the wall-to-ceiling bookcases. The record player was spinning a 78 of soft warbling classical, and I had the urge to rip it off, throw on

(*I'm*) *Stranded* by The Saints and test Mum's advice on Dad's hearing, as long as she hadn't thrown my old records out already. Instead I found an old standard in the bookshelves, *The Quiet American* by Graham Greene, and sat next to her, pulling the tail of her blanket over my legs.

'I don't sleep all that much,' she said. 'You know your dad built this for me?' I did, but said nothing as she looked around the room. 'He said he wanted culture and new things around here. Amateur dramatics in the town and chickpeas in the paddocks instead of wheat.' She closed her book, Japanese death poetry, and yawned deeply. 'You got the best of him in here though. When he wasn't with Alby out in the shed.'

'What will you do with the books?' A pile of flattened packing boxes leaned against her side of the couch.

'I was thinking of donating them. To the library. There's more than a few overdue in the collection anyway.' We laughed together, and shared a long silence, looking at the skylines of books on the shelves, everything from Shakespeare and Thucydides to how to do a sheep dip.

'I never wanted to stay,' Mum said. 'I only came for six months to Septimus. I was going to nurse in the city.'

I nodded and said, 'I know.' Dad was forever telling us how he wooed her by reading as many books as he could and blagging his way through conversations about literature.

'For some reason I did,' Mum continued. 'And six months became twelve and then nine more with Albert and then with you and now here we are.' Her book fell open, and she tapped a page. 'We've had a good life here, haven't we?'

I had the feeling I'd walked into a benevolent ambush, like being hauled aside by a friend at a party to be told to rein in the drinking.

'We had the best life here,' I said, meaning it, and hoping she noticed. 'We make choices and they lead to more. I just wanted something else.'

'We knew that,' Mum said, gesturing to the shelves. 'Kind of inevitable really. You were never a farmer.' She chuckled. 'Not in a million seasons. Albert used to beg us to drive the headers. You'd sit in the ute and read a book.' She swung her legs out of the blanket and patted mine, cinching her nightgown tighter as she stood and put her book back on a shelf. 'I'll go and make you and Sterlo some proper coffee. Set you up for the day. He's going to push you hard I think. You need to let him.'

I sat listening to the creak of floorboards as she shuffled to the kitchen. And right on time the screen door on the veranda creaked and Sterlo roused my room with 'righto boy', reliable as an alarm.

We set up a camp of fold-out chairs and tables under a shade tree Dad planted years back, a flooded gum that clawed the sky with widowmaker branches. The runabout utes would be parked there in what we called a 'laager', a word Dad said was a transplant from the Boer War, when white men from the district fought other white men in South Africa.

Sterlo's Datsun and Dad's old Toyota 70 Series would be used to deliver whatever was needed, then for driving the hands between paddock work and the holy trinity of smoko, lunch and dinner. The grain they stripped from the paddocks would be dumped in a bunker – a big U of corrugated-iron sheets angled at forty-five degrees that had already been smacked into the ground at the end of a nearby access track.

While Sterlo arranged the furniture, I hacked a patch of long grass with a machete, the whispering blade disturbing clumps of locusts flashing bright yellow wings.

'Think we'll get a swarm?' I called to Sterlo, who shook his head and spat into a circle of rocks that made a crude fireplace.

'Not been dry enough. Those are just remnants. We'll have to remember to put hessian on the radiators. They'll clog up quick if we don't.'

I slashed the machete down and hit a rock; the metal ringing swarmed my mind back to when drought and locusts crumbled all the crops and fodder at my uncle's place. It put him in the red. There was no money to keep the sheep, so he shot most of his flock. Bullets were cheaper than hay. Albert and I helped him scrape the carcasses into burial pits and set them alight with drizzled petrol. All that summer I carried the stink with me, from the farm to the coast, even in the dark under the saltwater breakers.

'I think it's best if I tell the fellas what's going on with your dad,' Sterlo said, standing close suddenly, and I startled backward, the machete in my hand flinching. 'Easy there, mate,' he said, hands up. 'It'll be Williamson and Murphy on the headers, and they've got a kid called John to drive chaser. He's across from Mingenew.' He pointed to his ute. 'I'll do the directing. You drive the taxi. Get fuel and do the errands. Nothing too hard. If I'm not on the CB, I'll be on the phone to the grain dealers or bringing in the semitrailers.'

'Suits me perfectly,' I said. I wanted to work, but didn't want any responsibility. 'Have you been back for those sheep in the bore?'

I meant it innocently, just a work question to pass the time. It disturbed him. 'Fuck, I forgot about it.' He peered across the paddocks, the direction of the waterhole where the three ewes were trapped. 'I'll do it this afternoon,' he said, grim with the task added to his to-do list.

We ate a scratch breakfast of boiled eggs and sliced white bread together, and watched clouds of dust fan up from the side roads. Flatbed trucks were driving header harvesters to the starting positions on all the properties in the area, and two threshers, one danger-red and one caution-yellow, were hauled into our laager as we mopped up our plates.

Sterlo got up and chatted to Williamson and Murphy in turn as they watched the truckies unload their machines. I hung back, trusting Sterlo to give my dad's condition the fairest hearing, and break the news that this would be their final harvest at Brockman's Place.

When the unloading was done, the three of them inspected the headers, rasping their callused hands over the great machines – each with four oversize wheels around an engine and glassed cockpit watching over a long octagonal comb that looked like a hollow corncob.

'Good to be back in the good land of Septimus,' Williamson said as he approached the camp we'd set up. 'And very good to see you, mate. Haven't changed much.'

I stood and shook his hand, still strong in the years since I'd seen him. Murphy was the same. They had seen more earth and done more miles, but they were still suntans and singlets, squinted eyes and rough humour.

'How is the big bad city treating you, son?' Murphy asked, taking a seat under the tree. 'Suppose you're ringing the damn place by now?'

'Thought I'd come back and have a breather,' I said, and they laughed.

'We'll sort you out,' Williamson said. 'Sorry about your dad. These things happen.'

That was all that needed to be said. I went to Sterlo's ute to fetch a thermos of tea and some mugs. When I got back, the three of them were deep in conversation about the plan to start at the top and then work their way down, Williamson on the left and Murphy on the right, with the chaser bins taking the grain to the bunker behind the shade tree. I doled out the tea and pretended to listen.

I wished I'd brought a book.

7

New day. Usual beginning. Sterlo's hand clacked the light switch as he said 'righto boy', and thumped off down the hall. Awake, dressed, coffees in hand, we drove in his ute to the laager where Williamson and Murphy were warming their hands over a cooking fire. Panes of dew dusted the canvas of their swags, the drops rolling into streaks as the rising sun warmed us. I breathed out mist and wished I were back in my bed at the homestead, then further away in my flat in Scarborough where the warmth of the ocean would be whispering through the windows.

'Best time of the day,' I said, and no-one responded. They were watching the land, preparing for what it held.

'No excuses today,' Sterlo said as orange light came. The banter of the previous day was gone. 'We've got to finish that bunker. Get all the augers into position. Make sure the trucks are all good –'

'We know what to do,' Murphy said. 'Same as always.'

Williamson tipped his coffee onto the fire to extinguish it. 'Let's get about it then. It's too early to stand around.'

Sterlo looked at me blankly, the face of a foreman. 'There's a pile of sheet metal, wire and star pickets behind the shade tree. I need that bunker a good couple of metres longer. Contractors shorted us. Make it six extra on each side.'

'How will I measure it?'

'Use your stride. Stretch to the limit and it should be two metres with your height. Lay it all out then call us over when you're done and we'll hammer it in.'

While I went to the shit job, the men turned their backs and spread a map on a camp table and poked it with their fingers, arguing over priorities and plans. It was like being sent to eat at the kids table.

Oil reservoirs got changed. Gaskets checked. Bolts tightened. Whatever Sterlo told me to do, I did it, swearing under my breath at the standard stuff a farm day held. Come five o'clock, I played the Mum card and drove back to the homestead, making a smooth turn for the gate and the highway instead of the front veranda. I went down next door's track, making my way to Alison's door, calling out as the dogs ran beside the ute's dust cloud.

'G'day, Bradman. Hello, Lillee.' Saying their names was tonic. I got out and patted their flanks and scratched their ears. They were dumb as rivets, but loyal. Lillee was a fine splicing of a sheep dog and a terrier, while Bradman was a genetic bitzer. They remembered me, licking my hands and jumping up for a pat, whining and clawing to get my attention as the sound of a door hinging open interrupted.

'They're terrible guards,' Mrs Chambers said, emerging from their veranda. 'They eat our dogs' food. And fart something wicked.' Her name was Maureen, yet I could never bring myself to address her as that. She came down the steps and patted them. 'They're good dogs.' She was an echo of Alison – the trace of her twenties still vibrant under suntan and stress. 'We're not keeping them though. Has your mum mentioned any plans?'

'Not to me,' I said, thinking of my flat's tight quarters. 'I'm sure she'll take them with her.'

'Old folks homes don't take pets. Especially farm dogs.'

That wasn't the plan. Not as I understood it. Mum would buy a home on the coast and get a nurse to take care of Dad. There'd be more than enough money from the sale for a place with a backyard.

'Whatever she wants to do with them I'm sure they'll be fine,'

I said, patting them again. 'If you want me to come and walk them or anything I'd be happy to.'

Mrs Chambers shook her head. 'You're busy enough.' She touched me on the shoulder. 'Harvest is always chaos. But you've got other things to deal with too.'

'It's just a few weeks.' I pointed to her paddocks. 'Got the work crew in yet?'

'Just the hubby and a few hands.' She looked away. 'Alison's driving a chaser bin. She's up there now testing it all.'

A stab of excitement hit my gut. 'I saw her at the pub. She told me she's living in Walpole now.'

Mrs Chambers pressed my shoulder again. 'Very happily.' She went back inside, leaving me to play with the dogs.

'Don't do anything stupid,' I told myself in the bathroom mirror. Alison and I had history. I was only in town for a short time. And it was typical of me to look for a complication. So while getting ready for Hoth's party, I jerked off in the shower – the new handrail was helpful – shaved my face and slapped on some of Dad's musky aftershave.

Mum had put him to bed early with a sleeping tablet so she could host a gathering of her own. Mrs Hoth, Courteling, de Groot and Slater formed a book club circle in our front room where I said polite hellos and hurried out the door, promising Mum that yes, of course I'd be back at a reasonable hour, and no, I wouldn't mess up the kitchen when I came back pissed.

Their gale of chatter faded when I hopped inside the ute. The donk started up first go for once and the vibrations shook a cloud of dust from the dashboard that nearly choked me. I switched on the radio and an AM station crackled to life, some bloke with a high-pitched voice complaining about government spending. 'You know what I think we've got to do,' he said, the tirade lighting up the road almost as bright as the headlights. 'These politicians don't know anything that goes on outside their windows. Give me five minutes with them behind the wheel of a tractor and they'd see the truth.' I switched it off and drove steady till Hoth's party appeared out of the blackness, a circle of utes with headlights shining onto a patch of cleared paddock where skinny kids were building a bonfire.

I parked and switched off the engine. The car body ticked and the party outside swirled as the flames licked the firewood and pointed skyward.

'Rowan bloody Brockman,' a voice yelled, and I waved through the windshield. I took a deep breath, ran a hand through my hair and dove in, adding my sixpack of beers to an esky full of ice and snipping the top off my first.

'We really should know better,' Peter Courteling said, stepping back to make room for me in the gentry circle. 'Should be tucked up in bed like my old man. Ready for the real man's work to start. But I do it better seeing double.' We all laughed and clinked our beers. Ryan Slater pulled out a deck of cigarettes and offered them around. When we'd all lit up, I looked over the rest of the crowd to see who'd turned up.

'Who are these kids? I don't recognise anyone.'

'That's because we're old, mate,' Michael Hoth said, pointing to the clumps of revellers. 'Younger brothers, sisters, cousins. All eighteen now. Well, a few of them aren't.'

'You're such a fucking toolie,' Walter de Groot joked, and Hoth nudged him sideways.

'Fuck off. Just because you liked her.'

'Hoth got with some high-schooler last harvest,' Courteling said to me. 'Dumb bastard thought she was twenty-five.'

'Did he think her pencil case was a handbag?' I asked, and a pause lengthened, broken by cackling that doubled them all over.

'Piss off, Brockman,' Hoth said. 'We only had a kiss. For the record she looked twenty-five. Only found out when her mum called mine.'

We oohed and aahed and swapped yarns and my six beers got sunk quick as the radio played old Creedence tunes and we sang along, mashing up the words, 'there's a bathroom on the right' and 'have you ever seen Lorraine?' getting the most play. No-one asked about Dad or Mum packing up the farm or shared a memory about Albert. We just drank and smoked and yarned and played cricket with a tin bin for a wicket and took turns jumping over the fire until Hoth wrenched his ankle and one of the kids got burning ash up his trousers.

I was going to call it a night when headlights swung across the paddock and Alison's hatchback parked up. Out of the doors spilled the girlfriends she'd met up with the other night at the pub. Out she spilled too. My pulse began to thud.

'Rowan, be a dear and get some cups?' she said, pulling a bottle of vodka from her handbag. 'There's a stack near the esky. And the orange juice too.' Her friends grinned, as though they were in on the conspiracy. I did a little bow and grinned back. When I came back with the supplies, she poured the drinks and took me away from everyone else.

'Tell me a story then, newspaper man,' Alison said, cup held up like a fan. 'Met anyone famous? Seen anything amazing?'

'Just car crashes and petty crime,' I said, pleased to be teased.

'No murders?' She moved closer. 'Serial killers or psychos? Tell me.'

I ransacked my brain. Found plenty to tell. 'You might get scared,' I said, teasing her back. I should have stopped there – changed the subject to her life, her friends, anything at all. I wanted to brag, seem tougher than my office pale skin allowed.

'Went to a car crash once that made me spew,' I told her, and she came even closer, putting a hand on my shoulder. 'Head-on smash between a semitrailer and a car towing a horse float. You can guess who lost.'

'Well that's just sad,' she said. 'I could tell you stories about Walpole. Strange things happen in the trees down south. I walked into a field of marijuana plants once. Had to run away so fast. I still get nightmares.'

'Did you grab any at least?' I asked. She told me to shut up, reached into her handbag and took out a palm-sized plastic bag. It held two white pills.

'I dare you,' she said, and walked over to where all the cars were parked. She found my ute and hopped up onto the tray. I followed, my legs melting magnets, sitting with my back to the cab and Alison Chambers pressed to my chest. She took the pills out, put one in my mouth and one in hers. We both swallowed, and she kissed me, harder and harder as the pill dissolved and that familiar stretch came to my stomach as the paddocks and the night sky and the town and the city and the harvest and the newspaper and the next day's demands packed themselves away into neat little boxes and all the lights switched off at once.

8

We didn't have sex. But I was fucked from the drugs and slept right through Sterlo's 'righto boy' alarm clock at five am sharp. Instead I woke to the steady klaxon of headers churning their way through the top paddocks, the noise carrying clear through bedroom curtains chinked with insistent sun. I dressed and dashed up to the vehicle laager with sweat like bleach oozing from my pores.

All I could do was watch and wait, helpless to help till the ten o'clock smoko came and the engines of the headers stopped. Silence ruled until Sterlo's ute came roaring across the open stubble of the harvest paddock, Murphy in the front seat and Williamson and the chaser bin driver holding onto the tray bar above the cab. The vehicle halted in a cloud of dust. They stared at me as locusts surged and snapped like castanets.

'I got on the piss last night and slept in,' I said. There was no point in lying. Half the town saw me. 'Sorry I missed this morning.'

'This morning? You missed the whole harvest,' Sterlo said, walking past me to sit on a folding chair. 'We've already stripped half of the first paddock. Dumped it in the grain bunker. Real yeoman's work.'

Murphy and Williamson sat down too, the kid preferring to stand.

'This is John,' Sterlo said, and we shook hands, his grip light in mine. 'He's from Mingenew. Proper farming country. He's come to teach us all a thing or two about growing wheat.'

'Nah, nah,' John said, embarrassed. 'I just drive the chaser. Slow and steady.'

'And we don't have much time,' Sterlo said, pointing to me, and then to the ute. 'Grab the sangers and the tea, mate. We've got a job for you.'

I passed out the snacks as though I were a waiter. When all the fellas had something in their hands, Murphy turned my attention to the header harvester paused halfway along in the furthest paddock.

'She chewed some rocks and a few of the teeth got bent out of shape. There's spares in the ute and a few tools. Be a sport and change 'em.'

The fellas laughed like weasels. It would take at least an hour to remove the nuts and bolts holding the teeth on, swap the blades and reassemble the binds. Shit of a job out in the heat and down in the dust. I had no choice in the matter. So put my hat on and stepped from the shade to the sun.

I spent the rest of the morning as the dogsbody – fetching fuel from forty-four-gallon drums in the homestead shed, then helping John transfer grain from his chaser bin to the grain bunker near the shade tree. My bones ached with the mothball comedown of amphetamines. The urge to vomit teased a waterfall in the back of my throat as I set up augers to spew torrents of harvested wheat to the top of the growing pile.

Just before lunch, Sterlo radioed, 'Rowan, go to the home channel,' and I switched the CB over to nine, what Dad had called 'the cricket channel', where an ashen hiss made my teeth itch.

'Don't have time for your shit,' Sterlo said. His voice was slow and deliberate, as though it were being pushed through a sieve. 'I need everyone firing. This is no place for passengers.'

'It won't happen again,' I said, and slowed to his pace. 'I hadn't seen the boys in a while. Lost track of the time I guess.'

'Bullshit,' he said, and paused a beat too long. 'If you just want to help your mum pack the house and take care of your dad then that's fine. I can get another hand. Like I said, we don't need passengers.'

I didn't really need to be there, let's be honest. It was a sop for Mum. I think even she knew it. 'Yes' formed in my mouth, but something made me swallow it, down to guts still turning from Alison's pill.

'I'll finish out the day.' I switched back to the work frequency where the boys were coordinating their work, John edging his chaser bin right up to Murphy's newly toothed header so he could strip the grain and dump it at the same time.

'Over a bit more. Keep it steady. Steady now. Further in.'

'Close as I can get.'

'Here you go then. Don't spill any. That's gold to us.'

Come five, I fuelled the headers up for the last runs of the day. Then drove back to the homestead to help Mum pack for a few hours before dinner, something I couldn't fuck up. So I took Albert's room.

It was a teenage museum – untouched since he'd left for ag college, then chucked that in for the big money on the mines. It was tidier than it had ever been when he was alive. Mum's touch. I packed his shelf of *Commando* comics first, then the books on cricket and footy – someone at the Salvos would snap those up. Then it was the posters of red cars, skimpy girls and shit bands blu-tacked so hard to the walls that paint flecked off when I pulled them down. Knick-knacks and trinkets. Trophies for sport, best and fairest, grand finals and country week down in Perth. Things that were so important at the time, coveted as proof of good things to come.

Finally I tackled the cupboard full of work clothes. They were all stained and creased, cut slim. I held a shirt to my nose and inhaled, smelling only dust and mothballs. There was nothing of my brother. Nothing of Alby. Just things going into boxes. I folded the shirts, shorts and trousers neatly into piles, then thought better of the order and threw them in haphazard so Albert's style would keep, even if the clobber just got cut up for workshop rags.

With just the bed to unmake, I sat on the floor and ran my hands over the grooves of the boards. We used to sit like that, playing blackjack with a deck of cards taken from Dad's liquor cabinet, betting with matchsticks when it was for fun, and with our turns for washing the dishes if we were playing for sheep stations. I slapped the floor, imagining the deal, saying 'hit me' for another card.

That's when I heard Mum scream, followed by a heavy thunk at the back of the house. Rushing to the laundry I found her standing against a wall, a shelf toppled over and snowdrifts of detergent across the floor.

'Don't move,' she warned. 'It's right there. By your feet.'

A snake. Long as a belt and dappled with brown and black diamonds. My roving mind focused with almost painful awareness on the reptile in striking distance of my ankles. Its stubby shark-like head considered me, the body coiled around, pure muscle instinct sliding from my boots to a wide gap in the floorboards.

'Oh no you bloody don't,' Mum said and strode across the floor looking ten feet tall, one arm reaching expertly to the back of the snake's head, the other around the meat of the body. 'Open the back door,' she barked, and I held it open so she could fling the twisting danger into the garden where it slid away.

'How in the hell did you do that?' I yelled, mind racing and heart melting, all the fear and excitement bursting through my blood vessels. 'I mean, you just grabbed it, and threw it. I thought it was going to –'

Mum hugged me and squeezed. I held her close, her head on my thudding chest. 'I've ruined your shirt,' she said, letting me go finally, foundation and mascara smeared together. She never let standards drop. 'Get another one and I'll put a load on. Do you have any others?'

I buttoned it off and she shoved it in a rinsing sink, busying herself with separating colours from whites and twisting the controls of the washing machine to the economy setting. In my cupboard I found another work shirt and grabbed a packet of cigarettes from the drawer beside the bed. I lit two, went back to the laundry and offered her one. Instead of scolding me for smoking inside, or smoking at all, she took it and inhaled a long drag.

'I saw that on TV once,' she said, laughing now, her latent fear mixed with relief. 'I just did it. Don't ask me how. And you're lucky I did. You were frozen in place. A very easy target.'

I didn't have the heart to tell her it was probably just a carpet python. 'Dad would have chopped its head off with an axe.'

Mum laughed. 'Pooh he would have. He was never that good with his hands. Why do you think the back door's still broken after all these years? That's probably how it got in.'

'Why don't we order pizza? It'll save you the hassle.'

She licked the fingertips on her ring hand, pinched the cigarette out and flicked it through a gap in the flyscreen door. 'Dinner's no hassle.' The washing machine clicked on its cycle. 'Sterlo tells me you need to have an early night. So let's get to it.'

She ran a bath for Dad while I went to finish packing Albert's room, folding bedsheets and rolling up the doona. The struggle to get the old man in the water muffled through the walls. 'No, no, no,' he kept saying, water splashing and sloshing, Mum's voice murmuring and soothing. With all that carry-on, I went out to the kitchen and dialled up the only takeaway joint in town. Three pizzas and a garlic bread, enough for leftovers the next day. When Albert's room was as bare as mine I found her in the living room with Dad, watching the six o'clock news on the long couch, holding hands.

'Pizzas will be ready for pick up soon,' I announced, and sat in the third couch seat.

'Cancel it,' Mum said.

'The order's done. It's being made now.'

'I said cancel it.'

Argument swelled, but I swallowed its heat and got up to call the shop. Mum turned down the TV volume with the remote. 'I'll make chops.'

She then turned the news up so loud I had to shout when the pizza joint answered.

9

Most of the farms observed a local tradition on the morning of the harvest's first Sabbath and downed tools. While Mum went to early mass, I resisted the urge to sleep in and took Dad's old typewriter and a sheaf of paper down to the creek behind our homestead. It was an ephemeral waterway that had once flowed high and wide after rains, now choked by irrigation and diversions. Lined with native trees and parched English willows, the creek banks dropped steeply to mud dried in octagonal plates like the armour of a snake. A few of the old trees bore teardrop scars where the Yamatji had harvested their bark. Maybe that would have made a good image to start Holt's article with. *They were the first people to leave this land, only without a choice.*

'Too intellectual,' I said, scrunching the idea and chucking it over my shoulder. I touched the notch of a scar tree and sat with my back to the apron of bark that remained, looking over paddocks of wheat stretching to the whitewash of the homestead walls. Locusts clicked, a header rumbled somewhere – someone ignoring the Lord – and I couldn't think of typing up anything for Holt beyond a bland report of a bumper harvest full of 'bloody farmer speak'.

Two hundred kilometres up the Great Northern Highway there's a turn-off for a small town called Septimus. The narrow strip of bitumen that leads there is hemmed in on both sides by oceans of wheat whose edges lap the road

shoulder. The land out there can be as flat as
a billiard table, featurelessness Xeroxed,
with the sky above so large and so blue
you can feel dizzy if you stare at it too
long. This is the true Wheatbelt-the place
where pioneer families established the great
farming properties after hearing what Banjo
Paterson called 'the master-word-And the
master-word was Wheat'.

Rip. Scrunch. Bin. 'That'll go above everybody's head.' I fed
another sheet of paper into the typewriter. Just tell the story.
Stick with facts. Ten paddocks at Brockman's Place and we'd
just harvested the first few. That would be a good starting point.
Set the scene. Then go from there.

Harvesting wheat is a lot like mowing the
lawn. The harvesting machines line up, and
then go back and forth till the paddock is
shorn of its growth of ripe grains. Sterlo and
Murphy and Williamson are the greenkeepers
at my parents' property near Septimus in the
Wheatbelt, and between them they've stripped
two paddocks worth of grain that will soon
become bread and flour when it's collected
and sold.

Rip. Scrunch. Bin. 'Blah, blah, blah.'

I thought back to the road smash I'd been sent to in my cadet
year. I had arrived at the scene before the gore had been covered
with tarpaulins. In the chinks of gloom between the red and
blue lights, the body of the driver of the car looked as though it
had burst like a red and white balloon. The experience horrified
me, but Holt praised my article as a 'ruthless distilling'. Now
its text came to my fingers, something memorised as if by rote.

Retired couple killed in highway smash

Rowan Brockman

Police are urging holidaymakers to drive with caution after a Perth couple was killed in a head-on smash with a semitrailer on Wanneroo Road. The crash happened near the Yanchep turn-off around six o'clock on Thursday evening in the lead-up to the Australia Day long weekend.

In a statement, police said the occupants of the sedan, both aged in their seventies, were killed instantly. The driver of the truck was treated for minor injuries.

'Matter of fact, bloodless and direct,' I said, hoping Holt's pithy spirit would help me. Another sheet, another go:

Western Australia's wheat harvest is one of the largest and one of the richest in the world. Every year it delivers on average more than ten million tonnes to silos across the state.

This colossal haul is contributed to by farms of all sizes, from the smallest hobby farm earning a yearly stipend to the immense conglomerates that fill hundreds of freight train cars with their grain.

Brockman's Place sits in the middle of these extremes. It's been part of my family for generations. So I have travelled home to help bring in the crops.

'The harvest is like one of those great big storms that builds up on a summer day,' I recall my father telling me when I was a child. 'We wait the whole year for it to come. Watching the wheat grow and grow, protecting it from fire and flood and pests.

And then it's time to harvest, and you can't work hard or fast enough.'

Rip. Scrunch. Bin. Where was the news in that?

When I crossed the creek back to the homestead, Mum was in the kitchen scrambling eggs while Dad sat mute on the couch watching *Wide World of Sports* on the TV. 'How was church?' I asked.

'Vicar went over his time again,' she said, humorously annoyed. 'Not just by a few minutes. By quite a while. And I'm sat in the front row so can I get up and leave? Plus the sermon was appalling. Why he has to use cricket as a metaphor is beyond me. I didn't understand a word. Saying we're all fielding at silly point or something when the Lord comes to bat.'

She noticed the typewriter. 'That's very traditional. Surprised it works.'

I put it down on the counter. 'It works.' I held up my fingers. 'These are a bit iffy. Work wants me to write an article. About the harvest.'

Mum didn't respond. She asked me to set the table, and between us we assembled Sunday brunch. Mum gave Dad toast and Vegemite, easier to eat, and as she filled my coffee cup she suggested, 'Why don't we go somewhere today? I'm sick of packing.'

'Why don't we take Dad into town later?' I suggested. 'Take him to a café?'

'I'm not taking your father to a café. For God's sake.' Mum went to the fridge, took out a tray of pills and fed them to Dad one by one in between bites of his toast.

'There's some rock outcrops out the back of the Hoths' place,' she said. 'They cleared some more bush to make a new paddock. You should see this one boulder. It's bigger than our house.'

Destination settled, I took a shower and shaved under the torrent of hot water, thinking of Alison, putting the razor down to jerk off, the handrail supporting images of fucking Alison against the creek bank, nails scratching my back like lightning.

I dried off in my bedroom and smoked a cigarette through the open window, looking at my naked body in the cupboard mirror. I'd lost weight, especially around the middle, even though I hadn't been on the tools very long – all that standing up and sweating in the fields instead of sitting down in dehydrating air conditioning, bashing out words with Holt setting the rowing rhythm. 'Deal in facts. Only facts. Use short sentences. Direct language shorn of sentiment.'

I thought about what Sterlo had said. 'This is no place for passengers.' Then Detective Lovestone, saying, 'This is no place for nostalgia.' Their voices chimed together. 'This is no place for you.'

The Hoths' paddocks were larger than ours. Their family came in the first wave of settlers, just like ours. They had been hungrier. 'She's been a great support,' Mum said. 'All those ladies have. I think it's what I'll miss the most. The community. Do you know your neighbours in Perth?'

'I'd rather be shot. You keep to yourself in the city.' Good advice. When I first got there I was saying hello to everyone like it was a country town. People looked at me as if I was crazy, or selling something. Where do you think you'll move to?'

'Maybe I can move in with you,' she said. 'I'll bet you have some nice enough neighbours if you'd give them a chance.'

'I'd really rather be shot,' I said, and slowed the car to turn onto a side road.

She said, 'Up here, right?'

'Left, then right. Right?'

'Let's hope.'

The wheat had grown higher than the car and the track that cleaved between the paddocks was more like a canyon. 'There it is,' Dad said, surprising us, pointing his hand between the front seats. 'Just up on the rise.'

And sure as he said it, the granite outcrop was revealed – a single monolith of solid dark rock mottled with green and red moss. I parked as close as I could get and helped Mum get Dad out of the car.

'What a magnificent sight,' he said, words bubbling and flowing. 'Our very own geological wonder. You see that, Albert?'

Mum glared at me. I swallowed the correction. Again.

'Millions of years of geological movement.' He swept a hand across the fields surrounding us. 'This is all fossil heart. The Yilgarn Craton. Dig down deep enough and you can find shells. The richest soil and best farm land you could dream of.'

Mum sighed. 'Here we go. The old tour guide never fades.' She rubbed his back. 'Why don't you stretch your legs? Have a walk around.' She nodded to me, and I kept pace with them, steering his feet away from clumps of rock and cracks in the soil. Up close to the rock I could feel its heat, all that sunshine trapped in this deep sleeping density too big to dynamite and cart away. All the Hoth family could do was leave it alone and go around, subtract its mass from their yield sums.

'What an ancient place,' Mum said, her hands on the rock. 'Makes you think, doesn't it?'

Dad put his hands beside hers. 'The Aborigines would have held this place in regard I'll bet. Till they were chased off.' He looked to me. 'We took the land and divided it up. Took ownership of something really never owned before. Burned the bush and chopped down the trees.' He put his back to the rock and looked out over the sweeping paddocks. 'They had teams of horses dragging whole tree trunks across the soil to churn away the brush and dig up the rocks. Fenced it all off and sowed wheat and ran sheep. When the Aborigines tried to come back, they forced them out. Then we went after more room. I remember my father hiring Italians to come and chop stumps out of the top paddocks.'

He levered himself away from the rock and walked off. Mum shook her head when I went to follow. 'Let him go,' she said.

'The memory will work itself out.'

'Is that true, what he was saying?'

'What did you think? They just up and left and we all moved in? Our town was named after an explorer who helped commit a massacre down at Pinjarra.' She patted me on the back. 'For a journalist you're not very inquisitive.'

'Steady on,' I said. She let the point go.

'The doctors said this would happen. His long-term memory is still very vivid. Ask him what the hit song was when he was ten years old and he might sing it for you. What he had for breakfast is a lost land.'

By the time Dad had circled the great rock a few times we'd run out of patience for a picnic. He refused to sit in the folding chair we'd brought him and wouldn't stand near to where we had spread a blanket on the dirt. It was like corralling a small child, one who said 'piss off' as I offered him a cup of tea from the thermos.

'The fresh air is doing him good,' Mum said. 'Just give it a little while longer. It'll wear him out anyway.' She watched him intently, her eyes never leaving the narrow frame of reference she had draped over him.

10

'Get that bloody chaser bin back here,' the CB radio blared. 'We're wasting time, fellas. Pull your fingers out.'

Sterlo was taking no prisoners. The mercury had risen above forty and the shire had telephoned around to all the properties to flag a possible harvest ban. One spark from a ute or a header or a cigarette butt could ignite the fields for miles around, and the hot easterly direct from the dead heart of the deserts to the east would fan it into a monster wave. If it stayed hot for long enough they'd call a halt across the district. Following regulations meant delays we couldn't afford.

'Rowan, get that fuel sorted. Murphy, watch your spacing, you're leaving channels between your cuts again. John, keep it steady. Williamson – foot to the floor mate, you've got to do it cleaner. Sharpen up, boys.'

'Okay,' came the terse responses.

'Will do.'

'No worries.'

'Over and out.'

Smoko was taken in the vehicles. I ferried cups of tea and sandwiches to everyone and slung diesel into the workers' tanks from a hand-pumped bowser strapped into the ute's tray. Murphy and Williamson looked like they had barely slept, while John was racked with nerves after he'd let half a bin's worth of grain spill out as he drove it to the bunker. 'If Sterlo finds out, I'm dead,' he said, eating the sandwich I'd given him as fuel fumes swirled around. 'Took that corner too sharp and I didn't latch the cover down tight enough.'

When the engines started up again and Sterlo resumed his CB haranguing, I hunted down the grain slick and scraped it all up with a shovel. The spillage would have been no more than a few bucks worth. But it all added up. So onto the pile it went. Fuel and oil and dirt on the grains be damned.

'Rowan, where the hell are you?' Sterlo's voice was another layer of static. 'I'm on a quarter tank and Williamson's got low radiator fluid.'

'Coming now.' I got it done. Ran the lunches out. Helped Murphy replace another pair of broken combine teeth. Fuelled the tanks again. Sweated and swore and fought through the heat. And by six o'clock we'd met the daily quota. Back at the laager, Sterlo took an esky out of his ute and passed out ice-cold beers.

'If the harvest ban comes in tomorrow we'll do running repairs on the headers,' he said, beer cap hissing between callused fingers. 'Until we know that for sure we just have to keep going. The moon's full enough that we can go late. So relax a bit now and then let's get on with it.'

'I'm charging overtime,' Murphy said. 'Already done ten hours in the cab.'

'You'll get what you're contracted for. We're here to work.' Sterlo looked at me. 'We're all here to work and get the job done.'

I walked away from the group, picked up a stick and started scratching letters into the dirt by the edge of a paddock. An old habit from older seasons, where I'd taken every moment available to shirk work and look beyond the farm gate to the world outside. Try to hate it as I might, I couldn't shake my admiration for it. The pure assault of the working day and the clear, simple task to sweat and push, the soil holding the ghosts of thousands of days filled with sore muscles and stiff backs. As much as I wanted the work to stop, I wanted it to burn.

We started up again at seven as the sun disappeared. The high beams of the headers reached out into the wheat making the ranks into stark decoupage. Sterlo didn't say anything on the CB. There was no need. Murphy and Williamson drove their machines with precise fury, and John and I served them like gun bearers. Strip. Offload. Dump the grain at the bunker. Fuel up. Repeat. The temperature cooled down as the waxing moon took over the sky, a blank of indigo blue with an immense halo around the bright light.

When Mum drove up to the laager with a surprise dinner, we'd been at it four extra hours. She called us in over the CB, parked her station wagon under the shade tree and served roast lamb, gravy, vegies and fresh baked bread off the station wagon's tailgate. Hunger is the best sauce. She could have served tinned spaghetti for all we cared. But the food was utter heaven, every mouthful enjoyed in total silence.

'Thanks for making dinner, Justine,' Sterlo said to her, as formal and polite as he could manage while she served up his plate. 'Could you cut me the burnt bit at the end? Best part.'

'It's my pleasure, Sterlo. And would you like some greens?'

'Of course. Got to keep my health up. We're nearly halfway done on this side of the highway.'

Mum heaped beans and broccoli onto his plate. 'This will help you see in the dark then.' She added a slice of bread. 'This will go nicely with the wine.' She turned to me. 'There's a couple of bottles of Côtes du Rhône on the front seat. Don't let the name fool you though. It's plonk.'

When all was served Mum packed her things up and drove off home to take care of Dad again, the headlights of her station wagon burrowing through the black tracks on the way back to the homestead.

We sat in the fold-out chairs with the moon brightening the paddocks around us. Mum left instructions for me to take the dirty dishes home and make sure there were no food scraps around. Wild dogs had been spotted in the district, and they'd linger longer if there were something to cadge.

'Lovely lamb, nice and rare,' Sterlo said, and let go a belch. 'I've still got to sort those sheep out.'

'Still?' Murphy wiggled his cup of wine. 'It's been days. They'll be well done by now.'

Sterlo changed the subject. 'Good work today, boys,' he thundered. 'We're ahead. Even if there's a ban, this late work will put us in a good position.'

The rest of the night passed in warm routine. We'd broken the back of the job – there was no need to push too hard. When knock-off was called Sterlo asked me to drive him home, admitting when the others were out of earshot that he had refilled his wine cup several times too many, and polished off the second bottle, and was in no fit state to drive. Not that it mattered all that much. We were in the country. I'd driven home so pissed once that I had to cover one eye so I could see double instead of quad. The local cops would sooner escort you home than throw you in the drunk tank. I wondered what Detective Lovestone would think.

'She's a good woman, your mum,' Sterlo slurred, rolling down the window. 'Doing the best she can. I get it. I really do.'

I murmured yes, and flicked on the high beams as we turned onto the highway, moths swarming as if pulled by magnets, flashing galaxies that kept pace even as I accelerated.

'Different place after dark,' I said, switching topics. 'Will we go late every night?'

'The forecast is for more heat. I'm being prudent.'

'I know –'

'Tight timeframe. It gets done or the crops rot. There's no negotiating with it.'

We reached Septimus town and I turned off the main drag into a side street pale with streetlights. Sterlo's place was a disappointing weatherboard home with a dead front lawn.

'Ever thought about getting your own land, Sterlo?' I asked, not able to help it.

'All the damn time, mate. But these days you either inherit it or buy it for top dollar. I'm in neither run of luck.' He opened his door and lolled out of the cab. 'My wife had land. She was canny enough to keep it. That's fair enough. It was hers. And it's not like your place pays the big bucks.' He shut the door and leaned inside the window, lowering his alcohol-tinged voice. 'I don't need to own, mate. I just need to belong. I figured that out a while ago. You need to understand that. I don't need things on paper.'

He bade me goodnight and told me to pick him up in the morning. I watched him pass through the front door, the inside as empty as my flat in Scarborough. I shoved the ute back down the highway, accelerating till the moths couldn't keep up with the headlight beams.

11

'Righto!' I slid my hand inside Sterlo's bedroom and flicked on the light. He was sitting on the bed, dressed for work, a cup of coffee in each hand. The weirdest thing I had seen in a long time.

'You're as predictable as your father was,' he said, bedsprings rocking in time with his mirth. 'No way you can get the jump on me.' The bastard laughed all the way to the laager, slurping coffee and tuning the ute's battered old radio with his free hand. 'You can't get the ABC on this thing? Radio National? Anything?'

'Sometimes. But it's pretty faint. If you go to FM.'

'I'm not listening to that shit. Least the ABC has the decency to play the classics and shut up.'

This was a revelation. 'I figured you for a talkback man. Calling up and giving the city folk a piece of your mind.' A road train came over a rise and I had to splay a hand over my face to shield its makeup-mirror lights. 'Someone's bringing grain in already. Really ahead of the timetable.'

Sterlo hit the dashboard and the radio warmed up with something jangly. 'T. Rex. Now this is how it's done.' The volume knob went round and round and the tune took over the mute grey scenery, drumbeat and guitar driving us along.

Sterlo rolled down his window and whooped at the rising dawn. Headers started up in fields on both sides of the road. Utes and trucks ran the maze of roads and tracks to deliver workers to their start positions. The whole web of activity that made the district hum and surge for a few weeks a year made a festival that played all day and late into the night.

'Forecast is for slightly cooler weather today. They must have changed their minds.' He leaned out the window, gulping the air and stretching as though it were laudanum. 'You've got to let it consume you. Harvest is a crazy time.' I didn't imagine I would, but the sentiment was tempting. I knew how to bury myself in work. Only this wasn't the job I could slump into. Sterlo seemed to sense my thoughts.

'You can knock off early today. We went pretty late last night, so if you need to help your mother, just go.' He switched off the radio just as the song worked to its climax. 'Did you speak to her? About the farm?'

'Haven't had the chance.'

Before he could say more, the laager swung into view with Williamson, Murphy and John sitting on the fold-out chairs, warming their hands around mugs. 'How did you sleep, mate?' Murphy called. Sterlo slammed the passenger door and took his place in the circle.

'Just heavenly. I dreamed that we finished the harvest in record time and went to the Terminus where they had Guinness on tap.'

'You really were dreaming,' Williamson said, and cracked up.

'It was a nice thought. But you're right. We'll have to make do with good old Swan Lager.' He switched a thumb at me. 'This idiot tried to get the jump on me this morning. Wake me up for work. Tell 'em what happened, Rowan.'

'Tell them yourself. I'm still traumatised.'

Sterlo relished it. 'He came to wake me up but I was sat there in the dark all dressed for work when he switched on the light. Tell you what boys, he near jumped a foot in the air when he saw me.'

'I've just never seen you so clean before, Sterlo.'

The others laughed. Sterlo didn't, and sat down on his folding chair to lead the discussion of the working day. As we ran through the timetable, a thick scatter of white cockatoos twisted over the paddocks.

'Rain coming,' John said, and wouldn't tell when.

Murphy's rig seized up at four, something to do with chaff getting into the engine box. He wouldn't let anyone else touch it, so Sterlo and John gave Williamson's header a lookover to make sure at least one of the crucial machines was ready for action next day. I drove back to the homestead and checked in on Mum and Dad – packing and sleeping like usual – and dialled the Chambers' place on the kitchen phone, flicking the rotary through a number long memorised. Mrs Chambers answered, and I asked her how the dogs were. Fine enough. When I asked to speak to Alison, the old girl hit me with a zinger.

'She's just writing a letter to her boyfriend.' A pause. 'I'll see if she can come.' The long wait drew sweat to my brow thicker than the sheen of the working day.

Boyfriend. The word stabbed its two syllables over and over. That had been me. Years before. Right the way through the first few years of high school and the senior years I did as a boarder in the city. When Albert died, I stayed away. And we withered. Of course she'd moved on. Seeing her, touching her, tasting her, I knew I hadn't.

'What do you want?' Alison said, terse as a hangover.

'Want to go for a walk?' The best I could think of.

We met at the creek in twilight and walked along the dry bed, meandering toward Septimus and the railway line that slid into the loading dock for the grain silos.

'Your brother's helping with the harvest then?' I asked, remembering what she'd told me.

'Yeah. He got some time off the rigs. He's earning pretty ridiculous money. Says it's all danger pay.'

'He's saving up to take over one day then?'

'That's the plan.'

'Yeah. That was ours too.'

'I know.' She touched my arm. 'At least I guessed it was.'

The sand squeaked under our shoes, suggesting a layer of water below the hardened armour of dried earth. The bankside trees whispered in the wind, and it felt good to be out of sight, deep in a furrow with the sky for shelter. Albert and I used to play at soldiers in the creek, pretending it was a trench that we'd defend side by side, lying on our bellies at the angled lip of earth to aim toy guns into the ranks of wheat.

'How's your work going?' Alison smiled. 'You remember how everything works?'

'Of course. I could do it blindfolded. It's not that hard you know.'

'I know. They kept me from it for years. Then I learned in a day and do it better than all the blokes.'

'What do you do in Walpole then?'

'Go back in time.' She punched me on the shoulder. 'I work at the school. Study. Cook and clean and run errands. Watch some telly. Read.'

'What do you read?'

'Nothing you'd approve of. I still have that book you tried to get me into. What was it? East of somewhere.'

'*East of Eden*. It's about farming. Well, kind of.'

'You can have it back. It's dreary. I'll post it to you.'

'It's a classic. Keep it. You might enjoy it one day.'

She sighed. 'I want to go back to uni. Finish my degree.'

'What did you study again?'

'Business. Same as Darren. He was senior year when I started.'

Darren. What a stupid name. 'Can you do it externally?'

'No. There's a campus in Bunbury. I could go back and forth.'

'And what will you do when you get the piece of paper?'

She punched me again. 'I'll be your boss.'

The creek angled up and ended at a landfill bridge that took the highway and the railway, with a stormwater pipe at the bottom of the span to protect these arteries from getting washed away in a downpour. We felt a rumble, deep and steady, relentless. A freight train. As we scrambled to the top of the banks, the front engine popped up from the lip of the flat horizon and grew and grew till a metal snake was clicking past over the bridge, ten cars, twenty, thirty, fifty, empty box cars on their way to the Terminus for loading with grain, then all the way back again to the port at Geraldton for loading onto a bulk carrier that would sail to Asia or the Middle East or Europe. While the final carriage passed I pulled Alison close and kissed her, both of us in plain sight of the fields and the town and the main road.

'Stop it.' She broke away. 'Just stop it.'

She walked off. The squeal of train brakes ground my mind to powder.

'Wait,' I called above the din, but she kept walking, her silhouette receding in the dark. My heartbeat surged as I went over what happened, the signs I thought she'd given, the meaning I had interpreted to draw her in. The train faded from view, and the silence that followed took all the steam out of me.

12

Despite the weather bureau's cooler outlook, the shire blinked and brought in a total harvest ban across the district. It was too hot and too windy to take a chance, and would last two days at least. So while Sterlo and the boys attended to the vehicles and did what they could to look busy, I hung around the homestead, trying to put Alison out of my mind. After breakfast, Mum showed me a clipboard with a list of jobs to do. At the top of my list was 'inventory the main shed'.

'I'm taking your father to town for a check-up soon,' she said. 'Let's get you underway. I don't want you saying I haven't told you what to do.'

The padlock was rusted with disuse and it took a few goes to get it to unlatch. Together we shoved the door sideways along its rail, opened the shed like an aircraft hangar, and inside we saw a clapped-out header harvester and a tractor that would fetch a good price in an antiques auction. A workbench with a lathe and a vice was set to one side, and a gun safe was bolted to the floor beside.

'You could get some good prices for the shotguns,' I said, approaching the gun cabinet, dialling 20-16-9-12, clockwise, counterclockwise, open. A pair of over-and-under Berettas and a pump-action Remington bookended a trio of .22 bolt actions. It was a decent battery for the killing of rabbits, pigs, foxes, wild dogs, galahs and anything else that was edible or annoying.

Mum walked about scribbling notes on her clipboard. She

patted the tractor and the header as though they were old horses, and picked up tools scattered across the concrete floor.

'I might just offer all of this as a job lot. Pick-up only.' She looked into the gun cabinet. 'Lord knows if any of them work. Sterlo does all the shooting.'

I pulled one of the Berettas out and hefted it to my shoulder. 'We could find out.' I swung it sideways, imagining a clay pigeon darting through the rafters. The trigger clicked dry.

'Put it away. It's not a toy.' She took it from me and broke the action open one-handed. 'Always check the chamber first. Never assume it's unloaded.' The gun snapped back whole inside the cabinet. 'I'd be happy to give them away to whoever wants them,' she said.

'They're worth a few hundred each, at least. They're pretty old. That could mean they're rare or something. I'll make some calls.'

Mum flicked a page over on the clipboard. 'Whatever. Just get it done quickly.' She scribbled a note. 'I've got a meeting next week with an agribusiness group. Seems their price could be right.'

'How much are they offering?'

She scribbled again. 'Enough. Best it's a simple deal. We strip the grain and keep the profits. Empty the house and sell all the assets. Away we go. They just want the land. They can have it with the price they're paying.'

Now or never. 'Why can't we just keep the property and get someone to run it? We'd still get an income from it every year. It would stay in the family.'

Before I could mention Sterlo's ambition, she backed away a few steps. 'You suddenly care about the arrangements? Look, Rowan, I get it. When my dad was dying I took care of most of the details, but right at the end my sister started insisting we did things differently. She felt guilty about not doing enough I suppose. Don't you do the same. Just bring the harvest in and help me pack. That's all you have to do.'

She strode out, leaving me to clean up Dad's tools, which were scattered around as if he'd just walked off the job and broken his own rule about a place for everything, and everything in its place. I picked up a hammer and smacked the workbench. I did suddenly care about the arrangements. I did want to do things differently. Mum asked me to come help. I had chucked three weeks of work away to do it. The moment I asked a question, it got thrown back.

I tossed the hammer aside and locked the gun cabinet, twisting the dial till the code was erased. At least that was straightforward.

Later that afternoon Mum came into the kitchen with a bundle of bills and pamphlets and a magazine from a university. She dumped them on the counter, said, 'I'll sort them out later,' and put the kettle on. She handed me a piece of fax paper, folded in half. 'This was waiting for you at the post office.' I opened it to find a scrawl of photocopied handwriting that shouted with Holt's unmistakable accent.

The number you left us had a digit wrong. Fax your story through by Friday. Happy harvesting. Thinking of putting you on the subs desk.

I muttered 'shit'. Crumpled the paper and put it in the bin. I was a field reporter – on the road, on the pulse. The subs desk was a graveyard for pedants and incompetents.

'Who was that from?' Mum asked.

'Holt. My editor.'

'About a story?'

'It's going to be a series,' I said. 'About the harvest. A big feature for the weekend editions.'

'You must be very excited.' She put tea bags in two mugs. 'You can do your real job.'

We took our teas to the living room where Dad was watching TV, eyes glassy as the screen. 'Is he having one of those days?'

'Of course he is.' Mum flicked through the channels. 'All clear from the nursing station. When I checked on him in his nap I thought perhaps he'd died. I couldn't hear any breathing. I'm ashamed to say it was a relief.'

Afternoon television was a choice of women bitching, men hectoring or children playing. Mum switched it off. 'I thought you wanted to write about politics,' she said. 'You made us subscribe to *The Economist* when you were ten. What does our harvest have to do with anything?'

'Makes a change from the police round.'

'I've never understood why you do that. You've always been so –'

'So what?'

She searched for the word. Settled on 'skittish'.

'After your uncle's sheep, you were a wreck. Now you're at the front of every bit of gore in Perth.' She pulled a pile of old papers from under the coffee table. 'The police stories are in the margins. Politics gets all the room. So why aren't you writing that kind of thing?'

A million reasons, all a variation of one stem – it was easy. 'Everyone likes a murder. A high-speed chase. Drug busts are good. Especially when they parade the perps. It's good stuff to write about. It's also what people actually read.'

Mum switched the TV back on. 'There's never anything good on.'

Dad started coughing, hacking through pained gusts like he was choking. Mum leaned over him and got a glass of water to his lips, patting his back till he settled. I made to leave, grabbing the keys for the ute.

'I'm going to town,' I said. 'Need to run a few errands.'

'Why don't you do something useful and mow the lawns?' she said. 'I don't think there's any risk of a harvest ban extending to the garden.'

The pause in work made Septimus a magnet for those with nothing to do. Utes and four-wheel drives were reverse-parked on both sides of the main drag. I eased the ute into a free space, and just missed scraping the side of a brand-new Land Rover.

'Rowan, come have a coffee, mate,' a voice called. Sterlo was with a mob of farmhands outside the café run by Nik, a Greek bloke who sent his kids to private school with the cash he made off two-dollar cappuccinos. 'Fellas, this is Bryce's son, you remember?'

All familiar faces, but I never remembered names. I said a few hellos and shook a few hands. There was a man like Sterlo at every property in the district, and it seems I'd stumbled into their knitting circle of gossip and venting.

I went inside to order, pushing aside strips of plastic hung to keep the flies out. There was no-one in there that I knew, thankfully. The aristocrats were probably drinking the day away at the Terminus. There was no sign of Alison and her girlfriends.

'Do you do them to go?' I asked the girl behind the counter, who looked at me with suspicion. 'I'll have an espresso then.'

'Why? Are you in a hurry?' Her face was absolutely deadpan. I laughed. She didn't. 'That'll be a dollar.'

I paid with a twenty. She twisted the dials of a long silver machine while I flicked through a day-old newspaper, scanning the pages for articles of anything interesting: housing developments on the front page, infrastructure bottlenecks in the middle, frictions between the government and the greenies at the back. Just a few pissant cop yarns scattered throughout, nothing meaty to worry about. The girl finished the machine's hissing process and I took a dainty cup outside.

'What kind of coffee is that?' one of the old hands asked. When I told him, he said the same joke as the girl inside, and everyone laughed.

'I remember your dad very well,' the joker said. He had a glass eye, and carried himself with the bearing of an oracle. 'Is that really true that he hooked up the generator on his ute to the pub when the power went out?'

'Dead right,' Sterlo said. 'And it was during his own son's wake.'

'We got free drinks for that effort,' I said, remembering the flash of lighting above the Terminus.

'He gave me a job a long time back,' the man continued. 'Even with the bad eye he didn't care. Always drought hitting some place or another. Salinity out in the east. Never in Septimus.' He leaned back in his chair. 'Tell you what, boys, for all our moaning about this and that, this is a good place to work. You catch a break in here and you've at least got something regular lined up.'

Sterlo winked at me. 'Yeah, as long as they lift the ban. I'm a day behind now. Two really. Man's made to work. Not just for sitting around.'

'Get us another coffee then,' the joker said, and we all laughed again.

'I promised Mum I'd cut the lawn,' I told the group, and took my leave, shaking Sterlo's hand as I went, then play-acted forgetting something important as I approached the ute. I crossed the street and went into the supermarket, walked up and down the aisles looking at bottles of detergent, tins of dog food and sacks of rice till the woman who ran the place asked me if I needed any help. Stalling, I said, 'I really need some gardening gloves,' even though Mum had a collection of them back home. The woman showed me to the section and I tried every pair on and compared the two styles available. By the time I got out of the store, the café was shutting and Sterlo and his mates had cleared off. No-one left to pin me in a conversation.

Back at the homestead I unlocked the toolshed and pulled out Dad's old push mower. The blades were blunt from years of use, and held a thick quilt of cobwebs. He would do the lawns every Sunday, his only day off. Work with his shirt off no matter the weather and have a beer when it was done. In the summer, he'd listen to the cricket on the radio. In winter he played a tape of The Moody Blues. 'Got to keep the blood pumping,' he told me when I made fun of the music. 'This lawn won't cut itself.'

I looked at my hands, still smooth from officework, and threw the new work gloves aside. The mower squealed as it was dragged over to the lawn in front of the veranda. There the handrail Dad used to help himself up the steps shone in the lowering sun, lighting my face with a warming gleam.

Push by push, line by line, the mower chewed through the grass grown as high as the top of my socks. The world contracted from the town and the paddocks and the creek and the homestead and Holt and Alison and Sterlo and Dad to the swishing, shaving, pushing blades lopping grass. In the cloying heat, my shirt became soaked in sweat. My muscles ached. The spicy tang of cut grass itched in my nose, and I sneezed with happy effort, raking the clippings into neat piles and scooping them into a garden bag. If the spotlights on the veranda still worked I'd have kept going till the dusk extinguished itself. But Mum came outside and announced dinner was ready.

'The shire called, the ban's been lifted,' she added. 'So you've got an early start again.' She made to go, then turned back. 'Looks good.'

'Try not to let it go so long next time,' I joked. She looked at me with an expression more deadpan than the girl in the café.

13

With the weather cooled enough for work, our days went through the motions: strip paddocks, cart the grain to the bunker, smoko, lunch, afternoon tea, work by moonlight with leftover lamb sandwiches wrapped in foil. Agricultural boredom multiplied by the digital clock on the ute's dash. Even the sight of a semitrailer taking a consignment of grain from the bunker was just another tick on the to-do list.

Williamson and Murphy had the best of it. They had to concentrate on the height of the comb as the harvester moved through the wheat, constantly adjusting its height and speed to match the terrain. With such an exacting task, they went deep into the rhythm of work like monks meditating. In between the bursts they smoked and drank caffeine to gird themselves for another casting of their spells.

John was always driving back and forth between picking up grain from the headers and dumping it at the bunker. He was too young to dare show he was bored shitless. Because Sterlo watched everything.

Come sundown, Sterlo said, 'Five paddocks down, five to go,' on the CB, acting the captain. 'But those were the easy ones. Now for the big ones. Odd shapes and angles in a few of them too. If there's any issues with the headers we need them sorted tonight.' He paused to let the unbroadcast groans pass. 'An ounce of sweat saves a gallon of blood, boys. Let's get it done. Tomorrow we can knock off on time. First round's on me.'

'It had better be,' Murphy cut in, his voice a slow drawl. 'This old girl needs an oil change. And that's thirsty work.'

'Grab the oil drum from the shed,' came Sterlo's quick order, and I drove along the homeward track as though it was a rally, threading the tired ute through the bends, headlights painting white pillars on the passing firebreak trees. The lights were bright at home, and as I pulled up into the driveway the kitchen window held Mum in a frame, head in her hands, shaking.

I rushed inside and she said, 'Take off your shoes. I just finished tidying the place.' Her eyes were red, streaked with tears, and the image of the sheep caught in the waterhole's mud leaped up as a prism refracting. I put that out of my mind and sat her down at the kitchen table and got the story out.

Dad had tried to hit her. She said he had a crop fire in his brain, and it would consume everything but the base functions. My mind made an unsaid link – that Mum had copped the basest of them.

'Can you have a night off?' I said, and she quickened with anger.

'For God's sake, it's not about me.'

Stop being a martyr. That's what I wanted to say. Dad's ship was going down and she was determined to meet the waves with him. Couldn't she see there was a bigger world?

'You could get Mrs Chambers to come round and look after him. We could go out and do something. Take your mind off it. I'll speak to Alison about it.'

Mum shook her head. 'Don't get any ideas. I'm still mending the fences. And Alison's got a fella now, you know?'

'We're friends. Nothing more. It's good to see her.'

Mum, like Sterlo, seemed to see everything. 'She's a good girl. You two were nice together. Whenever you were together.'

'One night isn't going to kill him,' I said, changing the subject back. 'Everyone I meet in town is concerned. Offers to help. Take it. For once, just take it. You and me can have a night to ourselves.'

She relented. 'It's not like leaving the dogs with someone.'

'Drug him up,' I joked, and she actually laughed.

'Oh, that's standard. I've been tempted to ask Sterlo to source me some horse tranquilisers.'

'And a dart gun?'

'Yeah, to use on you.'

Inside the fridge she took out a tray of pills and placed a trio of them on a plate. Red, white and blue, with a glass of tap water swirling with lime scale to chase it down. 'Make sure he takes them,' was the only instruction.

'You don't expect me to –'

'Yes. I do. Make sure he takes them.'

Come home. Help with the harvest. Help pack up the house. What use was I shoving pills down my dad's throat? This was her job. 'What if he refuses?'

'Then you make him.'

He was asleep. Skin grey and shining in the half-light streaming from the door. The days were forty plus and the nights not much different, yet he lay under a pile of winter doonas and quilts, his head clasped with pillows. Shaking didn't wake him. Nor did saying his name. So I left the plate and the glass on the bedside table next to a pile of books, all his old favourites, simple stuff like Sherlock Holmes and *The Wind in the Willows*.

Back in the kitchen, empty-handed, I explained Dad's state and excused myself to go get Murphy's oil drum, by then long overdue.

'I'll take care of it,' Mum said wearily, and waved me away.

I held my hands up to protest. She tapped the table. Scraped her chair back. Stood as if she was going to hit me. 'If you can't give Bryce a bloody bit of medicine then you're no good to me.'

I retreated, too late to try the pills again, too late to take anything back.

The only useful thing I could do was go back to the fields. The fellas were working late again. But they would keep. The house was barred to me while Mum cared for Dad behind their closed bedroom door. So I shed my workboots and paced the front lawn, savouring the glassy crunch of freshly mown bull grass blades. Then I lay down and settled into the stillness of dusk. Above, the sudden dip of evening sky. A white fraction of moon. Venus and the early stars.

'She'll calm down soon,' Alby said, lying beside me on the grass like he'd done so many times before. Mum would blow her stack and Dad would send us outside. While their storm thundered we'd kick the footy till we couldn't see it. Some nights we just stayed out and walked into town, cadging sly counter meals at the Terminus when we were underage. If it was warm enough we'd sleep on the lawn, waking in the cool before dawn to sneak back inside.

'He tried to hit her,' I said, and gripped the grass at my sides to stop the earth spinning too fast.

'It's not his fault,' Albert said. 'Mum can take care of herself.'

'That's the trouble. She can't see beyond it.'

My brother sat up, elbows on his knees, looking to the west with sure eyes, that pose he affected in all my memories. 'So show her.'

Wind rushed the treetops. Sticks and nuts scattered across the corrugated roof. I let go of the grass and let go of my brother. All I had to do was give the old man a handful of pills and make him swallow the collection with a sip of water. It was a simple task, one for an apprentice on the tools or a cadet in the office. And I'd fucked it up completely. 'Show her,' I said, making Alby's words my own.

I stood up too quickly. Blood rushed from my skull leaving pricks of light swimming in my vision. When balance returned, I crept back into the darkened homestead, walked automatically to my parents' bedroom door, knocked softly and pushed it open. 'We're going to the restaurant tomorrow, Mum,' I said to the darkness. 'I'll arrange everything.'

Mum switched on her bedside light and sat up. Dad was

snoring beside her. 'You've got an early start,' she said, arranging her pillows so she could read while reclined. She fetched her book from the bedside table, a paperback Agatha Christie, and narrowed her eyes to the task. 'Do your work. Then be home for six.'

I said goodnight, and left it at that. In the kitchen I made a sandwich and sat at the table watching the lights of the header harvesters roam up and down distant paddocks. At the bottom of the horizon the last carmine ebb of the sunset disappeared. The only thing I could do was survive another working day. Beyond it there was so much life left.

14

Pad thai. Green chicken curry. One large plain rice. Spring rolls for starters. Not quite an order, more an obligation. Tina had been running the only Thai restaurant in the district since I was a kid and her menu changed about as much as her banter, delivered in a voice that grew a beard whenever she laughed. 'Come inside. Lovely to see you. Our special tonight is a crispy fried duck with shallots. Killed fresh this morning. Ten per cent off if you find some buckshot, ha-ha.'

We stuck to the classics, uncorked a bottle of barbeque red and admired the silverware, arranged just so. Mum cleared her throat. Harvest. Crops. The weather forecast. Gossip from the town. Mrs de Groot was going to ask for a divorce, and Mrs Hoth was the rumoured reason, though Mum admitted her radar was a bit off of late. The new teacher at the school was very handsome. The student nurses and doctors at the little clinic were duffers. A runaway from the prison near Geraldton had been arrested on a farm in the next district. He'd been caught stealing food from another harvest crew's laager. Could I phone that in to the paper?

'Your father and I had a rule when we had our night off from you kids. We couldn't discuss you at all.' Mum drank her glass down, refilled it, and didn't offer me a top-up. 'Blimey it was hard. One time you kicked me in the shins when I put you to bed. I had to make up a story when he noticed I was limping into the restaurant.'

'What was the penalty? For talking about us?'

She sipped her wine and looked away, a small smile curling the corners of her eyes. 'Tina's a gem, isn't she? Everyone said she was crazy when she opened it up. Who'd go to a farmer's house for Thai food? And the gossip. The whispers. My goodness some of the people around here are narrow in the head.' She raised her glass to me. 'Not like us urban sophisticates. I'm sure you've dined in some pretty exclusive parts of Perth.'

Our glasses clinked, and my hesitation about being in the room and with the people in it vanished. Farmers and their wives. No-one that we knew, or at least knew well. Travellers with caravans seeking something decent away from a portable stove. A man eating solo, reading a book on the Battle of Long Tan that he held to his face like pince-nez.

'I met the mayor of Perth once for a meal at Council House,' I told her. 'It was a dining room on the top floor. Sweeping views of the river. I ordered a saddle of lamb and a waiter served vegetables onto my plate from a silver salver.'

Mum leaned forward as if in a conspiracy. 'What drink did they ply you with? I hope it was something top shelf.'

'Apricot nectar and soda water. I stayed off the booze. You need to keep sharp between the ears.' I snapped my fingers like some old gumshoe. 'The old man knocked back a bottle of French red. Probably expensive. Not like this stuff.'

'Come on now, Rowan. There must be something we can talk about other than work.' Mum made room on the table for the spring rolls, plonked down by a bored waiter with hair hanging over his eyes. 'Why are these things always too hot?' She broke one in half to let it cool on her side plate. 'Any girls?'

'No-one special.' Carol had been. Katherine too. Both reached the three-month mark – the deadline of making or breaking a habit.

'That's you all over, Rowan. You do live a charmed life.'

'Napoleon said, "Give me lucky generals."' I broke a spring roll in half and chewed a piece – far too hot. 'Long hours. Crap wages. Yes, I'm very fortunate.'

Mum laughed. 'You sound like your father.' I refilled the glasses and we ate the rolls in amused silence, blowing on them and chewing daintily, grinning at each other's careful dissections. The rough little fingers of chicken and vegetables and pastry had been homemade, like everything at Tina's, from the hand-stitched curtains to the lacquered tables crossed with white strips of filigreed fabric. This was her home, and she shared it easily, welcoming everyone and charging almost outrageously for the pleasure. Maybe Brockman's Place could be turned into a rustic restaurant. The notion vanished as Tina brought the mains to the table herself, balancing the platters on one arm as though she were a painter before an easel.

'One green chicken curry, one pad thai and one plain rice. I put some of the duck on the side so you can try.' She set it all down, clinking and clanking, and we took a serve of each, passing the spoons and plates between us till we each had a medley of vibrant intensity steaming high.

'We should be drinking white with this.' The remains of the bottle went into Mum's glass. 'It goes better with spicy food.'

'You know I prefer red.' She swirled the wine, held it to the dim mood lights and made a regal face. 'Interesting colour. And the nose is quite deep. Overall a nice little drop. Cellar for ten years I'd say.'

'Are you becoming a snob?'

'I watch Keith Floyd. The TV chef.' She put on a regal voice to match her poised face. 'A bit of wine in the food, and also some for me.' She quaffed like a bulldog, and that did it. We howled with laughter, drawing askance looks from all the other diners. We didn't care. That warmth, that sudden flowering of feeling, it glowed between us as though a chandelier had appeared above our plates.

'I'll update the will, in case you're wondering,' she said, changing from light to shade. 'You'll inherit the lot when I go.'

That was unexpected. She'd never mentioned money much. As far as inheritance went, I figured I could make my own money. It had never crossed my mind. So I laughed at her little joke, probably unconvincingly.

'The place is worth a few million,' she continued. 'The house is worthless. But the land is prime. Septimus is always top of the leader board in the grain count. And people pay for that...' She searched for a word. 'Reliability. Do you have any more wine?'

'I only brought one.'

'Pity. I'm just getting warmed up.' She called Tina over and asked her to open one from her own stocks, stepped-on price and all. A great flourish was made of uncorking and pouring, and though I smelled and tasted and pronounced it good, I hadn't the gall to say it was corked. The thing was to keep Mum drinking, keep Mum happy, keep Mum talking.

'And who knows?' she continued, her words twisting between gallows and humour. 'Your dad could die quick and the butcher's bill will be halved.' She drank down her glass and refilled it, sniffed the air as if about to sneeze, and her eyes glowed wet. 'He's always been a gentleman about things.' My throat thickened. The room pressed inward. She controlled it away. 'Not a bad drop. Shall we order some dessert?'

We debated the merits of fried ice-cream and homemade crème brûlée. Ordered one of each. Praised Tina's wine. Said a few passing hellos to the diners that Mum came to recognise. In a swift efficiency the bill was presented and paid and we were under the cool stars swirling with a pleasant drunkenness that would remain hidden from the local coppers by driving stealthily back to Brockman's Place.

Turning onto a back road, in the reflection on the inside of Mum's window, I could see her eyes shining with tears.

'You had a good time, right? Did I say something?'

'Sorry, Ro. I guess I just feel a bit guilty. Having a good time is hard. Before you say anything, I know. Just leave it.'

The radio in her station wagon worked just fine, switched to a city FM station scratchy enough to still be heard. Soft and bluesy. The smoke of a pool hall, secrets and glasses of neat whisky clouded with fingerprints. I wished I were drunker. Let the quiet river of her grief slide away dark and hidden through the dazzle of rock chips in the windshield.

When we got to the turn-off for the driveway, Mum ordered me to kill the headlights as we crossed the cattle gate, and I pulled over just before the tunnel of pines. The air was thick with harvest dust that made the world seem as though it was drawn in chalk, softening the shadows. She flipped her sun visor down and looked at herself in the mirror, aided by matte white moonlight coming through the windows.

'Best foot forward,' she said. 'Back to work then.'

I kept my eyes firmly on the track, concentrating hard, though I knew every curve and bump and could have done it blindfolded. As we approached the homestead Mum blew her nose and kissed herself a new layer of lipstick. She couldn't do much about the smudges of mascara, so she told Mrs Chambers, 'Not to worry, tears of laughter. He told me how much they're paying him.'

15

The heat came. True heat. The kind it was impolite to remark upon in passing. 'When will this end?' was about all you could get away with. The forecast stretched out north of forty degrees till the end of its measure. There was no wind. No easterly from the desert, no sea breeze from the west. Nothing that could fan any flames. So the shire couldn't halt the harvest. Not without a fight from a heat-crazed Sterlo.

At night it was remorselessly still. Sweating in my sheets, I thirsted for Alison, for the Indian Ocean down in Scarborough, imagining those cold rollers hissing in the low-tide shallows with glowing white foam lit by the spotlights of the surf club. Night after night I'd imagine a dark line rising from out the back and swim hard in the black sea, naked with her, both of us making for the crash zone where we'd dive under just in time, shouting water swooping over our spines as we collapsed under the hand of the moon's gravity. Up, up, up till we could breathe, make angels of our bodies on the surface, stars hanging fire in a sky made grey by the loom of city lights.

Sterlo had stopped being my alarm clock. He just expected me to be up and ready to work. So every workday I'd get up before the sun and eat a cold breakfast of Weet-Bix and chopped banana on the veranda. I'd drink glasses of water and mugs of coffee and still have no need to pee. As if to ramp up the weather, one morning Mum came outside and flung a work shirt at me – long-sleeved and thick, perfect for sun protection, murder for the heat.

'I packed up the sewing room already, so it's got some alterations I had to do best I could.' I unfolded the long-sleeved King Gee and saw a nut and bolt holding the middle button and eye together. She yawned as I put it on. I squeezed my nose past the metal pinch in the centre.

'Just like new,' I said. 'You know how much stick I'd cop if you ironed those pleats again?'

'It's a lost art. You should be grateful.'

'Made me look like a bloody newbie.'

Mum frowned, made a mocking face. 'Until you lose an eye fencing or have a thumb ripped off in an auger or roll a ute drunk and kill two of your mates then you'll never be an old hand.' She patted her sternum. 'I've been here what? Thirty years. I'm still some blow-in from the city.'

She went to the kitchen, poured herself a coffee and came back out, picking up where she'd left off.

'Not that I ever cared what they said. Let them talk. They'll be talking now. Oh, Mrs Brockman, I'm so sorry for what's happening. What will you do with the farm? A shame to sell it. A real shame. A shame you're a coward abandoning the land and chucking out all the noble sacrifices our noble, sacrificial ancestors made for us so that we may benefit forever and ever, amen. A real shame to give that up. I can't imagine how you're feeling. Do let me know if there's anything I can do.'

She was silent then, as if she'd emptied her lungs completely. I followed her back to the kitchen where in a steady production she made a big box of sandwiches and packed them into an esky, and boiled up enough espresso in a Moka pot to make ice coffee with, filling three flasks with the cold brew and condensed milk. While she worked I washed up the breakfast dishes with hot water straight from the cold tap. I swear it took five minutes till anything even resembling cold spat out the faucet. The pipes went deep underground, but so did the heat – Septimus was just a thin layer of topsoil on a bed of solid rock, an enormous radiator that Dad reckoned held temperatures old as the earth, working their way up through the shingles like lost waves patrolling some faraway ocean.

Chores done, we refilled our coffee cups and sat together at the kitchen table, both of us looking out over the early-morning land, muffled in blue light. 'It's going to be another scorcher,' I said, obviously. 'You can feel it. Even before the sun's up you can feel it.'

'It gets hot in here too. And only your dad gets the fan on him. Nothing for poor old me.' Mum held her coffee to her nose and let steam rise to her forehead. 'At least it's a bit cooler in the mornings. I've half a mind to get up even earlier. The days are getting longer anyway. It was so hot one year we did the harvesting at night. Started at four in the afternoon and went straight through till midnight. Then we set up long tables and served a dinner. Ice-cold beers. Rum punch. That was a good way to do it.'

'Why don't we do that again?'

She counted on her fingers. 'Insurance. Occupational Health and Safety. I can't be bothered staying up late.'

'Or getting air conditioning.'

'Toughen up. Officework's ruined you. Your great-great-grandfather didn't need air conditioning.'

'Yes he did. He just couldn't go to the shops and buy one. If he were alive today he'd have air conditioning in every single room of the house. Even in the toilet. Especially the toilet.'

Mum shook her head, eternally patient. 'The day I succumb to the air conditioner is the day I get a dishwasher. The good Lord gave you hands to wash with and sweat to cool with.'

I laughed. 'Did you practise that?'

'Of course. What else do I have to do around here?'

The sun came to light up thin streamers of clouds laddering the edge of our world. Like a great conductor's baton, the rising light summoned the tick, tick, ticking of a million and more insects, playing a layer of white noise that hummed through everything from the fillings in my teeth to the clicks of the living-room clock. My mind conjured locusts chewing the wheat and swarming the homestead, eating whatever they could to fill their hunger – oats in the pantry, rubbish in the bin, memories and time itself till there was nothing but a summer without Dad and a summer without Alby, Mum's station wagon driving through their bodies with a sound like fat drops of rain on the roof.

Right on time, Sterlo's ute drove up the driveway with headlights shining clear. I drank my coffee down, gave Mum a kiss and slipped on my workboots.

'Good morning, good morning, good morning,' Sterlo said, thumping across the veranda. 'When will this end? I never thought I'd say it. I'm hoping for another harvest ban. As long as there's no wind they'll keep us toiling though.' Mum asked him to stay for a coffee but he insisted on having it to go. 'No time to waste today, Justine. We're tackling the big paddocks. How is your packing going?'

'Steady,' Mum answered wearily. 'I'm a bit like you. I've done the small rooms. Now I've got to tackle the major ones.'

'Bit harder than what we're doing, I imagine.' Sterlo opened the screen door and looked around the place inside, taking in all the packing boxes and piles of junk ready for sorting. I saw what he saw, or imagined I did: the kitchen table where we'd hold Christmas lunch with the family and all the waifs and strays we knew, the living room where he and Dad would watch the Ashes, the kitchen and veranda that got such a thrashing whenever Mum held a party for a birthday or just for the hell of it.

'Let's get cracking,' I said. 'Time and tide wait for no man.'

Sterlo considered that. 'Suppose so.' He threw me the keys to his ute. 'You can drive then. I want to savour your mum's coffee. She brews it like no other.' They nodded to each other, telegraphs passing through a wire.

Out in the paddocks the temperature hit its maximum with the barest shove of sun. Parked under the shade tree of the laager, I checked my reflection in the ute's visor and rubbed dry white spittle from my lips. It was too hot to sweat. Too hot to move. But Williamson, Murphy and Young John were sat in a half circle of chairs by the embers of the fire pit, sipping scalding mugs of black tea with the sun blazing on their shoulders.

'Wonderful, wonderful stuff,' Williamson said, shaking himself like a man come in from the cold. 'This is nothing compared to Marble Bar. You know they hold the world record for consecutive days above a hundred degrees? That's the old Fahrenheit measure. A hundred days in a row. Imagine that.'

'Bloody paradise,' Murphy agreed.

'All well and good for you two,' Sterlo barked. 'You've got aircon cranked all bloody day in those headers.'

'Need to keep the instruments cool,' Murphy said, winking at me. 'And the beers. We brought a few sixpacks for later.'

'Later,' Sterlo agreed. 'Definitely for later. But for now.' He spread a map on a fold-out table arranged just so. 'These are the remaining paddocks. And they are whales. Worth two of the previous we've tackled apiece. It's going to be too much bother for us to do both sides simultaneously. So I'll need you blokes to strip side by side, with one of you staggered back so the other can overlap. Got it?'

I tuned out. Let them discuss the finer points of this formation flying. I was more interested in catching the news bulletin on the ute radio, so I walked over and hopped in to switch it on. Waterfalls of static rushed from the speakers. 6PR came in too quiet, local radio was too irrelevant, so I settled the dial on the ABC and its plummy-toned announcer who ran through the day's agenda: government corruption, new plans for the freeway, the progress of the America's Cup preparations, a shooting in the suburbs. No-one dead, so I hadn't missed anything. The rest was just a glossolalia of sport and economics and weather patterns, hot conditions over the Mid West and Gascoyne regions with no relief on the radar.

I played with the nut and bolt Mum had repaired my shirt with, twisting the metal pieces back and forth on their thread as if tuning in another radio. We were halfway done. In the paddocks and the house. All that was left to do was slog the rest of the way through, wiping sweat from our brows and enduring heat of a kind I would likely never feel again.

That was the forecast. Then the CB radio crackled.

'Sterlo, Sterlo pick up, it's Holding. Are you there? Over?'

I stuck fingers in my mouth and whistled like Albert had taught me. Sterlo spun to the sound and I waved him over, the others following, a sixth sense telling them something was up. He leaned in the cab, pulled out the handset and keyed his answer.

'Sterlo here, Michael. What's happening mate? Hot enough for you? Over.'

The reply hissed blankly. What sounded like laughing cut through. Then we realised. He was crying. 'They've taken them. They've got in and ruined the whole lot of them. All of them.'

Sterlo chucked the radio rules away. 'You listen, Michael. Tell me what's happened. Right bloody now. Who's taken what?'

'Dogs. They've hacked up the rams.'

Sterlo tapped his fist on the ute's roof. 'Shit. This is no good.' He leaned in and started the engine. 'Get on boys. We've got some business.'

16

We collected our tools from the homestead shed. Like a formal dance, we all knew the steps. Murphy and Williamson and John grabbed shovels and axes. I unlocked the gun cabinet and took out the shotguns and .22s. Sterlo got the over-and-under Beretta. The others got the bolt actions. As we loaded them with shells and cartridges, the weight of the pump action assured me we were doing the right thing.

'Keep those safeties on,' Sterlo barked. 'And hold them out of sight. I can't take a back road. Cops see us with these there'll be fines galore.'

I sat in the ute cab and the others rode in the tray. Sterlo could have driven flat out, yet he handled the truck like it was a Sunday outing. He even waved to a constable smoking outside the cop shop in the centre of town. 'Your mum said you're writing an article about the harvest,' he said, his voice switching from neutral to war. 'Don't put this in. People won't understand.'

An ancient wrought-iron gate that looked as though it was made from welded-together bedsteads hemmed the driveway of Holding's place. It swung greasily to reveal a swathe of fallow paddocks given over to grass and brambles and shocking purple thickets of Paterson's Curse, the invasive weed tourists often mistook for a wildflower. Holding was the only farmer in the shire not to grow wheat. Instead he ran sheep, and only sheep, and had a double-length cattle grid that rattled the ute's suspension against our bones as we crossed its ramble. Sterlo parked beside the simple homestead and when the engine cut out the silence of the place wrapped us completely till a low bleating came from somewhere.

We found Holding in the back shed. He was sitting on the concrete slab surrounded by bloated white bags streaked with red. Twelve merino rams with their scrotums torn open, testicles spilled, exposed as tumbles of wire around a smooth egg. A few were still alive, with swollen tongues lolling from their mouths. Whatever their vitals they were all useless now.

'I found them like this in the top paddock,' Holding said, patting the reddened wool of one of the dead rams. His voice was calm and even, a strange contrast to the shock written on his face. 'Dragged them back here one by one.'

Click. Clack. The break action of Sterlo's shotgun swivelled open. He took two shells from the barrels and replaced them with two more from his pocket, a little ritual perhaps to calm his nerves. 'We'll get them. They'll be going after others if we don't.'

'A hundred thousand dollars,' Holding said, looking over his flock. 'A hundred thousand dollars. Ten years. Ten bloody years.' Tears swelled on his cheeks. As we split up into two hunting groups I quelled the urge to ask him why, if they were so valuable, didn't he have a guard dog?

Sterlo and I took the bottom paddocks and the others took the topmost. No order was given, we all knew the words: shoot on sight and shoot to kill. The wild dogs wouldn't have gotten too far. He led the way down access tracks that skirted the wide fields of grass gone brown and dry. The sun had reached its zenith so we cast no shadows. The ticking and clicking of locusts and cicadas masked the crunching of our boots on loose soil and rocks. I felt part of the landscape. Baked into it. A dusted and unforgiving animal with a shotgun cradled under one arm, the other wiping sweat and shielding eyes against the glare.

'They'll be at the dam,' Sterlo said. 'They'll be red as the devil and playing in the water.'

Holding's place bisected a creek just like our place, only his was fed by an underground aquifer that kept it trickling almost right the year round, independent of the district catchment. If he grew crops instead of tinkering with sheep he could irrigate his land rather than wait for rain. Some men do it differently. Even when the cards they're dealt are ones others would kill for.

'How much time is this costing us?' I asked, making conversation. Sterlo stopped and jabbed a finger into my chest.

'As much time as it bloody well takes. You don't quibble when a mate asks you for help.'

'I didn't mean anything by it,' I said, stepping away.

'Your dad would do the same as me. Exactly the same.'

He went to say more. Stopped himself. Just pulled his hat tighter down on his forehead and walked off again, giving me his back to follow.

We found their tracks close to the dam. Two dogs. Dabs of blood and saliva streaked a tunnel through the long dry grass, and then met up with a trail of paw prints leading to the water. At a signal from Sterlo I checked my shotgun over, racked the slide back and forward to load a shell into the chamber and pressed the safety button to the firing position. I did these things automatically, pressing my own feelings of protest far down. It was a job to do. And in a skirmish line we approached the rammed-earth walls of the dam, which held all that water beneath the shade of weeping willows.

Two dogs slept in the slanted sun. Just as Sterlo had predicted. Streaked with blood and dirt. 'I'll fire left,' he whispered. 'You fire right. Then work your way in.'

We crept closer. A few metres away I raised the barrel. The iron sight piked a sleeping head.

'Wait.' It was impossible. I couldn't do it. 'Wait.'

'No,' Sterlo whispered. 'It's okay. I'll do it.'

He pulled the trigger. Straddled the bodies with a rain of buckshot that kicked up geysers of water in the dam behind. He pulled the trigger again to make sure. Then he dropped his empty gun, took mine from my grip and pumped another shot across the red ruin. I couldn't hear a thing. Then as if the sound of a movie was on mute, I watched Sterlo take a pocketknife and cut collars from the ruined dogs. He handed me two leather straps with gold engraved discs.

One said *Lillee*. The other read *Bradman*.

Holding thanked us profusely. Sterlo told him the dogs were truly wild – not someone's farm dogs run amok – which made the old sheep-breeder feel righteous as the victim of misfortune rather than someone's neglect. The others came back full of questions about the gunshots they'd heard as dry snaps of champagne corks, the sounds of celebration.

I wanted to vomit. They were good dogs. Lillee and Bradman. Our dogs. Loyal and stupid and full of love. How could they have done that? I shunted those thoughts aside and told Holding of Sterlo's heroics. How he'd led the hunt and pulled the trigger without hesitating.

As I spoke, Sterlo wouldn't look at me, as though horrified by the mask I'd pulled over my face. He had saved my family from shame. From paying out a hundred thousand dollars. Perhaps more in lost income proved in affidavits and testimony in the courts. Whose fault was it? The Chambers were looking after the dogs. They were ours at the end of all of it. Mum's responsibility. Mine. They were family pets that cadged scraps from the dinner table and hunted rats in the toolshed. What had made them do that?

We offered to help bury the dead sheep, but Holding refused. The ones still alive were too badly injured to survive. He wanted privacy to extinguish their lives. We paid our respects, said our goodbyes, and Sterlo drove us away, talking to himself. My forehead burned as I filled in the gaps, imagining what he was saying with fears I held to be true.

Bloody useless good-for-nothing city-dwelling arsehole holier-than-thou pleated-trouser soft cock. Can't even shoot his dogs

when they've gone berserk. Leaving me to do the goddamned
dirty work.

We got back to the shade tree with a whole afternoon of work ahead of us. Again we were all silent, all knowing the moves, what had to be done.

Just before the engines were fired up I took a piss against the tree, and followed the course of my slash down the bark and across the roots till it settled black and shining in the topsoil. It looked like blood. I saw Lillee and Bradman again. Their bodies torn apart, jaws shot off, eyes smashed and tongues shredded. If we didn't do it, someone else would. I put a hand in my pocket and touched the collars with the dogs' names engraved on brass discs.

Another secret for a place composted with them.

17

Dry blood congealed in my palms as warm water from the garden tap jetted through my fingers. I went over the story, again and again, lest I tell Mum the truth. I settled on a version that could be taken as rote – Lillee and Bradman wandered from the Chambers' place and got hit by a passing road train.

'Stupid bloody dogs,' she ruled as I handed her their cleaned collars. 'They were always roaming around, weren't they?' She took a deep breath, balled her fists, and changed the subject. 'I can't be bothered cooking tonight. Cold meat and salad?'

Meat. Blood. Bone. 'How was Dad today?'

Mum sighed. Wet a sponge. Wiped down the kitchen counter. 'He's alright. Asleep. So you missed the fun.' She wiped in circles, clockwise, then counterclockwise, over and over. 'He was a pain in the arse. A real pain in the arse, you know?' She ran the tap and wrung the sponge under it. 'How was Holding?'

'Upset. He loved those sheep. The wild dogs we killed were real mongrels. Maybe ours saw them and tried to follow them.'

Mum shrugged. 'We'll never know. I was going to see if someone in the district could take them when we left.' She held their identity discs up to the overhead light – two more items to pack or discard. 'In the scheme of things, it's a mercy.'

My body felt bruised all over. I slumped into a chair at the kitchen table and held my head. Not even two weeks had passed, and I felt a year removed from a desk at the paper, from my shitty flat at Scarborough, from the cooling ocean that washed away every nerve of feeling after every shift.

'I'll go to the Chambers. Tell them what happened.'

Mum picked up the phone and dialled. 'I can just call them. I'd say they already know from the bush telegraph. In fact, I'm surprised they haven't called already.' She listened to the receiver a while and hung up. 'No answer.'

'I'll go around and see them after dinner.'

'Go now if you like. I've changed my mind. I'll do pasta with sage and burnt butter. My sage has come up nicely in the heat.'

I grabbed the keys to the ute and gave her a kiss, and she pulled me in for a hug. Held it a second too long and ruffled the back of my head. 'They were good dogs. Your father loved them. Idiots though they were.'

The ute revved its guttural voice as I swung her onto the highway for the quick run to Alison's. I let the turn-off pass and gunned the speedo till it hit a hundred and the high beams cleaved a channel through the wheat, the windscreen harvesting bugs, their bodies making a phosphorescent wake across the black tarmac. Hands tight on the wheel, the straight road rushed under the tyres for kilometre after kilometre after mile after mile after hectare after hectare. Direction easting, further inland where salt lakes digest the topsoil. *Fuck this place.* Thoughts thundered. *Fuck it. Fuck all of it.*

Killing the dogs was the right thing to do. So shoot them once, shoot them twice, shoot them a third to make sure, make the grass grow with the blood of blighters that had licked up my scraps under the dinner table and guarded the front door without fail. That was the fate of us. Sell the house and bulldoze the grounds. Make it like it never existed. Let Dad fade away in some hospital bed. I'd go back to work. Mum would live on the coast. And we'd try to forget our job lot of unpleasant tasks.

I wound my window down and screamed, sending the yell into the rushing air, roaring rubber, revving engine.

Beyond the town, the pub, or the paddocks, there was only one place I wanted to go, and it drew me back along the highway with magnetic fascination, back to within striking distance of our homestead, next door at the Chambers' place. Theirs was just like ours, an island of lamps shining in windows, colonial and majestic, held together with fading paint and shadows. When I knocked on the door, Alison answered, her eyes two flames in the cold veranda light.

'I heard about the dogs. I'm so sorry. I don't know how they got out –'

'They were old. It was their time.'

'Hit by cars?'

'A road train. Not much left of them but the collars.'

'That's terrible. I'm really sorry.' She lowered her voice. 'Shame about Holding's sheep.'

'Yeah. Worth a fair bit, he said. He was pretty broken up.'

'Well, you would be.'

A train moved along somewhere, rocks rolling in a river. And there, caught on the landing between her world and mine, all the pressure that had built in my skull drained out in a single smooth motion. I didn't have to pretend with her. 'Want to go for another walk? It's a nice night.'

'That's pretty corny.' She shut the screen door behind her. 'You were always such a dork.'

'You dated me. So what does that make you?'

She punched me on the arm. 'Foolish. Lead the way.'

Our feet crunched the driveway, muffled the grass and slid down on the riverbed's fine powder dust. The moon was far down, just a sliver of silver on the low sky. I looked up and breathed in the Southern Cross, and there was the False Cross, the lines of the constellation a lookalike that could steer you astray. Down in the dry river hollow all the light skidding the blackness of the flatlands was gone. My hands found hers and I pulled her close and kissed her mouth, fingers through her hair, swishes of calligraphy over her hips and the dimples of her back. Words bubbled up – I need you, I want you, stay with me, take me away. I kept them quiet and kissed her and lay her down on a shiver of dry grass on the riverbank where we shed our clothes and felt the warm night air coating our skins as we rubbed friction chest to chest and hip to hip till we unravelled a million miles away.

We fell asleep for a while, and then woke with sudden gusts rushing through the trees above. We dressed and climbed back up to the flat land where the wind shook the wheat in undulating rows of worship. The veranda lights of the Chambers' home and Brockman's Place burned to the north and south with us in between. I kissed her on the forehead, tasting sweet sweat.

'I needed that,' I said.

She punched me on the arm. 'Still a dork.'

'We're behind schedule again. It's going to be hammer and tongs from now on. I don't know when I can see you next.'

She sighed. 'I'm not in love with you. Not anymore.' Her head went to my chest, her hands to my back. 'This is just the harvest. Your last one.'

She would have heard my heart accelerate. 'Why didn't you tell me about your boyfriend? I'd have kept away.'

She shook her head. 'No. You wouldn't have. You think I'm yours to save. That's what you used to do when you came back from school. Only you never took me with you. I was never part of the plan.'

'Did you want to be?'

'Sometimes. When I couldn't think of anything better to do.' She took my hands in hers. 'I love coming back here. My life is down south now. But my home is here. That's what I don't get about you. It's not about you. It hasn't been for a long time.'

'You wouldn't understand –'

She lifted her head. 'Because I'm a girl? Not in a line of succession to take over?' She grabbed my face and shook it side to side. 'Stop complicating things. Just do the work. Help your mum. It's a straight road.'

We walked to the flat land on her side of the creek. I wanted to say something definite to her, something that would explain the knots in my heart. 'What are you doing tomorrow?' was all I could think of.

'The usual. Help Mum. I might even go drive the chaser bin for a while. Much easier than driving the header.'

'You'd be good at that.'

'Steady hands,' she smiled, and put them around my neck. 'This is a dream. We'll wake up soon. And you'll be gone. It's going to be weird coming here and not having you for a neighbour. Seeing some new family in your homestead.'

'Don't worry. Whoever buys the place is just keen on the land. They'll knock it down. Or let it rot.'

No kiss. No hug. We just went our ways. I steered myself to our veranda where moths revolved around the bulb. The darkness flicked when I switched it off and sat on the edge of the deck. In the distance the light on Alison's veranda switched off too.

'Shit, I've left the ute there,' I said, and laughed. I'd just have to get it in the morning. And maybe get to see her again.

18

No such luck. Alison was up and gone with her work crew by the time I walked over. So the rise and fall of the sun bookended another hot and hurried day for the Brockman's Place mob as we made up for lost time. The line of our advance moved ever closer to the homestead. It cost us more time to drive back to the shade tree for breaks, and more and more fuel for the chaser bin to dump its loads at the grain bunker and come back for more. We ate on the go at all times, with Dad's ute becoming a constant delivery wagon for sandwiches and drinks as well as jerry cans of fuel and tools and oil.

When the ABC news theme blared from our CB radios at seven o'clock we knew Sterlo was calling it a day.

'Thirsty work, fellas,' he said, and drove around to each of our vehicles so we could pile inside his and drive to the pub. I sat in the tray with the boys instead of taking the seat in the cab. A shiver came suddenly.

'Kind of like getting out of the sea on a hot day,' Murphy said. 'Even if the water's warm, you still feel cold.'

Sweat cooled on our backs as Sterlo drove the five kilometres to town. More utes piled with workers drove ahead and behind us on the grid straight road. We all seemed to have the same idea as if by intuition. At the Terminus, the car park was full, so we stopped on the grass paddock behind it. The old pub's veranda was festooned with coloured light bulbs, mixing a palette of orange, green, red and yellow. As we crossed the threshold, I imagined they were a sunset, and found the night inside.

'Fellas, good work today,' Sterlo began, sitting on a bar stool so his bulk was on our level. 'John, you're becoming an expert.' He clinked glasses with the young bloke from Mingenew, who grinned with pride. 'Murphy and Williamson, you haven't stuffed up yet, so keep that up.' They clinked and laughed, old friends beyond compliments, and he turned to me. 'Nice and steady, mate. Nice and steady.' I clinked cautiously, and we all drank half our beers down.

I should have taken him aside. Had a word to straighten things out. But what word? 'Thanks' – that was impossible. Not for a bloke like Sterlo. He was younger than my father, yet definitely of that generation, whose pride in deprivation made them curious bundles of nerves. Like the coppers down in Perth; for all their toughness they were sensitive as stubbed toes.

He didn't need reminding of doing my dirty work. So I bought a second round and spun along with the merry-go-round of our conversation. Cricket. Rugby. Paul Keating in question time. The danger of Labor. The heartlessness of the Libs. The incompetence of the Nationals. Round and round it went – blokey talk of nothing in particular. More men from the fields came in and the circle widened and the noise increased to compete with the usual Cold Chisel tunes thumping from the speakers in the ceiling.

'Me missus was saying the yachts have started arriving,' Murphy said, and we all looked at him with confusion. 'The yachts. You know? For the America's Cup. Down in Fremantle. They've started practising.' I had completely forgotten. And in a flash, I saw Holt drumming his fingers on that great desk of his, crossing off items on a to-do list with my name next in the queue, his eyes darting to the subs desk where he'd threatened to bury me.

'I don't know the front end from the back,' Williamson said. 'When that little white pointer crossed the line I fair jumped through the roof.'

John chipped in. 'Stayed up with Mum and all the cousins

and uncles and we had a party that morning. Got to skip school.'

Sterlo put on his best Bob Hawke voice. 'Any boss that sacks a worker for not turning up today is a bum.'

Everyone laughed, but I kept quiet, watching for my chance to talk to Sterlo, and when he ducked out for a cigarette on the veranda I followed him to the darkened decking where the silence of the land could be heard.

'Plenty of fresh air out here,' he said, exhaling a gust of grey. 'Jeez we talk a lot of shit, don't we?'

'I thought that was the point.' I cadged one of his smokes. 'What else are we supposed to say?'

'Back in my day we did bush poems. You know? Like Banjo Paterson or Henry Lawson. Blokes would just make them up on the spot. Compete with each other to get the biggest cheers. And we'd play two-up. Right there at the bar.' He pointed through the greasy windowed doors. 'No-one would say anything. Not even the coppers. They had a go too. They were good at it.'

I laughed and shook my head. 'So I missed the glory days.'

'You sure did. But every old fella says something like that.' He was sharper than I gave him credit for. I think he knew when to remind me of it.

'Forget about the dogs,' he said. 'That was duty.' I acted dumb, and he waved it away. 'I can read you like a book. Don't worry about it. It was just something that had to be done.'

'That should be my family's motto,' I said, and we both laughed.

'Your dad always said "Better to ask forgiveness than permission". That's a better saying to live by.'

He flicked the red end of his smoke into the darkness, clapped me on the back and went inside, the arc of the door letting out a gust of raucous noise. I stayed out there awhile, looking up at the stars and the light bulbs burning on homestead doors spread through the district. I was about to sneak off home when the door swung again and Sterlo called to me.

'Come on back inside, professor. The old times are returning.'

There were women in the pub. Their presence triggered the sucking in of stomachs, the straightening of backs and louder voices at the bar to usher in the monthly pub meal get-together of the Country Women's Association – the CWA. The real bosses of the country.

'They're done with the formalities,' Sterlo grinned. 'I love these old ducks. They're great value. Just watch your swearing around them.'

A silver-haired woman stood apart at the bar playing her long red nails on the counter as the barman prepped a battery of shandies and pints and white wines with chipped ice. She turned and I saw it was Mrs Chambers.

'I thought you were Alison for a moment,' I said, all charm. 'Where's she tonight?'

She looked me up and down and lodged her tongue behind her teeth. 'Tucked up. Safe in bed. Where she should be.'

The barman slid her drinks order over on a tray. She thanked and paid and went to balance the load but I beat her to it. 'Where are you all sitting?'

'In the farthest, darkest corner away from all these Neanderthals.' Not a joke. She led the way through the crowd, which parted for her easily; the Neanderthals had good enough manners, and gave me winks and sly looks as I followed in her wake. A table was choked with the merry women of the shire, all practical hair, workboots and jeans, women who could cut you to the bone and make soup with it. I set the drinks tray down and said a polite hello, which was returned with polite questions, polite smiles, and a polite inference that I should bugger off.

'Tell your mother I'll come around tomorrow and give her a hand,' Mrs Chambers said. 'I expect she needs it. Sorry about the dogs.' She squeezed my arm. 'These things happen.'

I nodded thanks and strode off, shoulders squared, feeling a bit ridiculous. Back at the bar the boys slid me another glass of beer and I blathered along as best I could. Sterlo caught my eye and raised his glass. I raised mine. The big man cleared his throat.

'All along the railway line the riders came ariding.
And at dusk of every day they camped along the siding.
To war, to war, to war, they cried, Mother England's calling.
So down to Perth, join the Light Horse, we ride hard in the
    morning.
How many came back from that dusty track? The one that
    led to war.
They disappeared, never came back, said nothing evermore.
The railway line became a scar and the sidings a mausoleum.
But we remember the horses' hooves forever, galloping
    without fear.'

The chatter of the pub resumed. The blaring music had never faltered. For a minute Sterlo held court, his poem a breeze on our skins, a relic from another age.

'I made that up myself,' he beamed, and took a few handshakes. Even Mrs Chambers had listened, smiling at us Neanderthals from her table.

'Anyone got a reply?' Sterlo asked. No-one did. He raised his glass again, catching light in the liquid.

19

Late in the working morning, Mum called me on the CB and asked if I'd swing by the house. I asked her what for, she wouldn't say, so I promised the boys I'd bring back biscuits and left them to their drudgery.

'Take however much time you need, mate,' Sterlo said, labouring a point he'd made so often. 'You don't always have to be out here with us, you know?'

The homestead was as quiet as my arrival those short weeks ago. Shirts and sheets semaphored from the washing line. The windows were darkly reflective. As I tacked across the driveway and went up the veranda stairs, I gripped the new handrail that helped Dad's step, bolted tight, permanent as the chimney.

'Get inside,' Mum hissed, materialising at the top of the stairs. She lunged back through the flyscreen door and let it slam behind her.

In the kitchen she paced up and down, sweat plastering flicks of hair to her forehead. 'He can't have gotten far,' she said, words tumbling and rasping. 'Not at his age. Not in his condition. Not in this heat. He can't have gotten far.'

In the master bedroom the blackout curtains were drawn tight. A greasy odour cut with bleach and lavender hung thick. I sat on Dad's side of the bed and saw the world as he would: bedside table, books, a lamp casting its glow onto the wall where a framed print of Hans Heysen's *Droving into the Light* held a man on horseback, upright in the saddle, herding cows into the sunset.

Heat. Work. Dogs. Now this. Anger burned in my throat. I wanted to scream again, let it out and bash around the house thumping the walls. The rotting of my Dad's speech had left him a mix of dumb and verbose – could he explain himself if I found him? If I called out his name, would he even know it?

Back in the kitchen with Mum, the ticking of the dining room clock thudded with my pulse in counterpoint. Cartoonish scenarios rolled through my mind: Dad wandering in front of road trains, getting stuck in the mud at a waterhole, straying into the path of a thresher.

'Get on the CB and call for help,' I ordered. Mum folded her arms.

'I don't want a fuss,' she whispered. 'It's enough of a burden.'

'Everyone will want to help.'

'This is our problem,' she yelled. 'Yours. Mine. Our problem. We'll deal with it. The Brockmans.' Her words were a sudden storm. 'Search the garden and the top paddock and the creek and everything else within striking distance of the house.' She grabbed the keys to her station wagon and jangled them like a jailer. 'I'll do the eastern half. You do the western. Meet me back here in half an hour. He can't have gone far.'

As I went to go, Mum stilled me with a raised hand. 'I thought about your brother today for a long time.' She pointed to the screen door. 'I was standing right there, just at the door. I remembered everything about him. Everything.' Her voice quivered. 'And then I felt arms wrap around me. How do you explain that?'

I couldn't. There was no time to dawdle. I shoved through the screen door and left it banging on the frame.

There was no sign of Dad having passed through the dry creek bed. Just footprints from me and Alison and the scuffling marks of kangaroos. From there I could see the lay of the land rise gradually to the top of the property, with all the paddocks on one side of the highway neatly shorn. In the light of midday, the earth looked ironed flat, but it was coursed with shallow troughs that could hide a man from view even twenty feet from the edge of the homestead's front garden.

Standing in the dry creek, I remembered a story I did for the paper on an offshore sailing race, riding along on a boat to get the inside details. As the yacht surged through midnight waves off Fremantle, the skipper had grabbed me by the harness and hissed, 'Don't fall off, whatever you do.' He pointed out. 'Look there, what do you see?' Black waves. Black sky. Black world. 'We'd never find you.'

More possibilities played while I trudged the access tracks: I'd find him shivering in a ditch and the dementia would be oozing out his pores in veins of black mud. When enough of it had passed from his flesh, he'd go back to how he'd always been, checking the fences for breakages and cursing the wobbly tracks left by Williamson's and Murphy's harvesters in the paddocks. 'Measure twice, cut once,' he'd say. 'The shortest distance between two points is a straight line. Deviations are the devil. Even the slightest wavering can add up the costs in fuel and time.'

The home paddock was clear. So too was number two and number three. It was so bloody hot. Flocks of pink-and-grey galahs were wheeling over the wheat stubble. Their screeching hid my calls to Dad to stand up, to show himself, to come back. Whenever I tried to raise Mum on the CB there was no answer. Stuff asking for permission. I switched to the harvest channel.

'Sterlo, come in, it's Rowan, over.'

The radio hissed and whined and dialled in his blaring voice. 'Yeah, what's going on? Over.'

'We've got an emergency. Dad's gone walkabout. Sometime this morning. I've looked in the home paddocks and Mum's had a search by the house and the road. We can't find him. Over.'

Hiss. Pause. Sterlo barked 'shit' and fumbled for a few moments. 'I'll raise the alarm with the district. If he's not near the homestead then he could be anywhere. Why didn't you tell me earlier?' Our chat became a garbled mess.

'Mum didn't want ...'

'... could have found him by now ...'

'Thought it best ...'

'... be there in ten. Out.'

There was a windmill out by the machine shed that drew water up from an artesian bore for the livestock. Its rusted ladder offered a way up to the highest point on the property. That was where perhaps I should have begun my search. You only think of these things as they come.

The view from the platform made a compass dial of the earth. There were curls of dust coming toward our homestead from all points: utes ripping up access tracks from neighbouring properties, men and women, neighbours and blow-ins, all gathering on the driveway at Brockman's Place. The sun was a light without shadow, and for a long and drinkable moment I paused time, breathed in bursts of dusty air, and remembered: Dad in the fields, Dad in the toolshed, Dad in his pomp and power and pride. He'd have been touched by this sight of solidarity, of the community coming together. I dreaded what Mum would think, opening the gates of our private crisis.

Down the ladder, each rung stung the new calluses hardening my grip. Mum came out on the veranda and tried to wave all the people away, saying it was all under control, that he couldn't have gotten far, that we could find him just fine. I put my hands on her shoulders and spoke in a voice that was far from my own.

'He's been missing for a few hours now. There's no sign of him in the paddocks close to home that we can see. Let's split up and take the far paddocks. Then go over the close ones again. Search the neighbouring properties. Wherever a man could get to walking. Take your utes and use channel nine on the CB.'

There were at least thirty people gathered: our work crew, the Chambers and their mob, plus the de Groots and Hoths and Slaters and Courtelings and people whose faces I could place but not their names. And there was Alison, a high note amongst the dull, her eyes finding mine.

'What's he wearing?' Sterlo asked.

Mum thought for a moment. 'Yellow pyjamas.'

'Think of it as hi-vis,' I said, and a few laughed. Turning my back to Mum, I let them know the rest. 'Some of you may or may not know this. It's nothing secret.' I searched for the words. 'He's got dementia. He may not remember you. He may be confused.'

'He's not dangerous,' Mum begged, calling out as the group dispersed. 'He's as you remember him. Just talk to him if you find him. Say it'll all be fine.'

20

The weeping willow on the front lawn swayed in a breeze. Utes crept up and down the paddock tracks. Clouds of dust wafted over the wheat stubble. After checking the home paddocks again, I went back to the homestead to look under the veranda, in the cupboards, in the library, the laundry, the bedrooms, madly thinking he'd been overlooked as part of the furniture. The CB in the empty kitchen crackled with reports that all amounted to the same thing – there was still no sign of him.

Dusk was approaching. I felt detached, as though a fever was ballooning my senses. Sweat circled my head, my breathing became ragged, and I had to hold on to the kitchen counter till dizziness passed.

Then I knew it. Typed bold as a headline. Dad was at the boulder. The outcrop of ancient granite in the Hoths' paddocks he had been so drawn to the other day. Where he had been so vivid with his old way of being, steeped in recollection, a place where perhaps he really could remember himself, tap in to that seam of knowledge and enthusiasm that had so rarely burst through his sickness, bright and sure, making us feel for a moment truly in his presence again.

'I'll get a dinner on,' Mum said, bustling into the kitchen with Mrs Chambers at her heels. 'Get on the radio and tell everyone to come up for something to eat. It's going to be dark soon.' She clattered pots and pans in a quick *mise en place* and whacked a pair of lamb sirloins in the oven with a splash of olive oil and rosemary. I made my mind small and focused on making orders, one word in front of the other, bolting them together with the nonchalance of a council worker.

'Searchers at Brockman's Place, this is Rowan at the homestead. Come up for something to eat when the light goes. We can resume with torches and floodlights afterward. Over and out.'

Call made, Mum satisfied, I went outside where the falling light made bas-reliefs of the garden trees and turned the paddocks into distant seas. The sound of engines approaching was all around, and faint voices continued to call Dad's name, pushing its alliteration across the fields.

'Bryce Brockman.'

'Come out, mate.'

'Bryce Brockman.'

'Where are you?'

'Bryce Brockman.'

They were looking in the wrong place. I was sure of it. I fired up the ute and drove along the driveway till I saw a pair of headlights shining through the sentinel pine trees. I slowed to a crawl, wound my window down and saw Sterlo at the other wheel. He looked wired, like someone who'd stayed up past the need to sleep.

'Where you off to? Didn't you say to come back?'

'I'm checking the back paddock again,' I said. 'It won't take long. Save me a something will you?'

'We'll find him. Hook or by crook. We won't stop. Your mother can cook all she likes. No-one's going in.'

I waved him off and planted my foot on the accelerator. The whine of the turbocharger brought a memory of summer, of Dad fanging a rented four-wheel drive through sand dunes close to a beach shack we'd rented. 'Don't tell your mother,' he said to us boys, and Alby and I promised, happy to share some danger together, thrilled to break the rules. 'Simple science driving on sand,' he'd say. 'Keep the revs up and don't let the wheels stop.'

On the highway, driving to the rock, the sound of waves came humming past the spattered bodies of locusts on the windshield, drawing me deeper into times when nothing was lost.

The sky was full of pure white clouds with the sun's pale fire painted at their edges. The tide went out, waves flattened, and the sea breeze withered to a caress. Albert, me, Mum and Dad, we all walked together on the sandy flats looking for something interesting to scoop into a bucket. Shells and squid cartilage, old glass polished into cloudy jewels, anything we could string onto fishing lines and make a wind chime with for the garden.

'Maybe we'll find a message in a bottle,' Dad said, grabbing me round the waist, hoisting me onto his shoulders as though I didn't weigh a thing. I looked down at Albert and waved, a king on a sedan chair, and he ran up and jumped at me, missing and laughing, coming after us, begging Mum to hoist him up.

'You're too heavy, Alby. Why don't you pick me up?'

In a flash he did. Scooped Mum up with a fireman's strength and put her on his shoulders. 'Come on then, fight!' he cried, and came at me and Dad. 'First one down does the dishes for a week!'

Push and pull and twist and shout, an almighty battle of hands and legs and arms. Mum smiled like I had never seen her smile before. So I let her win. She pulled me from Dad's shoulders and I fell to the ground where Albert kicked a wave of sand over my chest to mark the victory. Off they went down the beach, my brother running fast as he could go with Mum on his shoulders, swishing her right arm behind her like a jockey.

'Better luck next time, mate,' Dad said. 'It always pays to hold on tight.'

We walked together in the warm shallows, away from Mum and Albert, heading back to the shack in the dune where our dinner was bubbling in the oven – a red sauce for crabs we'd catch at dusk.

'Why journalism?' he said. 'I thought you'd do a commerce degree. Something political and dry.'

I had a line well practised. 'If I'm going to do hack work, I want to be paid poorly for it.'

He nudged me with his shoulder, pushing me into the path of water rising up the sand. 'You can always come back for the harvest. Earn a few bob for the summer.'

'Dunno, Dad. I'll have exams probably. Work experience to do. You know?'

'Fine enough. But the offer stands.' He stopped and picked up a rock, threw it into the sea where it skipped once, twice, thrice. 'It's nice to forget about the place for a few weeks anyway. It's good here. Timeless.' He picked up another rock and hurled it far out to the flat sea where it kicked a single splash. 'You can always come back,' he said, and fetched another.

There he was as if in a painting. Man on the rock, distinct to the dark as the headlights washed over his arms and legs and face and hands, yellow pyjamas, black leather slippers and white skin. He was sitting in the pose of a thinker, looking out over paddocks lit by the moon and the Milky Way. I killed the engine and the lights and climbed up there after him, finding the way by easy instinct. Up on top, I sat beside him and said nothing.

There are only a handful of moments I can truly say that the whole of my attention was focused, where no stray ounce of feeling was on autopilot, rendered of any distraction. Up there, on the rock, the ticking of all the clocks stopped. A great bubble of calm projected out and made a new country that only I could see. Bulldozers skimmed their blades across the topsoil to make foundations for housing estates rising into the naked sun. An apartment block towered where Brockman's Place once stood. The whole of Septimus was gavelled to developers who'd turn it into a retirement village and a brace of starter homes. Suburbs expanded up the coast from Perth to Geraldton, bobcats felled banksias and grass trees and mulched the saltbush while ditch witches sucked the scum from sewerage pipes, the veins of progress making the soil into weathered skin. And at the source, a great tower rose and put my apartment in Scarborough in shadow, a spear of the Gold Coast planting its roots on a western beach.

'When I was a young man, this was all bush,' Dad said. 'The

Hoths hired some Italians to clear the scrub for a few bob a week. To expand their holdings. So they diverted the creek bed and chopped down the big trees for firewood and hacked the rest out with axes and crowbars and chains. Took a good three months to get this paddock into a billiard table. They had to leave the rocks of course. This is just the latest they've revealed.'

He patted the boulder between us. 'What brings you here, mate? You from the harvest crew?'

'I'm a last-minute addition,' I said, knowing to play along.

'I know all about them,' Dad said, smiling at me as if to make a friend. 'My family's been on this land for generations. Right back to the days of John Septimus Roe and the expeditions to map the potential of the state. We're rusted on.'

He checked over his shoulder, then leaned in. 'A mate of mine told me when he went over to France and saw their farm land, blood fair rushed to his head. Then he says he picked up a sod of the black soil and ate a pinch of it. He could chew the minerals in it, you know? Think of all the centuries of death and decay in it. Then the millennia of life all churned into it. What do we have here? Sand. Gravel and drought. God knows what they saw in this place when they clapped eyes on it.'

He put on a posh accent. 'Oh this would make jolly fine farms. All we have to do is run the natives off, cut down all the scrub and find some fools to do all the work for a pittance.'

He paused a while, then stood slowly, turning in a circle. 'If I had my way I'd let it all go fallow. Let the bush reclaim it. We have no business being here.' He looked down at me. 'You got a cigarette, mate?'

I did, and lit two. We smoked in silence, sharing the view, and I kept a hand on the boulder to steady my balance as the world spun faster and faster, louder and louder, till I felt like a rock tumbling through the air.

21

Dad climbed down with spidery ease, ignoring my offers of help till he reached the final ledge and let me take the weight of his step to the ground. He sat in the cab of the ute with mute patience, watching me with the interest of a child as I started the engine and switched on the CB. I listened to the hissing search band for a while, monitoring the crackling reports of 'no Bryce here, over' and 'nothing in the bottom paddocks, over' while the prize himself reclined in the vinyl beside me, seemingly with no idea of what was going on. I keyed the handset, licked my lips to talk, but held fire.

This was the first time I'd had him completely to myself since I came to the harvest. No-one knew where we were, no-one was in the next room, waiting for a turn, watching me to see that I said and did the right things. I couldn't think of anything to say to him. Nothing that really counted. I knew how to sum the day up in twelve-point type.

```
An elderly man suffering from dementia has
been found safe and well after going missing
for several hours. Bryce Brockman, 64, was
found by his son on a neighbouring property,
and is said to be recovering well.
```

'You ready to head back?' I said. 'It's well after dark. They'll be looking for us soon.'

He shrugged. 'Not if we don't have to.'

Dad put his window down, grunting with the effort of winding the handle. 'Where is there to go around here? It looks like there'll be something interesting over the next paddock. But there's just another paddock.' He pointed through the windscreen to the rock, stark in the headlights. 'I'd rather be left there. Suppose yeah, duty calls. We'd better get back to work.'

I wound my window down and let the night in to my side of the cab. The heat of the day was still in the air, mixing with a breeze salty from the distant sea. I could tell him about Scarborough, my place by the waves, the nights I spent seeing the worst of things, and the days sanitising them with words, pushing on the phones to get the next one, and the next one. To him I was Albert, or I was a stranger. I wanted to punch him. To kick him to the dirt and leave him behind, this husk of my father. What use were words with him? He could nod at the right moments, maybe prompt a question or two. I'd be better off speaking to myself.

I drove home on autopilot. My mind a blank of pressure and white noise. At the homestead, the veranda was alive with people come in from the fields for a meeting. As I drove up, I could hear Sterlo's voice carry above all the others, giving instructions, leading the way, and knowing what to do as he pumped them up for a new sweep of searching.

It seemed a cheat to say I'd found him. Before I could get out and announce it, Mum ran up to the ute and pounded on the bonnet, the headlights making her face a mirror of shiny tears.

'I'll kill him,' she said, choked between relief and anger. 'I'll handcuff him to the bloody shower rail.'

Mum kicked everyone out, even Sterlo, who offered to stay and do the dishes and clean up and do anything else the CWA women hadn't already done themselves or ordered done. Mum got Dad into bed and when the last pair of headlights had swung onto the highway she shut the veranda's flyscreen door and then the back door, swinging its neglected hinges to a bolted full stop.

'What a nightmare,' she said, covering her face with her hands.

'We need a drink,' I said, moving toward the couches. 'Is there anything strong going?'

Still holding her head, Mum shook no. 'I'm going to bed. The house is dry anyway.' She yawned deeply and wiped her eyes. 'You've got an early start. Sterlo says the timetable's getting tight.'

I stamped my foot. 'Really? We can't have a day off? After all of that?'

'After all of what? He's back home now.'

Coughing hacked through the walls. Dad spluttered and retched. I made to go help him. Mum stood in my way. 'He's fine. He always does that.'

'We should get him away. Maybe go to Geraldton.' I thought of the coast, of Dad holding me on his shoulders in the warm sea's shallows, Mum and Albert trying to tackle us down. 'It would do him some good to get away. And you too. We have plenty of time left.'

Mum went to the kitchen, poured a glass of water, moving slowly through the motions, giving herself time to think. She stood at the sink for a few seconds, hands on the splashback, looking at the neatly cut lawn illuminated by the moon.

'I said I thought about Albert. Saw him in the doorway there.' She nodded at the flyscreen, then me. 'I felt arms wrap around me. Maybe it was a trick of the brain. I don't believe in that sort of thing. But I know what I felt. That's what got me through today. I'm glad you found Dad. Now we have to get on with it.'

I wouldn't let it go. 'Let's take a day. Just the three of us. Go out to the coast. Settle ourselves down. This will all still be here.'

Mum wouldn't be moved. She switched off the lights to close my suggestion.

'You know what I miss about Albert? He always knew the right thing to do.' She walked past me, a black figure creaking along the floorboards.

Sweating in my bed that night, I dreamed of an Indian Ocean that was frigidly cold. Long arcs of beach and wind-blurred sand dunes stretched to a white vanishing north and south. It was a sunlit limbo, where I couldn't hear above the wind and could barely see through the glare of the sun. Long, languid rollers crashed onto the shallows and hissed foam that smelled of rotting seaweed.

'Race ya,' Albert said, paddling in the bow of a sea canoe, and from the seat behind I matched his strokes, paddling hard as our momentum built and we flew through the flat water, hissing over menacing banks of seaweed refracted in a high noon sun. Down below sharks and rays and sea snakes and God knows what curled to strike. So I paddled harder, dipping the paddle deep with my left arm like the bloke who rented it to us had said. *Dip, dip and swing. Dip, dip and swing.*

I looked behind and the land had become a horizon. Out ahead was trackless water. I dug the paddle in sideways as a brake. 'Alby, stop, we're going out to sea.'

'Don't be a bloody wuss,' he barked. 'We're going good.'

'Nah, stop. Turn us around.'

He stopped. Then laughed. 'I don't know how to turn it around. Do you?'

The canoe slid along under momentum, slow, slower, and settled over a dark patch, a sitting target for all my fear. 'I don't know how either.'

The bloke had showed us how to row forward but not how to turn. A balloon rose in my belly and my lungs grabbed for air. I looked behind again and saw we were moving sideways. The current had us. My mind raced – we'd be dragged out to sea and a container ship would crush us beneath its wave breaker bow and we'd tread water till a tug of teeth pulled us under.

'Relax, Ro,' Albert said. He pulled his oar in across his lap and put his hands on the gunwales. 'I reckon it's like a tank. Or a bulldozer. Anything with caterpillar tracks. They brake one side and drive on the other and the turn happens.' His oar went in on the right side. 'Paddle my side. Paddle like crazy.'

I did, and we moved forward again, and slowly the canoe swung around and faced the land and we climbed down from the sea, paddle by paddle, back to safety. When the bow touched the sand I jumped out and collapsed my shaking knees into the wash of the waterline. Albert took my oar and dragged the canoe back across the beach to the shack where we got it. I watched him laugh with the rental bloke, pointing out to sea, nodding at me, and clapping the man on the back.

As we walked back to the beach shack, he asked, 'You weren't scared were you?' and I said no. Of course I wasn't. I was with my brother.

22

Before first light I woke ahead of my alarm, turned it off and crept into Mum and Dad's bedroom to check that the old man was still there. Mum had her arm over him, her bare flesh and his swaddled chest rising and falling together. I watched them sleep till the red pips of the digital clock beside Mum ticked to 05:00. A country song played and she got up to switch it off.

'I can stay with you today,' I whispered. 'It's no trouble.'

Mum put on her dressing gown. 'Go to the fields.'

Dad stirred, coughing sharply, a trifecta of hacks sharp as razors.

'You sure he's okay? You could take a few days off.'

'He's fine.' She ushered me from the room and closed the door. 'He just needs to rest. That's what you wanted. So let him do it.'

She led the way to the kitchen and put the kettle on, its rising whisper waking me fully. I switched on lights and saw the CWA ladies had tidied all the packing boxes into a neat wall, making our work in progress look almost organised.

'We're going well on the headers,' I said, trying to make conversation. 'Even with the interruptions we're pretty well on schedule.'

Mum yawned and rubbed her eyes, still as puffy as the night before. 'That's a harvest. Controlled chaos, your father called it.'

'I wish he was out there with us,' I said, thinking it the right thing. Mum clinked enamel mugs on the counter and assembled our coffees, going through the steps as if I wasn't there. Dad's words on the rock came to me as if scribbled in a notebook.

If I had my way I'd let it all go fallow. Let the bush reclaim it. We have no business being here.

'Did Dad ever want to be anything else?'

Mum clicked her tongue. 'He wanted to be all kinds of things. He had all the dreams when I met him. Architect. Pilot. Agribusiness consultant. Anything but raising crops on a farm.' She slid a mug to me over the counter. 'His father willed it to him. Just as his father had willed to him, and so on backward. So there was a link that couldn't be broken. Sounds very old-fashioned, doesn't it?'

'You wanted Albert to take over.'

'He gravitated toward it. You didn't.'

I said nothing. That was enough.

'We were angry when you chose the city.' She gathered more words and said them carefully so there was no misunderstanding. 'This is a difficult life. No-one really chooses it. It's either thrust upon you or it calls you. You're our son. So of course there was expectation. Especially after Alby died. It doesn't mean we love you less for choosing another way. Your father admired it. Though he would never have admitted that. Every chance he got, he told everyone in earshot what you were up to.'

'Then why didn't he ever say anything to me?'

Up went her hand.

'You know the joke – what did the farmer say to the other farmer?'

'How's your farm?' I said.

Mum sighed a bitter note in the back of her throat. 'Got any of those cigarettes?' I sparked up two and handed her one, which she puffed up to the ceiling, the smoke curling against the rafters. 'Get to work. I'll handle things here. It won't take much longer.'

'You're on chaser bin,' Sterlo said to me up at the laager, then nodded at John. 'He's going to town.' With that arranged, the young bloke hopped into Dad's ute, turned the keys that were left in the ignition and drove off in a slow cloud of careful dust.

'Got a sick aunty,' Sterlo said as I scuffed my boot on the dirt.

'Mum wants to crack on with everything,' I said, veiling my complaint in a light tone. 'I asked her to take a day or two out. Wouldn't even think of it.'

'Well, mate. That's life. Maybe I'll see if she wants to have a drink or something later. Maybe we could all go to the pub. Just ease up on her. Let's get the work done.'

Sterlo turned to Murphy and Williamson and gave them their orders. They were good enough not to mention Dad going missing and the time on task they'd missed because of it. When they were out of earshot Sterlo came up so close I could tell he hadn't had a spare moment for a shower.

'Nice and steady with that chaser. I don't want any spillage. And you need to be quick smart between the loading and dumping at the bunker. We're tight on the timetable as it is.'

'I've got plenty of leave left –'

'Good for you. We don't. We need to get it done quick as possible.' He looked to the sky and rubbed his mangled hand across the stubble on his chin. 'There's rain coming. Forecast says so. And all the old-timers say so. We need time at the end of the day to waterproof the bunker. So get on with it.'

I stood there for a second too long, staring at the cloudless blue on blue. He tapped the brim of my hat and snapped the fingers of his good hand. 'I'm a man down today. Murphy's rig is doing its usual technical-difficulties bullshit. Williamson's back is playing up. Be the least of my worries.'

Engines started, the work of the morning began. Up the paddock, down the paddock, and when the headers were full, I drove a tractor alongside to catch a torrent of grain in the chaser bin from their holding tanks. When the bin was chocked I drove to the bunker and tipped the grain in a pile inside its U-shaped mouth. The second I returned to the paddock I had to go through the whole process again, and then again, and then again, breaking the holy rule of the ten o'clock smoko to work right through to lunch without a break.

'Eat quick and get going as soon as you're done,' Sterlo said over the CB. He was really cracking the whip. I opened the door of the tractor and sucked in lungfuls of itchy air thick with wheat dust and dirt. I'd stopped on a fence line next to the bitumen road and could see the Chambers' work crew still going strong in the paddocks opposite. Alison would be there – did she have a CB? I got back into the tractor and switched to channel 40, the one for truckers and caravans. Maybe she'd be listening.

'Alison, it's Rowan, you there? Over.'

Static. Nothing.

'Want to have some lunch with me? I've got soggy sandwiches and a room-temperature Coke. Tempted? Over.'

Her voice crackled, then came into focus. 'Sounds very inviting. Over.'

More voices came on, workers from other harvest crews within transmitter distance. 'Yeah, save some for me.' 'Why are they soggy, mate?' 'Got any Diet?'

Alison told them to shut up or she'd 'tie their dicks in a knot' – and they did.

'Where are you?' she said.

'Edge paddock of ours. Are you in a header today?'

'Yep. The red one.'

'Yeah, I see you. Walk to your western fence line and cross the road. I'm right there. See me?'

I sat on the engine cowl of the tractor and watched her walk to me. From a distance she looked like any other man on a farm with her wide brim hat, checked shirt and jeans. Up closer the orbit of her hips quickened my pulse, and when I held a hand out to help her up, the soft skin of her palm took the heat of the day away. Down the shallow rise of the land I could see Sterlo's roving ute parked next to Williamson's header with Murphy's just beyond it. There was no chance of anyone sneaking up on us. I wiped sweat from my nose and said, 'It's hammer and tongs round here,' in my thickest country accent. Alison blew a raspberry.

'Your crew worrying about rain too?' she said.

'Yep. Stupid if you ask me.'

'We didn't. It's worth heeding.' She put a finger to my hairline and wiped sideways, smoothing my sweat-wet hair. 'If it comes, better we get it in. And if it doesn't, well then the job's done quicker. So either way we win. Harvest is for working.'

The engines of her work crew switched off and the paddocks whistled to silence all around us. Locusts ticked in the long grass. Birds screeched somewhere. I ached to hold her. For her naked warmth to obliterate everything around us, erode that great rock Dad had perched himself on and silence his words of doubt.

'How's your dad?' she asked, as if reading my mind.

'Sleeping last I saw.'

She shifted in her seat to move closer, but still kept herself apart. 'We checked our property all over for him. I was so relieved when the call came in. Was he really just wandering around the Hoths' gate?'

'That's where I found him.' I took a Red Delicious from my lunch bag and bit into it – rotten to the core. The apple arced through the air like a cricket ball and splattered in the wheat stubble. 'When I found him he didn't know who I was. He thought I was one of his work crew.'

She stroked my arm. 'What did you do?'

'Went along with it. Drove him home.'

I leaned to kiss her. She leaned away. *Not here. Not now.* She checked her watch and hopped off to the ground. 'I'd better get back. Don't want to start any rumours.'

'Hang on.' I grabbed her arm. 'When do I see you again?'

Alison's eyebrows rose. 'When I let you.' She jumped from my grip and walked off, never looking back.

Back at the house, Mum was in a foul mood sorting through the mess in the kitchen. Three generations of Brockman women had left a strata of crockery, utensils, time-saving gadgets and gaudy knick-knacks crowding the cupboards. She'd been playing at arranging it all for weeks, but a sudden frenzy to get it done had taken hold.

'I booked the movers,' she announced, hair tied back and damp with sweat. 'They come a week Monday. So dive in. Pack anything that looks modern. Set aside anything that looks antique. If you're not sure pile it on the kitchen table. I'll sort through it.'

Wordlessly I followed orders, working at the opposite end of the long bench that held most of the knee-height cupboards. A golden oldies station played motown hits on the radio to blur the need for conversation, and both of us worked happily for an hour or so, lost in the rhythm of wrapping plates in newspaper and stuffing mugs and glasses with napkins. Now and then I'd snatch a glance at her; eyes narrowed to the task, brow creased with concentration. She looked beautiful and dangerous, as though coiled to strike. So I chose my words carefully.

'Sterlo's going to the pub tonight. Said we had a hard day.'

'You go then,' she said, quickly and without looking up.

'He asked if you wanted to come.'

She looked at me like an eagle sighting prey. 'What about your father? Someone's got to look after him. Want to swap for the night?'

I nodded. 'I'm happy to do that. You only have to ask. But no – that's not what he suggested.' Bless that man. He knew it was best to come from him. 'He suggested we bring Dad. It could be good for him.'

She stared out the window for a long while. I looked too, and just made out the line between cut and growing grain we'd moved ever closer to the finish line of the homestead. Maybe she'd notice our hard work. Or more likely it just looked like the same old view to her, the same paddocks, growing or gone.

'That's a very good idea,' she said finally. 'What time did he say?'

'He didn't. Around seven I'm guessing. I can get him to pick us up.'

'Make it six. Your father tends to have a witching hour around eight so the earlier we eat the better.' She stood and turned up the radio, Aretha Franklin singing about her 'Chain of Fools'. 'If we're going to get on it, I want this mess sorted. Forget the plates. Concentrate on the back shelves. That's where all the crap is.' She came over and reached into the cupboard I was working on, pulling out a mismatched set of Peter Rabbit dinnerware and Royal Family serving platters. 'Your grandmother had hideous taste, bless her. These are heirlooms. Heaven knows what I'm going to do with them.'

23

By six o'clock dark clouds had blown in, stepping low across the district. 'Looks like rain' was the refrain, and sure enough it bucketed down just as Sterlo turned his ute onto the highway with Dad safe and dry in the front cab's passenger seat while Mum and I got soaked in the back tray.

'Good thing I wore my best dress,' Mum shouted, holding on to her hat in the soaking slipstream. 'Just be thankful you've got so much of the crop in.' She pointed to a passing property where men were scrambling to cover their grain bunker with tarpaulins, dragging the blue sheets behind them as they climbed up and over piles of wheat darkening with moisture.

'This is just a quick storm anyway,' she said, shifting her finger to the clouds. 'They're moving too fast and too low to hang around.' Thunder rumbled clear above the throttle of the ute. 'It's a heat storm. Just the earth blowing off a bit of steam.'

After five minutes on the highway we drove clear of the rain and rolled through the town with the itching smells of wet grass and ozone from lightning strikes somewhere. The wet on our clothes and hair quickly dried to damp in the rushing air.

The Terminus was blacked out. The rest of the town too. People ambled around the streets as if there was a great pause. As we parked up, I looked to Dad to give the signal, to tell us to back the ute up to the rear of the pub, start the portable generator bolted to the tray and connect it to the mains. Sterlo's ute didn't have one. The old man's mind didn't have the signal. He sat facing the pub, waiting for someone to get him out.

'I'll grab us a table,' Mum said as we climbed down from the tray, her hands fidgeting with her handbag, then wringing out her hat and hair. Two men stood smoking near the door, watching our arrival. They didn't smile. Didn't move. Just stared as if expecting us to do something for them.

'Not that you need to book,' Mum continued, her voice becoming babble under their gaze. 'They always have room. He was a regular, wasn't he? It's not exactly busy.'

'It's fine,' Sterlo said, taking her by the elbow. 'I've booked. We've a booth at the back. There'll be a sign on it. Why don't you go inside?'

She nodded to the smokers, who parted to let her through. Once she was inside the darkened pub, Sterlo opened Dad's door and gestured for him to get out, which he did in one smooth motion, no need for the hands we offered to him. For a fleeting moment he looked himself again, straightening his belt and re-tucking his shirt, looking up at the pub and the smoking strangers, smiling like they were all his oldest friends.

'Righto boys,' he said to Sterlo, imitating his catch phrase. 'Let's see if they'll serve us.' He glared at the starers. 'Unless these bastards have a problem.' They looked away, and stayed away as we ushered the old man inside.

Candles flickered from behind the bar to light the power-cut room. I knew it by feel, one long counter with rings of stools around the support posts, then a dining room beyond with a few wooden booths and chipped tables. Pale sun glowered through blinds drawn over the west-facing windows, letting us know the weather was clearing. The beer was still cold in the lines. The kitchen ran on gas. Nothing could stop our evening.

'I'm getting the parmi,' Mum said, handing us menus. 'No need to even look really. And I'll guess the rest.' She pointed at us in turn as we helped Dad sit down on the long leather seat next to her. 'Rowan will get the fish and chips, and say something like "we're not that far from the sea, so you know it's good". Sterlo will have the steak. Well done and with peppercorn sauce. Your dear old dad will have the hamburger. Though I'll have a quiet word to the server and change it to one of those vegie patties for his health.'

'Spot-on for me,' Sterlo said, nudging me as he sat beside, the two of us facing Mum and Dad like it was a business meeting. 'Let him get the burger? Not like he's in training for the Olympics.'

Mum laughed – a little forced, a little too loud, but she seemed to be relaxing. 'I'll get them to put a fried egg on it. He loves that.'

Dad picked up the knife and fork arranged at his place, hefting the silverware in his fingers as if to inspect its qualities. Round and round he turned the tang of the knife, catching the reflection of the candles at the bar in their dull surfaces.

'It's a nice touch,' he said, looking up at me. 'They don't put on the dog in here. Not for anything. Not for anyone. They serve on plates and give you this nice silverware.' He looked to Sterlo and smiled, his voice wavering as though confused or needing to cough. 'My dad used to tell me about the drovers who would come in. The prospectors and jobbers. Blokes without fences to keep them in. All dirty from the bush and hard living. They'd come in here and wash their faces and scrub their hands and put on the one jacket they carried over the top of their work clothes. They'd drink till they dropped and eat every skerrick. They never smashed a glass or cracked a plate.'

He stood and shuffled out of the booth, walking over to the bar with his weight creaking the floorboards. Mum inhaled sharply, and we all watched to see what he would do.

'It was here,' he said, pointing to the floor below the beer taps. 'It was right here.' He bent down slowly on one knee and smoothed his hand over the floor, fingers plucking a handle from the flush of the floorboard. He grunted, pulled and a panel swung upward.

'Whoa, stop that mate,' the barman said, walking around. 'What are you doing?'

'We used to siphon it off,' Dad said, laughing to himself. 'When it was busy and they couldn't see, we'd tap the beer lines and have a few on the house. Bit of a design fault having the access here.'

Mum went over and picked him up. The lights came back on and the pair of them looked like they were ending their night rather than starting it, Dad slurring and stumbling while Mum went red in the face. I made to get up but she cut me a look of *don't you dare*.

'Sit down, love,' she said to him, and he obeyed with the reluctance of a schoolboy, winking at Sterlo and me, mugging that he was in trouble with the missus. 'I'm getting the food now. Did I get your choices right?'

She had. And while she spoke to the barman with the order, Sterlo leaned close and whispered, 'Talk to her yet?'

'Kind of. Haven't had a chance to mention you though.'

He patted his silverware and straightened them. 'Not to worry. I might find the moment tonight.'

'We didn't drink during the harvest in those days,' Dad said, commanding our attention. 'The tradition was to have a big blow-out the night before it started.' Sterlo nudged me, and I tasted bile in my mouth, Alison's pill from the party at Hoth's farm, my stomach like boiled orange peel the morning after.

'Then we'd go until the job was done,' Dad continued. 'The trick was for everyone to finish on the same day. That was a tall order with some of the other mobs. They were pretty flash with their work and sometimes we'd have to flog late into the night to keep up. Course our property is a bit smaller than the others so we had some wiggle room. Then whoever had finished came down here and we had an almighty piss-up. It was on for young and old. No women, mind.'

Mum sat back down and patted his leg. 'What were you saying, love?'

'No women. Not back then. You wouldn't have been allowed inside. To protect your scruples.'

She passed us cardboard beer mats. 'I ordered you some pints. There's a bottle of red coming for the table.'

'Who's driving?' I asked, and she tapped her table place.

'We'll get a cab. I'm in no mood to be the designated driver. Scruples or not.'

By the end of happy hour the bar was full of farmers and workers, blow-ins, and rusted-on regulars. A few of the farmers' wives came over and said hello and gave Dad pecks on the cheek and shakes of the hand, saying good to see you back, good to see you out. The men stayed away. Men who had been Dad's friends for years stayed away. As if he was infectious.

Because sickness was one thing. Failure was another. Selling the land. Getting out. Giving up. My mind ran and ran with judgements, resenting these men who drank their pints and looked away whenever my eyes crossed theirs.

Beside me, Sterlo gripped his knife and fork as though he was conducting a dissection. Mum was chatting about the packing, getting our life to fit in boxes, and though we nodded, neither of us was listening. When Mum's words petered out, Sterlo excused himself from the booth and went and had a word with the men. Hoth, Courteling, de Groot. Slater and a few more of the older generation. Whatever he told them, they looked abashed. He came back over and told me to come have a yarn, and took Dad by the elbow too.

'Don't worry, Justine. They're just shy is all.'

'They'd bloody well better be,' Mum murmured, and took her wine glass to a table of old friends. Maybe it was my imagination, but as we came over to the bar every man there seemed to be looking right at us, pausing their chatter for an awkward moment to have a good look at the man they'd heard was crook in the head and heart. Even in his addled state, with pain clouding his eyes and thoughts unravelling, Dad sensed it too, and rallied at least the flavour of his old spirit.

'Which one of you blokes has finished?' Dad asked, shaking

hands with each of his old friends in turn. 'Sterlo here is more than halfway done. Ready to knock off by next week, right?'

'If the plan goes.' He accepted a beer and knocked its head off with a few forceful gulps. 'We've got a ragged crew,' he said, looking to me. 'They're doing well. When they focus on the job.'

'I'm sorry you're going,' one of them said to Dad – I think it was Hoth – and they all murmured their assent. 'It's come as a bit of a shock. Come a bit quick.'

'We used to carve it up, didn't we boys?' Dad said, leaning back on a wooden beam. 'Right in here. In this bar after a hard season. Just in time for the summer.' He raised his glass and looked at the roof. 'I don't know what else to say. I really don't.'

That was it. I put my arm on Dad's shoulder and led him away.

Sterlo drove, saying, 'Bugger the cab, I'm sober enough.' Out on the highway, with the bright lights far behind, the stars sharpened above the paddocks. Mum leaned against me as we rode in the ute tray with our backs to the cab. High beams lit the way behind us, spilling light to the side of the ute as though we were a meteorite burning through the black.

'No-one wants to look at your father, do they?' Mum said. 'That's why I don't go out. All that attention.'

She stood and slapped her hand on the ute cab's back window. 'Stop the car, driver.'

Sterlo braked and crunched the wheels onto the gravel road shoulder. Dad swung around in his seat and looked at us, lit devil-red in the glow of the brakelights.

'What's the problem?' Sterlo shouted, rolling down his window.

'We didn't have a toast,' Mum yelled back. 'For the harvest. For the bloody end of things. It's bad luck not to.'

'I'm not going back.'

'I'm not asking you to.' She reached into her handbag and

pulled out a bottle of dark rum. 'I took this from the bar. When the lights were out.'

'Mum, that's terrible. How did you do that?'

She nodded at Dad. 'He casts a long shadow.'

The bottle's cap cracked and she took a swig, then offered it around. When we'd all had a drink she took a few steps to the back of the ute tray and hurled the bottle at the distant lights of Septimus.

24

Up at the vehicle laager, Williamson and Murphy had strung their swags up on a washing line, drying the canvas beside the cooking fire stoked to brightness. The contrasting cool of the morning was made sharper by the skin of rain still clinging to the topsoil. As we warmed our hands on mugs of ember-brewed coffee, John drove up in my ute, throwing me the keys before looking to the ground, his eyes heavy-lidded and tired.

'She died,' he said. 'My aunt. Had a heart attack.'

'Sorry to hear that,' I said, offering him a coffee, which he refused. So I offered him another standard. 'If you want to take some time away, you can. Do what you have to do.'

He shook his head. 'Nah, no worries. Funeral's next week. So I can finish up here and then go.'

Sterlo patted him on the back. 'Whatever you want to do, mate. We're glad to have you.'

John joined the circle, eyes still down, ignoring the sympathy of Williamson and Murphy, who looked to me and shrugged – *what can we say?*

'Let's get into it then, I'm not used to this cold,' I said. For once, Sterlo held back the whip.

'We need to wait for the wet to dry out. We'll do vehicle haul-overs and make sure the bunker's tight. John – give the tractor a once-over.' He picked up the coffee pot from the fire's ashes and topped up our mugs. 'Finish your brews first. We're going to go late today. Make up for all the lost time.'

Silence then. We stood still like men always do when there's something more to be said, but isn't. I glanced over at John, who seemed relieved, holding his hands to the fire's glow, his fingers curling in and out. How could he take a blow like that and still show up, as if nothing were amiss? Maybe he wasn't close to the aunt. Or the benefit of a swift sickness and clean death was less shock, more resolve.

Warm wind blew at my back, promising heat, and a sweating day of work. Nothing would stop the timetable. Not even death. Would my father's? I imagined going home for lunch to find Mum crying on the couch, the old man's rigour under the pure white bedsheets.

'Back to work,' she'd say, and wipe her tears away with a twist of packing paper.

By ten o'clock the paddocks were steaming like horses in winter. All that evaporating rain seemed to lower the altitude of the clouds, restoring the flat land to the summit of high crags it had held in ancient days.

'Oil checked, combs checked, systems all okay, over,' Williamson said on the CB, words acknowledged and then copied by Murphy. They were sitting in their headers, keys in the ignition, with John in the chaser bin tractor and me in the ute, waiting for the good word to get stuck in.

Sterlo made a big show of walking into the waiting wheat, his hands making metronomes of the stalks as he inspected them for damp. Dry enough was not good enough. They had to be good as they were before the rain, or close as possible to it. Though we wanted to rush back in, we knew wet wheat would clog the machines and spiral us into a cul-de-sac of bullshit maintenance, pulling clumps of sodden grains from every intricacy of the threshing maws.

I watched Sterlo make his inspection through the ute's windshield, the glass all streaked with water stains. 'Thumbs up,' I said, strangely wanting the work, as something to do, something to distract, something I could feel. He raised his hand.

'There it is, over,' Murphy said, his voice on the CB distorted by the ignition of his header, the big pistons puttering like rain on a roof. 'Get ready for a shit of a day, over.'

'Lost time is the best time, over,' Williamson said. 'Still get paid.'

'How many times do I have to say it's a fixed rate?' Sterlo said, back in his ute. 'Break's over. I want this paddock done by lunch. Then we start on the home run. No more fucking about.'

Strip, dump, strip, dump, nothing more to report. I drove like a robot, ferrying fuel and tools and food to the machines, helping John at the grain bunker, smothering whatever little piece of annoyance Sterlo threw my way. 'More diesel. Broken tooth on Williamson's rig. Cup of tea, two sugars.'

At one o'clock Williamson held a mutiny and called lunch, stopping his header in the middle of the paddock to lie on the ground and stretch his back out. Murphy and John and Sterlo walked over to join him, making a circle under the sun to eat and chat and have a minute without all cylinders firing. I waved to them from the shade tree, happy to be alone, looking over the land to the Chambers' place for any sign of Alison. They were working the other side of their property. I didn't dare try to call her up on the CB.

A gun fired on another property. The shot pulsed sharp and wide, chasing a scattered palette of cockatoos and galahs and rosellas away from the bunkers of grain they were preying on. White wings threaded across the paddocks to the shade tree, and as the flock of cockies settled in the boughs I tasted bile, smelled cordite, saw Lillee and Bradman get torn apart by Sterlo's accuracy. I walked to the next paddock, into the wheat, where I could light a cigarette out of the wind, fingers pinching the filter to my lips.

The heat hit forty. Sterlo pressed the accelerator. 'We've got four hours to make up and I don't want to be doing this in the dark.' He drove beside Murphy and Williamson in turn, acting like some mad foreman, making sure the combs of their headers were at the perfect height to catch all the stalks and lop off their heads. While those blokes stripped the crops, John and I dumped the grains at the bunker, him reversing the chaser bin with one-fingered expertise while I scraped the tipping container with a shovel.

On yet another run back to the line, the CB crackled and hissed with one more of Sterlo's whims. 'Rowan, go back to the homestead shed and grab a rasp,' he said, all officer. 'Murphy's combine needs a bit of sharpening up.'

I snapped a quick 'righto', and braked hard in the wheat stubble, sending a cloud of dust into the firing line. The heat subsided as I swung the ute along the access track, and when I got back to the homestead, Mum's garden enveloped me in cool greenery. Her station wagon was gone. She'd probably taken Dad for a check-up at the clinic in town. I went straight to the shed, pretending my old home were the property of someone else, and me just another workman with an errand.

The shed door slid along its difficult rail. Inside was still a mess. Dad's tools were right up the back, hidden behind some cabinets and old chairs Mum had stuffed out of the way. I squeezed myself into a gap and shuffled through. There was a bank of rasps neatly arranged in a holder nailed to the back wall. 'A place for everything, and still everything in its place,' I said, and pocketed a bastard file, half for its name and the sharp ridges it offered. In the gloom, behind all the junk, there was a big old machine, blood red and scabbed with rust. The bonnet logo said MASSEY FERGUSON – Dad's old header harvester. It hadn't run in years. Maybe a collector would come and take it. Or we could shove it in a paddock and make it the next owner's problem.

Back outside, the ute was idling with a patient purr while the CB hacked high-pitched words. 'What the fuck is that smoke?' Sterlo said, his anger garbling electronically. I looked to the sky above the shed. 'Everyone shut down. Extinguishers. Blankets. Whatever you've got. Let's go.'

My fingers pinched the bastard file from my pocket and threw it on the passenger seat. 'I'm on my way,' I said into my handset and kicked into gear. 'Shit, shit, shit,' I said, 'fuck, fuck, fuck,' while a black river rose from the paddocks, cutting the windscreen's view into two ragged halves.

25

When I got to the scene it was all over – just a few hundred dollars worth of grain charred into the smell of brewing beer. Utes from properties all over the district had driven in with trays full of workers who had beaten the flames down. Sterlo shook hands with some of them, saying thanks for coming so quick. He was too calm and too curt, as keen for them to quit the field as the captain of a losing cricket team. I stood beside him watching the utes leave, both of us hacking away gasps of smoke stuck in the back of our throats.

'Good there wasn't much damage,' I said, bowling a stock ball. 'So how did it start? I was in the shed when you called.'

Sterlo spat on the dirt. 'Cut the bullshit.'

'What do you mean?' I said, words flicked as a quick left jab to create distance between us. Sterlo didn't flinch. Didn't move. His mouth smiled, a shark sensing prey, while his eyes kept their level.

'If we didn't put that out as quickly as we did, the whole paddock would have gone up in flames. Then it could have spread to the bunker. Then let's say it jumps the road and burns out the neighbours. Every live body able to swing a blanket would get called in. By then it would be too late. Some of us lose a year's harvest. A few of us might even get killed.'

A finger from his mangled hand stabbed me in the chest. 'I thought I saw you smoking. At lunch.'

He looked over to the shade tree where Williamson, Murphy and John were standing, arms crossed and scowling. 'We joked about it. Said you were just taking a piss. You walked into the wheat with a naked flame, didn't you? Jesus Christ, boy. You bloody well know better than that. What have you got to say for yourself?'

My mind lurched as though I were riding a steep slide, caught in a swing of gravity between launch and landing. I couldn't deny it. I could only acknowledge it. The words wouldn't come.

'Gutless shit,' Sterlo said, hammering the insult's three syllables. 'It's plain as day to see that you don't want to be here. You don't have to be. So let me make it clear. Fuck off. I'm not pretending for you anymore.'

He left me facing a wall of shirt backs, all of them sweat-stained and streaked with the ash I'd summoned. They went back to their machines, started them up and got back to work.

'Fuck this place,' I said, scuffing my hand on the ute door's latch. It wouldn't open smooth. So I yanked it hard and flung the panel through its arc, climbed up and slammed the door back again. The biting lip of the door caught the seatbelt clip and smashed its plastic cover. I cursed and mashed the gearbox into first.

Mum was packing knick-knacks in the dining room when I got back to the homestead. Dad was in the lounge room watching TV. Both of them were glazed with blank expressions made even more placid by the ticking of the hallway clock.

'Hear about the fire?' Neither of them blinked. I had to tell her, before Sterlo did. Sweat ran thick in my armpits. I wanted to drive back up the access track and tell Sterlo how sorry I was. That it was a stupid mistake that wouldn't happen again. He could trust me. All I managed was, 'We put out a crop fire near the vehicle laager. Nothing serious.'

Mum looked at me and nodded. 'I go to town one time and you mob try to raze the place to the ground.' She sniffed the air and sneezed. 'There's a fire every bloody year. And I always miss them. One time I saw the smoke from the house here and drove up to help. I had blankets and spades and all kinds of tools in the back seat. When I got to the fire all the blokes helped themselves to my gear.' She laid her accent thick, drawling, 'Oh, thanks, Mrs Brockman, good thinking. You saved us the hassle.' A single 'ha' punctuated her response. 'It was no place for a woman back then. Just load the guns like a good wife and keep the kitchen fire stoked.'

She held an old china plate up to the light and inspected its underside. 'This one would have come over from England in someone's packing case.' She wrapped it in newspaper and laid it in a box. 'Probably end up at the Salvos.'

I went to help her. She waved me away. 'I've changed my mind with the sale.' She reached into her pocket, pulled out an envelope and slid it to me across the dining room table's varnished top. 'Take a read. I think you'll like it.'

When I'd read it through twice, she walked to the kitchen, switched on the CB radio and keyed the handset. 'Sterlo, bring the boys in to the homestead. I've got something to discuss with you, over.'

He acknowledged, and five minutes later all the distant engines went silent. The flesh on my chest throbbed where he'd pressed his finger, and the pain got louder and louder as the dust cloud of his ute approached the veranda.

We sat around the dining table. Dad was at the head with Mum to his right, then me on the left, Sterlo opposite, Williamson, Murphy and John rounding out the rest. It was like an annual general meeting, only the air was thick with dust and sweat and the agenda had just one item – the sale – from which a spider's web of possibilities flowed for everyone waiting. Mum cleared her throat, and Sterlo leaned forward in his seat. He looked to me, eyes wide, telegraphing a question – *did you finally talk to her for me?* Mum went on before I could indicate anything.

'I was going to let this property go to a city consortium,' she said. Her voice had taken on a formal tone, slashing away the hints of farmer argot she sometimes let slip. 'They wanted to add it to their portfolio and bring contractors on to run it.' She squeezed Dad's hand as if to make him listen. 'I've had a lot of time to think lately. And I got a letter that made me think twice.'

Sterlo was quick off the starting block. 'So you're not selling, Justine?'

'Still selling. But to a university instead of a company. They need a research facility. Brockman's Place is perfect for that.'

'How do you mean?' Sterlo said, immediately sceptical.

She drew in a breath, kept her measure. 'They are going to rehabilitate half the property. Bring the old kind of bush back. Make that dry creek run again. Bring back all the birds and the animals and rip out the fences and make it like it was before the settlers came. They say it's an investigation into keeping salinity down.' A strange smile dawned across her face, one just south of happiness.

'The other half will still be a farm,' she continued. 'In Septimus I imagine even half a farm is worth as much as a whole one somewhere else. Even if it's for crop research. They've got new kinds of grains to test. Drought-resistant stuff. Higher yields for less effort.' She grabbed my arm and squeezed. 'I always wondered what the place looked like a hundred years back. So did Bryce. I'll get to find out if they ever let us back for a visit. What do you all think?'

Words unspoken, I let my thoughts dwell on what Dad had said at the great rock standing on the Hoths' property, that perhaps we shouldn't be on the land, that things could be done differently. That the master word for us was not wheat.

Sterlo spoke clearly. 'That's a bad idea. You won't get what the place is worth. Plus you'll do us out of any chance of a job.' He looked at me and narrowed his eyes. 'Your son was going to discuss it with you. Now I'll say it. Keep the farm. Let me run it and we can arrange a split of the profits. That way nothing really changes –'

'We've been over this,' Mum said. She laid both hands on the table, splaying her fingers as if to still its movement. 'I just want out of it, Sterlo. I don't want to have to burden you with it. There are other properties that'll take you on.' She looked around the table. 'All of you.'

'Think of the generations that have worked this place,' Sterlo said. 'It's a hell of a thing to let go.'

'My mind's made up,' Mum said. 'Bring in the harvest. Then we'll see what other good this place can do.'

She stood to break the meeting up. Sterlo wasn't finished. 'We've worked for you for twenty years.'

'And you were well paid,' I said.

Sterlo stared. 'What did you say?'

'You were well paid,' I said again, thinking him deaf.

He got out of his chair. With swift strides he was around to my side of the table. 'Say it again,' he said, standing over me.

I inhaled to speak and his fist cracked my jaw. Mum screamed. The room skewed sideways. I landed on the floor beside Dad. He looked from Sterlo to me and back again, staring blankly as the man walked out.

26

Mum took Dad to bed. She didn't pick me up off the floor, offer an icepack or a word of sympathy. Perhaps she was right not to. I shouldn't have said what I said to Sterlo – even though it was the truth. He was a hired hand, not family. When I started at the newspaper, Holt had told me, 'Remember, you will come to love this place, but the place will not love you back.' No man was irreplaceable. No job was either.

'He'll calm down,' Murphy said as I walked the rest of the mob down to the driveway. 'He's pretty attached to this old heap. Nothing lasts forever.'

'Exactly,' I said. 'It's ours to do with as we like.'

'There's more to it than pay packets,' Williamson said as Murphy shushed him. 'No, fuck that, mate. You were out of line, Brockman. Every property in the district wants Sterlo on their crew. He's stayed with your dad and your mum for years. Ask yourself why.'

I jangled the keys to the ute. 'I'll give you blokes a lift.'

'I'll walk,' Williamson said, and started to, followed eventually by Murphy, and then John, who gave a wan smile to substitute any involvement.

'See you in the morning then,' I said, talking to their silence as their footsteps crunched the gravel.

Back home I ran the shower cold. Held my face under the stream till the bruise went numb. Scrubbed my body with soap and one of Mum's loofah sponges, raking the roughness over my skin to get the dust and dirt and itching traces of clipped wheat out. In the mirror, the bruise was a jagged island. The punch hadn't connected fully. The humiliation did. It burned through me. Dad hadn't stepped in. Because of course he didn't, he was too addled and sick. Still the son in me wanted him to rise up and roar and smack the table, intercept the fist, wither Sterlo down with just his eyes and voice.

The light on the veranda at the Chambers' place burned softly through the darkness, giving me a waypoint to aim for as I scuffed through the dry creek and then the short stubble of their harvested paddocks. Every few steps I had to stop and sneeze away the dust clogging my nostrils from the exposed topsoil. It smelled of death and decay, of the potential for new life, tired and spry at the same time, as though the sandy soil was soaking on the interchange bench for the blood rule.

Dogs barked as I crossed an invisible perimeter. I approached the house directly, cutting across the front lawn to the veranda light where Mrs Chambers opened the door, looked at me then yelled inside to her husband that it was only me. 'What's that on your chin?' she said as I went under the loom of the bulb.

'Just the price of work,' I said, playing it off as field injury.

'Good to see you getting into it then.' She held the door half shut. 'It's late.'

'No it's not,' Alison said, bustling through. 'We'll take the dogs for a walk.'

Mrs Chambers shut the door, muttering that farm dogs don't need walking. We took them anyway. A pair of rusty kelpies who knew the way better than we did, back over to the creek, along to the railway track and the distant view of the grain silos at the Terminus, tall cylinders capped with white paint, the effect of a mountain range without the majesty. The shine of the railway tracks drew in starlight, becoming two lines of a lead pencil. While the dogs sniffed through fields and gullies, Alison and I stood in the shadows, private in the darkness.

'Does your jaw hurt?'

The ache was a blade of cold metal. Yet I pulled up my shirt to reveal a bruise spreading along the bow of my ribs. 'This one's worse. Got it hauling jerry cans into the ute tray.'

'You'll live,' she said, and touched my chin at the edge of the fresh bruise.

'How did it happen?'

'I don't want to talk about it.'

'Yes you do. What else are you here for then?'

I considered lying. Considered a joke. Alison looked at me and arched her eyebrows. I told her about Mum selling to a university, making a research farm, and Sterlo asking her to keep it in the family, to think of all the years he'd worked for her. That I told him he was well paid for it.

'You are very punchable sometimes.' She cocked her fist and made to strike. Her laughter made a murder of crows fly from their roost in a dead river gum. 'I'd have done worse than punch you for saying that.'

'Taking his side?'

She kissed me hard so the bruise flared but I didn't break away. I needed the oblivion she'd bring. My hands moved to her waist, under her shirt to the skin of the small of her back.

'Not so fast,' she said, and pulled my grip back. 'Earn it.'

She ran her hands up my spine to the back of my head, ruffling my hair as she pushed my mouth down. I pulled her jeans off, then her underwear, my touch over her dusty skin. She was rocks at the beach, salt on my tongue, fingernails electrifying the train tracks. I huddled in her body deaf to the world, muddled to everything but the quickening of her pulse and the quickening of her breath till she compressed the calluses on my hands and led me deeper into dunes, darker into forest, quieter into the sea, a place where everything was her. We would never do this again. She would never be mine.

The harvest didn't exist. Septimus was abandoned. I had no name. Just an arm around her back and her hand on my chest.

We lay together listening to the dogs pad around about us, sniffing the soil and scarpering after each other in the darkness.

'What are you going to do now?' she said, and I woke from my illusions.

'I guess I'll just have to step up,' I said, knowing how ridiculous that sounded, yet saying it anyway.

'You could apologise to Sterlo. Ask him to come back.'

'He walked out on us. Punched me –'

She covered my mouth. Shushed and pinched. 'I don't want to hear it.' The pressure released. 'Sort it out. That's just what you have to do.'

'I could come work with you.' I shifted my hip against hers. 'Have lunch breaks together.'

'I'm not an excuse.' She sat up and rearranged her shirt, clasped her bra, did the buttons on her jeans. With two fingers in her mouth she whistled to the dogs and they ran over to sit at attention before her. When she stood they walked at her heels, leaving me behind, half dressed in the dark.

The keys to my car hung on a hook on the inside of the homestead's back door. The serrated bit slotted easily into the ignition as I gripped the steering wheel and checked the angle of the mirrors in the weak light. The key turned through two stages to switch the electrics on. One more click would ignite the engine. The edge of the trigger. A centimetre twist. I'd be on my way back south.

Mum stood on the veranda. She looked spectral in her nightie. Her arms were threaded across her chest. The key slid back, and I got out of the car and locked the door with a quick click.

'Testing the battery,' I said. 'Hasn't been turned over for a bit.'

'I thought you were a thief,' she said.

'Who'd steal this heap of junk?'

She came down the steps and held out a hand to me. Didn't say a word. I placed the car keys in her palm. She nodded. Went back inside. The screen door swung shut behind her with a smooth thunk.

'Great work, mate,' I said, and went to where Dad's ute was parked, drumming my knuckles over the bonnet, still making a pantomime of mechanical inspection. I doubt the oil had ever been changed. It would drive till it stopped. There were half a million k's on the odometer and the suspension was so loose the whole left side tipped as I hauled myself up into the tray. Settling back, I looked up at the clear ink of the sky, then the stars. A chain of meteorites burned down six angles like a spread of signal rockets.

'Did you see that?' I said, looking around for someone to share it with, Albert, Dad, anyone. 'Did you see that?'

I rested a hand on the space to my right, where Alison had sat during the harvest party at Hoth's, putting a pill on my tongue to start our thing again. Her darkened face appeared in my vision. 'I'm not an excuse,' she said again.

As if I needed another.

27

'Righto boy' woke me the next morning, but it was only imagined. Real was the bruise on my left cheek. Another cold shower numbed it and woke me to the new day, one without a leader, and all the work to do.

'Just keep your mouth shut,' I said to the mirror. 'Get on with it.' I dressed in my dirtiest change of clothes – the khaki shirt with the nut and bolt for a middle button and shorts streaked with splashes of diesel. At least I'd look the part.

Williamson and Murphy were sitting in their headers when I arrived at the laager. Only John was beside the campfire, warming his hands over the last of its embers. 'You look like shit,' he said, and went to get in his tractor. 'Don't worry. We know what to do.'

I raised surrender with my arms to signal 'engines start' and pointed to the next paddock's nearest edge as the starting point. It was all very obvious, but the wiser version of Dad I kept recalling told me that every orchestra needed a conductor, no matter how familiar the tune. Sterlo had spent most of his days on the CB and the satellite phone checking grain prices, negotiating contracts and communicating with farmers on other properties. Every now and then he'd show us how to do our jobs, bark out some orders and run his work gloves over the shine we'd put on. His job was to be the whip. In my hands, it was a flannel.

'Straighten up there, Williamson, you're missing some. Can you go back?'

'I'll get it on the next pass. That's how it's done usually.'

'Murphy, you're slowing down. Does your comb need a fix?'

'Nope. It just needs to be left alone.'

'John, you on your way back?' Silence. 'John? You coming back? We need that chaser bin.'

'Yeah, I'm coming. Just getting a tea. Anyone else?'

'Earl Grey for me,' Williamson said. 'It's smoko.'

'No, it's nine o'clock.'

'We're taking it,' Murphy cut in. 'Make up for the others we missed.'

I gripped the handset like it was a grenade with the pin pulled. 'Fine. Just we need this paddock done today.'

Williamson coughed. 'What's the rush? You're not paying us by the hour.'

'Don't you want to finish the job?'

Murphy laughed. 'We've got nothing else to do.'

Come lunchtime I left them at the laager and went back to the homestead. I couldn't pretend to be their mate in the circle. I was the officer, and they were the men. Let them gossip. Let them vent. At least at home I had a fairer fight.

Mum was washing the dishes with the old man asleep on the couch. I was still mad at her for saying nothing when Sterlo hit me. My temper loaded itself, shells in the chambers, ready to fire. She looked frazzled, with her hair tied back in a rough knot, bags under her eyes and the clothes she wore the night before still on.

'Sterlo arranged with the co-op for the grain to be off by next week. He was pretty well on track. How is it going today?'

I ran a hand through my hair. 'Okay. We're a bit behind.'

She frothed the dishwater and slid two plates into the bubbles. 'Grain prices are hitting a sweet spot. If we can get the crops in then we make good money. If it's late then we make worse money. And we can't afford that.'

'I thought the sale would cover everything.'

She looked at me like I was an idiot. 'It'll cover the debt. Maybe leave a bit left over. The crops are the ticket. They always were and always will be. So you need to get Sterlo back. He's the ringer of the shed.'

'He hit me.'

'You deserved it.'

The clock ticked. The roof beams cracked. She drained the dishwater and picked up a tea towel to dry them off. 'Your editor called just before.' She nodded to a bank statement on the counter where she'd scrawled the number. It was one digit less than the balance we owed.

Holt's words crackled through the telephone line, precisely shaded, as though he'd rehearsed every syllable.

'You thought you were immune, didn't you? That you could be impartial with something by all rights you should have recused yourself from.'

I had called him back from the phone in the study where the rest of Mum's paperwork was scattered: bills and statements, letters of demand, contracts from two decades ago to the present. It was a web of worry, and Holt was its out-of-time narrator as I rummaged and listened, read bills and tried to hum yes and no in the right order as he spoke in that way of his.

'You think you're too close to the story to tell it right. I say impartiality is the conceit of all hacks. We ask the questions and make the judgements. Direct the lens. Strike the keys. Rarely does the spotlight swing to us and cast our shadows distorted.'

He laughed, and there was the sound of scribbling. Was he writing that quip down for later? The telephone cord nervously wrapped itself around my knuckles.

'When my father died I remember feeling quite detached from it all. Our little family home back in England so pokey and dark. Priests flapping about in black giving the last rites.

They rang the church bells at the funeral. Bells cast in the sixteen hundreds. Quite amazing really. It was theatrical. Each of us had a role.'

He sniffed, cleared his throat, and got to the point. 'Look, my boy, let's just forget the article. It's clearly getting on top of you.'

I held my breath. Any sound I made would be agreement. And I didn't know what to say. The long black highway pulled from the gate at the bottom of the driveway, down through the coast road and the saltbush country and the wind-bent trees to the junction and the freeway and the city buildings scraping the navy sky where the newsroom was clanking and thumping and swearing on its daily kamikaze to the five pm deadline.

'It's very kind of you,' I said, stood up straight and forced my shoulders back. 'I'll get it done. We've just been busy. I don't want to intrude on my family too much.'

He cleared his throat. 'Oh yes you do. But fine then. Show me brave farmers battling the elements and doing good old Aussie hard yakka. Have you been down the pub yet?'

Of course I had. 'Once or twice.'

'And were there any fights? Bush poems? Sun-wrinkled wisdom?'

Mum came in, pointed to her wrist.

'Look, I've got to go.'

'I say when you go.' He paused, scribbled again. 'You are a good young reporter. When you miss deadlines it's disappointing. Deliver it by Friday.'

The article was a red herring. Eight hundred words destined to be a piece of fish-and-chip wrapper. Like a fool I'd promised it – needed a mission as an excuse to come home and do my duty. If I couldn't pack the house or lead the harvest, then I could bloody well tap out some bullshit.

'No problem whatsoever, you can count on it,' I said, and cringed at sounding like a used-car salesman.

'See to it that you do. Stories evolve and change as much

as circumstances. I do understand that. Be warned you're approaching becoming a three-time Charlie now. First is a mistake. Second is carelessness. Third is incompetence. I've been more than generous. Even with your circumstances. News is a beast and must be fed.'

He rang off, and I held the beeping receiver to my bruise. The newsroom was five hundred kilometres away. Holt could only touch me through telephone wires. Yet his voice had lashed me hard as Sterlo's fist. I should have called him straight back, told him I'd changed my mind, to shove the deadline up his arse, that he'd get the article when I wrote it, and it would be about whatever I bloody well wanted it to be. Trouble was I'd already thought of a lead.

28

The blokes knocked off at five on the dot and went to the pub where no doubt Sterlo was brandishing the fist that he would brag 'knocked some sense' into me. He could say whatever he wanted. I'd type the printed version in my home field, the homestead library, and decide the run of things with proper punctuation. I cracked my knuckles and bashed the keys.

```
The  rudest  question  a  visitor  can  ask  a
farmer  is  'how  many  paddocks  do  you  have?'
It's  the  country  equivalent  of  asking  how
much  money  they  make -
```

Dad stomped in. 'Hello there, Rowan.' My fingers froze their pads against the Bakelite letters. He filled the doorway, made it a frame for what had been his exact essence. 'Good to see you're back. What are you up to?'

Rowan. Not Albert, or Alby, or mate. My name. He sat beside me on the couch, jetted a tired breath, and reached to the nearest shelf to grab a random book – *Moby Dick* by Herman Melville. 'Abridged version,' he said, flicking through the pages till a dried leaf fell out. 'Just where I left it. I can't stand the full fat version. I know what a bloody whale is. Just show me the hunt and the flensing.'

I watched him as though he were a museum exhibit. He began to read, appreciating the words with a private whisper till after a few pages he swam back to the surface. 'There's a bottle of scotch in the bookcase. The middle one. Behind the encyclopaedias. Your mother put it there years ago. Thought I wouldn't find it.'

I put the typewriter behind the couch. Holt's article could wait. Everything could wait. Behind the dusty books I found Laphroaig ten-year-old, its white label and green bottle smooth as glass on the beach. I snuck out to the kitchen to get some tumblers. Mum was watching TV in the lounge room, deliberately oblivious, never once turning to the sound of my rummaging. Back in the library I poured doubles and we clinked them together, the first sip hinting at sweet seaweed.

'What are you writing?' Dad twisted in his seat to face me.

'Just an article for the newspaper.'

'The paper?' He took another sip. Then another. 'For the school?'

I was half a memory. Times and places all mixed together. I remembered Mum's advice – don't correct the record. 'Yeah, for the school,' I said, and held the drink up. The whisky tipped warmth down my throat, fading the pain of my jaw to the background. 'What do you reckon?'

Dad knocked his back like a shot. 'Don't mind this stuff.' He held his glass out, and as I poured more measures the room seemed to shrink, the walls growing darker and thicker till my vision was clouded beyond Dad, the couch and the bottle in my hand.

'You coming for harvest this year? Albert's booked himself a block of time off. Be good to have you both on the tools. Maybe all go away for the summer. Like we used to.' Dad looked away, out the window, through his reflection. ' "The years that the locust hath eaten." Churchill said that. One of his speeches. All those missed chances to make peace.'

I'd come back a few times while I was at uni, then cut the pilgrimage off after my brother died. There was always an excuse with an ember of truth: an assignment for the paper, shifts I had to cover, Buckley's chance of getting leave approved.

A month away to work my guts out at a job I hated wasn't much of an invitation. So what did it count to alter the record, even just a bit?

'Sure thing. I'd love to.'

Dad clinked his glass to mine and knocked the drink down his throat again. He coughed hard as the booze stung his throat. 'Give me another,' squeezed out half breath and half order.

'You've got to sip it, Dad. Appreciate it. Slowly.' I raised my glass to the ceiling and admired the amber glow the table lamps gave it. Then I sniffed the top of the glass, wafting the rim side to side to catch the aroma. 'Robert Louis Stevenson said it best. "The king o' drinks, as I conceive it, Talisker, Isla, or Glenlivet."'

'You bloody wanker,' Dad laughed. 'It's a drink. Do you do that with a beer?'

'Depends on the brew.'

'Give me a tin of Swanny D every time. Don't mind this stuff though. It quickens the job.' He cleared his throat, hacking something up and swallowing. 'My old man used to give me a nip whenever I looked like getting a cold.'

A pause came. Grew and waited. I could have asked him about what his dad was like. About the shape of the life he'd led growing up in the same house I did. I could have asked him about anything. Instead I yawned, and he took that as his cue to leave. 'Better let you finish your work,' he said.

I should have refilled his whisky glass again. Dragged the moment out. Kept him engaged. I let him go. When I picked up the typewriter again the bruise on my chin seared with pain and I tasted white chalk in the back of my nostrils. Images played, again and again, me and Dad driving together to a waterhole, talking easily as father and son, nothing to hide between us. I couldn't write – only remember, holding on to a memory of a man unable to make any more with permanent ink.

'Flyboy's Waterhole,' Dad had announced and pulled the truck off the highway onto the gravel shoulder. He'd speared the bonnet down a scrubby track and parked under a gum tree shading a mustard-brown waterhole. The rumour was that an RAAF bomber accidentally dropped its load during a World War Two training flight and ruptured an underground stream to create an instant swimming pool.

'Brought us some beers to take the edge off,' Dad said as we got out and stretched our legs. 'You did well on the tools today. You barely made a complaint.'

We set up a little drinking spot beside the ute with folding chairs. The engine ticked as it cooled down, the metallic clicks mixing with the sounds of the bush – swaying leaves, cicadas, unseen insects by the million. A rope swing hung from the thick boughs of the gum tree, swaying in the wind, a big knot tied to its end so you could hang on and launch into the muck to prove your bravery.

'Cheers,' I said to Dad and we clinked the necks of our beers together. 'This is absolute piss you know. Could have sprung for something imported at least.'

'You cheeky bastard. Nothing wrong with Swan. It's got WA in it.'

'Probably why it gives me a headache.'

'We used to come out here,' Dad said, switching from banter to philosophy. 'Me and me mates. You know them all as misters and missuses now. Back a few years they were just like you and Alison and all the rest. No lines on the forehead or skeletons in the closet yet. We'd drink and jump in the water and fool around and drive like bloody maniacs and do our best to forget that we were kids stuck in the middle of nowhere.'

He looked to me, then looked away, continuing as if talking to himself.

'I always had the feeling that things were going on everywhere else. I was stuck on a calm island, you know? Robinson Crusoe of the Wheatbelt. So I'd drive to Geraldton or down to Perth and see the bands and chase sheilas and all of that. It only made the feeling worse. Then you know I'd always meet some bloke or girl in the city who'd look at me with big eyes and say, "Wow, the country, I've always wanted to live there." Like they were missing out on something too.'

I sighed and wiped my lips with the back of my hand – dismissing him. 'So the grass is greener –'

'No, mate. Stuff the phrases. You have to make your own luck and make your own fun where you are. No-one will give it to you just for showing up. The happiest days of my life have been out here with you and Mum and Albert. You don't have to go chasing things. Most of the time they're right in front of you.'

I changed the subject. 'Are you going to go for a swim?'

He snorted. 'Do you know how many dead cows are in that thing? Probably a few murders too. I doubt even a bunyip would make it a home.'

'Should we go then? We'll want to be back for dinner.'

He leaned over. 'Stay awhile. Just enjoy it. The here and now.'

Galahs chattered above, water shimmered in front of us, and blue sky and gold land lay all around. Still, I wanted to leave.

Dad's coughing woke me just after four am. Through all the walls and closed doors each group of hacks sounded like he was shouting 'how, how, how', and they got louder and closer together. I listened at my bedroom door. When Mum screamed I forced the handle and swung it open.

Bright red blood spackled the sheets. He coughed and coughed and bled and bled. 'Don't just stand there,' Mum yelled. 'Call an ambulance.'

The operator on triple zero talked me through it with calm despatch – yes he was breathing, yes he was conscious; no the pain level didn't seem too high. She talked to her colleagues and then told me it would be two hours wait for an ambulance to come from Geraldton. Then we'd have a two-hour trip back to the emergency department where he would be admitted. My objections were demolished one by one: the job was too low-grade for the Royal Flying Doctor Service, the nursing post in town wasn't staffed that night, and the ambos wouldn't break the speed limit for what sounded like simple pneumonia. 'We'll drive him in,' I said, and hung up.

The exit happened in a rushing smear. Mum packed bags. I dragged Dad to the station wagon, him leaning against me like a wounded soldier. I covered his shivering with a blanket, put a towel over the top for any more blood, and helped Mum shove the luggage in the boot. We didn't say goodbye. See you soon. Good luck. She switched on the engine and slammed herself inside. I stood at the veranda and watched the red taillights till they vanished over a crest. All around the dawn was rising. Another working day. Mum to the hospital and me to the harvest.

I went back to the library and stood in the bay window, watching the sun rise through the crops, casting rays I imagined were flames stoking in the paddocks as Mum's garden melted into kindling for the ember attack. Dad stood in front of me, blocking the heat, smacking the pane with his hands.

29

Birds chattered. Locusts ticked. The day's ignition revved high. I kicked my flip-flops off and walked on the dew-soaked front lawn. The slick cool brought a shiver to my spine that wouldn't connect to my skin. Inside the green perimeter of the homestead, everything was a held breath and time stilled. I could have run down the driveway till my feet bled. Or jumped in the ute and driven foot to the floor west with the sun in the rear-view mirror.

'Hold the fort,' I said instead, and crossed the phrase out midair with a subeditor's red pen.

I went through the motions: got dressed, made coffee, ate breakfast, looked up the rise of the paddocks to the shade tree where the distant figures of Murphy and Williamson and John were rising and readying. I would be no use clogging up a visitor's chair in the hospital waiting room. We had four days to strip the rest of the grain and get it on the way to the customer Sterlo had lined up. He and Mum knew the details of the deal. I just knew the deadline. And I knew how to hit those.

I was heading out the door when a pull of what felt like magnets grabbed around. 'Where are you going, mate?' Albert said – imagination giving him life. His old bedroom was all packed up. Every trace of him had been removed from display. Yet the house was more his than mine. It always would be. I could add clutter to the bookcases. Shed dust to the kitchen rafters. But he was the one who'd installed the new roof beams, working with Dad in the summer heat of the school holidays to knock out the old lengths of jarrah and hammer replacements in.

'They still look good, even unvarnished,' he bragged in my mind. 'See the colour? Medium rare. We never got around to staining them. When the place gets knocked over I'm sure they'll make good kindling for some lucky tradie.' He talked like Dad – to himself and an audience, and then to you.

'Dad's in hospital,' I said. 'His lungs are giving him grief.'

'That'd be the whisky you fed him,' Albert said, fucking with me, my conscience disguised. 'He's an old man, Ro. Wheels are bound to fall off sometime.'

The brother remembered by my mother was invincible. The captain of the ship in a storm. Mine was the merry prankster, his face unburdened by the sun lines and scars it bore when he was alive.

Alby's death had been sudden. Dad's would be slow. Really what was the difference? There was nothing I could do about either.

I told the blokes what was going on and they rallied around the job, said they were sorry to hear it, that Dad was a good man, and then did their work with diligent neatness till knock-off. Sterlo had dumped a satellite phone in Murphy's swag as he stormed off the property, and I used it to call the hospital at every break to check on Dad's condition then broadcast it over the CB. Hang the expense.

The word was that Mum had got there around eight in the morning and the nurses stabilised him till a doctor could be assigned. He had a touch of pneumonia, just like the triple zero operator had guessed, was still in a bad way at the last check, five o'clock, which I ruled as the end of the working day and drove the boys back to the laager for their dinner.

'If you need to go, you need to go,' Murphy said, wiping grease from his hands to his overalls. 'We can crack on without you tomorrow.'

'Like they've always done,' my brother's voice said, and I smirked, shaking my head to clear him away.

'I appreciate that. I'm staying out till Mum tells me otherwise.'

Williamson looked to Murphy, who raised his eyebrows and went to the campfire, kneeling to get sticks of kindling arranged over a cloud of crushed newspaper pages. 'Do what you have to do, mate. We'll stick with it.'

'I need to go to my aunty's funeral,' John said, cutting in. 'I think it's in a couple of days time.'

'Think or know?' I said.

'I'll find out for sure tomorrow.'

Great. Another man down. I swallowed my anger, knowing it wasn't right, that he needed understanding, not the small print of a contract. Mum should have let us take a trip to the coast. Perhaps we'd have detected Dad's illness sooner. We'd at least be closer to the hospital. And I'd be with him.

'Do what you have to do, John. I could drive chaser again, no worries.'

We needed Sterlo back. My jaw still ached from the punch. Murphy saw me rub the spot, and flicked a match to strike the fire. 'Stay away from him. He's still on the boil.' He fed thinly split logs to the crackling base, and when the flames caught, he placed an iron pot with their prefabricated dinner inside on the frame. 'See you in the morning, boss,' he said, the last word close enough to sincere.

Taking a notebook and pen I went to the front lawn where weeds were springing up from the cut I'd given the grass. There were two chairs at the edge to choose from, and I took the right-hand seat, Dad's seat, where he and Mum would have evening drinks and leave me and Albert to do the washing up on pain of death for shirking. Even with the house empty, I felt the anger he'd cast if our farm went idle, out of sync with all the other properties pushing their machines late every night.

I got lost in work, scribbling notes for Holt's article, trying to make some sensible news of the clusterfuck the harvest had become. The flow of the pen on the paper focused the world away from the crunching of tyres rolling toward the house, masked the bang of a car door slamming.

'What are you still doing here?'

The spell broke – Alison stood over me.

'Your Dad's really sick. My mum was on the phone with yours for ages. They were both crying.' She stood over me and held my chin in her hand, inspecting the bruise on my jaw. 'You writing in your diary about it?'

'It's a notebook,' I corrected, swallowing hard, keeping my cool. 'Just sketching a few things for my article.'

'Well, you should go see your dad.' She sat in the chair beside me. 'My dad's hit the roof over what you're planning for this place. Said the bush brings the wild dogs back.' She put on her old man's voice – a posh jackeroo. 'Then it'll be the insects and the flies and then it'll be the Aborigines wanting a native title fight. Mark my words, Alison. If one falls, then so will the rest.'

Out in the east a curtain of dust rose above the land where Hoths' place lay just over a shallow hill, hiding that old granite outcrop that drew Dad in like a magnet. It would have been hot to the touch, pulling in the sun as it had done for thousands of years or more.

'When it's done, I suppose they'll see the sense of it,' I said, imagining the return of the trees, the return of shade and the animals and free-flowing water. 'I've always wondered what it would look like to see the bush as it was around here. Imagine what Australia was like before we got here.'

'You're such a nerd. I'm sure you'll be back to write another story about it.'

'That's not a bad idea.' I set the sketchbook on my knee and pretended to draw her, making her squirm. 'It's just me here you know? You could stay for dinner. Believe it or not, I can cook.'

'We're not in a relationship.' She looked away and the breeze caught her hair, making it a mask. 'We would have been good together, you know? Our parents like each other. We could have gotten our own place nearby. Probably had kids by now. Sent them to school. Have holidays.' She looked at me, and held the gaze. 'The thing I always wanted to see is what the ocean looks like without the water. Just find a way to lift all the water up and see what's underneath. Like valleys and mountains and all the things hidden away. All things we can't ever see. That's what I'd like. You can always bring the bush back, Rowan. You could never lift the sea.'

I saw her at sixteen, happy to see me back from school. At eighteen, cautious that I was back from uni, then coldly mature at Albert's funeral, dressed in colour as a bulwark against grief. Now she was older, and I knew I had missed everything good.

'Do you mean that? That we'd have been good together?'

She laughed and delivered the punch to my arm she'd telegraphed. 'Of course we'd have been good together. Look at us sitting like a sexless husband and wife in the garden. All we're missing is the tea and biscuits.' She hesitated a moment. 'He knows.' Her voice was steady and measured, as though she were reading a psalm at school mass. 'He knows because I told him. And I told him because I know about his woman. So I suppose that makes us even. He said he'd break his off. I said I'd do the same.'

'Like you say, we're not in a relationship,' I said.

She held up a hand, demanding the space. 'You told me that no-one ever tells you the truth. That your mum and dad never said anything to your face. Never told you how they really feel or what they really think.'

'When did I say that?'

'Albert's funeral. When you left during the wake.'

The memory intruded: she'd intercepted me in the parking area behind the Terminus. The drinks were flowing again after the blackout thanks to Dad's move with the generator, and I told her I had to get back to Perth for work, that I couldn't get any time off. I wanted to be alone in my apartment. Drink down beers and smoke a pack with the TV turned up. Be anywhere but a place where people could ask me when I was coming home, when I was going to take over, all while smugly knowing the answer was never.

'I just told you the truth,' Alison said. She pushed her hair back. 'I told you how I feel. At least say something yourself.'

'I've got work to do,' came as a reflex.

'Oh, is that right?' She looked at me with fury. I held her gaze, clenching my jaw to stop myself from saying anything more. My feelings were clouded with poison, the words all shaded and blunt. She shook her head to break the stare.

'I suppose I'd better let you get back to it then. I know how important all this is to you.'

I watched her go. She looked back at me every few steps till she reached the dry creek.

30

Tick. Tock. Tick. Tock. The hallway clock played baroque notes and chimed on the hours, swinging its pendulum through smooth progress. *Tick. Tock. Tick. Tock.* The two-step usually measured me to sleep. That night it pulled me apart, inflicting a lassitude where I couldn't tell if I were sleeping, dreaming or thinking too quickly. Thoughts grew as jungle creepers: Dad in the front seat of the car, slumped under the seatbelt, Sterlo looking at me from across the dining room table, asking if I'd spoken to Mum, Lillee and Bradman licking his hands, begging for the scraps of a dinner Mum was serving from those hideous bone china plates we couldn't find a place for. Harvest. Heat. Holt. White noise twisting an auger screw to pick up grains and dump them in the bunker.

At the strike of two am, I yelled, 'Shut up!', ripped off my sheets and bashed out to the hall where I twisted the standing cabinet away from the wall, pulling the batteries from the back of the mechanism to stop time at thirty seconds past. I had to be up to work in just under four hours. I couldn't get back to sleep until I knew. The phone in the kitchen seemed to dial itself.

'Hello?' Mum said, brightly awake.

'How is he going?'

'No change. Same as before. He's stable.'

'I'm coming to see him.'

She exhaled. 'Not a good idea. You need to stay with the harvest.'

'Alison came over. She said you were talking to her mum. You were crying.'

'Of course I was. Doesn't mean it's all that serious.'

I put the phone down on the counter, rubbed my eyes, and held it to my ear again. 'Look, I just want to come. The boys can handle me being gone for one morning. I'll drive over now and get going back in the morning.'

'It's late. Visiting hours are over.'

'I'll talk my way in. It's what I do for a living.' I hung up before she could say anything else.

'Shut up,' I said, to the homestead and its silence. 'Just shut up.'

The registrar looked me up and down and frowned. Should I have brought flowers? A book? Snacks? Maybe a sixpack of beer would have been in order. Not even a servo would be open. She told me the floor and room numbers, reminding me to wash up before I went to see him. Inside the elevator I checked my reflection in the mirror. All of me was sunburned and wheat dusted. My palms had new ridges of calluses, the nails were blackened with soil. 'You look like a farmer,' I said to myself. 'Or at least a decent impression.'

Up the elevator went, slow and steady, humming and creaking as if with exaggerated care for the patients it usually bore. That tiny moment of lone quiet lasted till the bell dinged and the doors clattered open and I walked down a corridor filled with nurses making their rounds. The doors counted down till Dad's appeared.

I knocked twice. Mum answered. 'He's sleeping. Come in.'

White stubble frosted his chin. The skin of his face was grey. That great body was swaddled in blankets hiding connections for tubes and bags. The faint sucking of machinery and electronic beeps filtered his ragged breathing through a clear mask.

'Is he on life support? Is he dying? What's going on?'

'Slow down, he's out of danger,' Mum said. 'Go sit down.'

Her cardigan was hung over a chair closest to Dad. I dragged another from near the window and sat to watch the steady rise and fall of his chest. My old man was six foot tall. His right hand consumed yours when he shook it. He had a booming voice from a chest that was two axe handles across the shoulders. He was not that shrunken thing.

'There you go, white with two.' Mum handed me a polystyrene cup scalding with tea. An electric kettle steamed on the windowsill next to jars of tea bags, UHT milk and a stack of white cups. 'I've been living on the stuff.'

Green walls. Blue floor. Everything clean and bright. Enough to make you sick. The tea tasted of metal. I took it to the window where a framed view of downtown Geraldton's squat buildings was silhouetted by the waning moon. The busy ocean behind them was chinked with white and black. Directly down eight storeys the deserted greens of a bowls club were bathed yellow by streetlights. Dad would have played if he had retired to Geraldton. He'd have been a fixture at the bar, revelling in pint prices not seen since the days of Empire, using his coal-shovel hands to cup the bowl ever so lightly and send it down the green with supple strength, though he could likely still have thrown the thing clear over the club roof and smashed a windscreen in the car park. Mum would pick him up after she'd gone shopping or had a tea with her friends and they'd drive to their home on the shipwreck coast in one of those new suburbs perched in lonely dunes.

'I'm going down to the cafeteria,' Mum said. 'They open in a minute.' She came to the window and put a hand on my shoulder. 'Do you want anything?'

I didn't, but asked for a choc milk anyway. 'What happened?'

Her voice was as metallic as the tea. 'He developed pneumonia. Probably took hold when he went walkabout. They've given him antibiotics to clear it. Seems to be clearing.'

At his age. In his condition. 'Will he recover?'

'No. He won't. Not fully. There's complications –'

'You're taking care of him. Nursing him back to health.'

'No I'm not. I'm managing the end. That's all I've been doing. For years.' She moved to the doorway. 'Talk to him. He's still there.'

If I could have, I'd have torn down the hospital walls to let in the air and space. Let that be Dad's medicine. He lived outside. Life-support machines buzzed, heart monitors clicked and his breath distilled into a plastic mask.

'I wish I could tell you my life was the way you wanted it.' My voice was a low murmur, as though I were masking an insult. 'No girlfriend. Not at the moment. Nothing serious in the offing. So you'll have to wait for grandkids.' I watched the heart rate monitor. Steady mountains. 'Fuck this. I mean, are you even listening?'

I ran hands over my hair. Scratched my knees. Fidgeted in place. Watched the door and prayed for a nurse to come in and interrupt this ridiculous confession, a confected heart-to-heart. 'Mum said talk to you, so I'm talking to you. Pick a topic. Cricket. Politics. Rainfall. What do you want to know?'

His skin was so pale I imagined him turning to stone, calcium for the topsoil if we scattered his ashes over a paddock.

'I don't even know what's really wrong with you. Every time I ask Mum how you are it's like she's talking about the weather. Like it's nothing to do with me. That she can handle whatever's being thrown at her.'

I took the chart from the end of his bed and scanned the notes. *Myeloma. Inflammation. Metastatic.* It might have been hieroglyphics for all I knew.

'You asked me once why I didn't like farming. I was ten. I said it was because it was dirty. You laughed and told me about Lawrence of Arabia. He said he loved the desert "because it's clean". Why couldn't I see it like that? That utes are supposed to be speckled with mud. Work shirts are supposed to be held together with nuts and bolts and have wrinkles.'

I took his hand in mine and pressed the glove of calluses he'd earned. He opened his eyes. Cleared his throat with a hacking cough. Then whispered, 'Bring me water, boy.' I shifted his breathing mask and lifted a full cup to his lips. He gurgled some down and went back to sleep.

A daze of minutes went by where I listened to the quiet efficiency of the hospital. Nurses chatted at their little desk station. Air conditioning hummed. Bells chimed softly somewhere. I whispered all the words that defined my father's life – thinking it would revive him.

'Salt. Metal. Rust. Rain. Cloud. Sky. Stars. Rock. Dust. Soil. Calipers. Torque. Header. Bastard. Auger. Chaser bin. Terminus.'

No response. I pulled out the bedsheet and wiped my eyes, kissed his forehead and went out to the corridor. Mum walked up with a choc milk carton and another cup of tea in her hands, looking at me as though I'd just smothered the old man with a pillow.

'He's fine. I need a moment. Been a long day.'

'And a longer night,' she said, and handed me my drink. We went back inside to sit vigil, her taking the nearest chair and me the view out the window.

'Give it to me straight,' I said, and nodded at the doctor's chart thick with notes. 'There's more than bad lungs and fading brain.'

Mum frowned. 'It's in his spine. Cancer.'

The shock of the word pulsed my stomach. Mum sat on the edge of her seat with her knees slanted downward, as though she were about to sink to the floor and beg.

'I didn't want to burden you with it. Come home and help with the harvest and pack a few boxes.'

'You didn't tell me he had cancer.'

'Keep your voice down. He's sleeping.'

I couldn't. I wouldn't. 'He's going with you to the coast. He's going to live a few more years. We have time.'

'No. We don't.'

'There's treatments. Chemo.'

Her voice slapped with sudden heat. 'Don't lecture me. We went through all the options. He refused them. The lookout was pretty bad when it first came anyway. He's held on till now.'

'And now?'

'It's been progressing. His wish is to leave it to do its work.'

'Then why didn't you tell me before? I came home to help you pack up. Set up a new life. Not to say goodbye. You should have trusted me.'

She cleared her throat, breathed out hard, and made a cresting wave of words.

'He wanted to keep it quiet. So did I. All of this is going on right in front of you. Just ask me a question. Isn't that your job? You stay away for years. Come back and get drunk and run around with Alison and sleep in and slack off. You've pissed Sterlo off right when we need him the most. Eat all my food and never say thanks and then leave the bathroom floor wet every night. Even if you knew, how much help would you be with this?'

She tucked Dad's bedsheets in, smoothing the creases I'd made in them, adjusted his breath mask. I wanted to scream at her. To smash the window and let the wind in to sweep the room clean. 'You don't let me in,' was all I could muster. 'I offer to help in the house and you refuse. I'm no good in the fields.'

She shook her head. 'If he remains stable then they'll discharge him in the morning. He's taking up space here. There's a nurse who can look in on us if we request.'

'You're taking him home to die?'

She nodded. 'What will we do when he's gone?'

I went to the door. 'I don't know. Call me when you leave.'

31

The bow wave of a passing road train shook me awake. The dashboard clock said 07:44 – just in time for the ABC's big radio bulletin. I switched the key to turn on the electrics and the broadcaster's majestic fanfare marched through the speakers, announcing the reader's vacantly correct tones. She told of a triple-fatality car smash, a budget forecast for the state government, selection woes in the cricket and a chance of a thunderstorm for the Mid West and Gascoyne regions. Nothing I was missing out on. I turned the engine over and crawled out of the culvert by the side of the highway. The old ute chugged up to one hundred and ten with both windows down to catch the last of the early-morning cool. One hundred and fifty k's to Septimus lay ahead, where I hoped the blokes would have sense enough to start work without me.

The intention was to go home. Past the turnoff, past the town, the paddocks faded and the land was bright and empty. I kept going. A kilometre, then another, till I slipped into country where the salt had come to rule, further and further east, where the soil had become poison. Where there were few trees. No birds. Just the crumbling brickwork of abandoned homesteads and the slow turning of windmills left to rust.

'If I had my way I'd let it all go fallow. Let the bush reclaim it. We have no business being here.'

Dad's voice again. An earworm that wouldn't shake. I tried the radio. All I got was static, on both AM and FM. Too far from any transmitter. So I hummed something made up and let the warming air numb the passing minutes. I had the feeling of being a teenager on the run. What did I care what Mum did with the farm? It was hers to dispose of. If her wish was to flog it to some university and let the grass go wild again, then I'd let it be. Alison would keep. Like she said, we weren't in a relationship. It was just fucking. The farm was just work. Mum was just angry. Dad's cancer was just a fast-forward button.

'Sterlo, go to the private channel,' I said, keying the CB handset. I was miles from any receiver or repeater. Getting nothing but static. So I spoke to the sky and the clouds.

'We can't do it without you, mate. I have no idea what I'm doing.' Once I'd said that, the rest came out of me like rope. 'Dad was right. I'm no farmer. Alby was. With him gone there's just me to do the business. I'm fucking hopeless.' I looked at my hand on the steering wheel, lifted the palm to reveal all the blisters and cracks. 'If he was alive, he'd be running the place now. He'd hire you no worries for the rest of your life. You'd run the place well. You and him had all the ideas. I visited him once in Kalgoorlie. Finally got my act together and took the train out. He met me at the station at night and walked me straight into a bar where all of the barmaids were topless. I think I blushed like a schoolboy. Never seen anything like it before. He got a kick out of that.'

Static. Nothing. Just the white noise of dead stars bouncing through the atmosphere. I looked up through the windscreen and pictured Albert when he took me to the top of Mount Charlotte after we had our drinks. The place where the waterpipe from Perth terminated. From the lookout we saw black land and black sky scattered with constellations and the late-burning lights of mine sites. He told me he came up there when he couldn't sleep. Thinking about home and what everyone was doing.

I keyed the handset again and broadcast it to Sterlo, who would never hear it. 'I once asked Dad what he'd do if we ever lost the farm. He said he'd get another one. That he didn't have words. Or maths. Or brains. All he had was his hands. That's all you need on the land.'

A sign flashed up from a dip in the road and I had to brake to read the words smearing past. *Sealed road ends 10 kilometres.* The edge of the map. Here be monsters. 'Meet me tonight at the Terminus,' I said to Sterlo. 'I'll shout you a beer.' Maybe he could hear me. Maybe he couldn't. But that had to be promised.

When I got to the end of the sealed road I saw two strange things for that part of the country – a tall gum tree green with life and a man thumbing a lift from its strip of shade. The brakes squealed and the fella approached my door.

'G'day, Rowan,' he said, hat brim lifting. It was John, from the work crew. 'Reckon you could get me over the salt lake?' He threw his swag in the tray and let himself in the passenger side. 'What are you doing out here?'

I told him I was just going for a drive.

'We wondered where you went,' he said, and explained how Murphy and Williamson were carrying on with the harvest, taking turns to drive their headers while the other drove the chaser bin. 'My aunty's funeral's tomorrow. It's going to be back at my dad's place. He's just in the next district.'

'You were going to just walk there?'

'Don't have a car. No-one could give me a lift. Except you. Just follow the track and I'll let you know where to go.'

We lapsed into silence as the greyed bitumen turned to limestone gravel and got narrow and slippery. Rains had been through recently. There were long seams of white and grey mud churned together as though a plough had coursed along. Further in, the salt lake grew from the land inch by inch, its edges humming white like the ring of sand shoring a Pacific island.

'There's something calming about it,' John said, sniffing deeply on the acrid stink of rotting weeds. 'I come out here when I stay with Dad. It's like limbo. Something like that.'

The horizon was a dark strip, the folded flap of an envelope, splitting the stark haze of the salt lake from faded blue of the sky. The track finished at a shore of the vast expanse where I parked the ute on a shock of samphire plants, figuring their weave of electric green would hold the axles out of the mud. We got out to look at the view, and John picked up a stone and held it in his palm.

'Reckon I could skip it?'

'Nah. Too shallow. It'll just stick.'

He chucked the rock sideways. It hit a thin layer of water hovering above the salty mud and flicked skyward. 'Should have put a bet on,' he said, and in a mad rush we stooped and picked up more and hurled them at the lake, driving each other on, good throws and bad throws, whooping and hollering till streaks of mud painted our hands and shirts. When I couldn't find any more rocks to throw, I sank to my haunches and trailed my fingers in the mud. Fatigue seeped through me.

'Are you really going to walk across? It's pretty far, mate.'

John threw his last rock. 'It's a shortcut. Saves hours.'

The salt lake was at least two kilometres across at its widest. The land all around it was a harsh table of rock and mud and dead trees. John had his swag, which I guessed had water and food wrapped up in it. Maybe he'd live off the land. Yet all around us was dead and dried. It would be no worries giving him a lift across it all.

'You're Yamatji, right?' I asked. There was something about his demeanour that welcomed such bald curiosity, something so disarming, so calm, that I felt he was the oldest friend I had, though I barely knew him.

'Mum was,' he said. 'Dad was a stockman. They met on the Canning route. I guess they needed something to do.' I laughed at his quip, which felt an old family joke, and John seemed to appreciate my getting it. 'He's still going. Come over sometime. There's always people dropping in to his place.'

'I've got to get back. Get this harvest finished. If I can.'

John laughed. 'It's pretty easy, really.'

'Not without Sterlo.'

'Nah, he's just good at bollocking us. We know what to do. Just point the blokes at the paddocks and tell them to strip them. It's not that hard. You used to work with your dad?'

'When I was a kid. I left for the city. Not much of a farmer.'

'Yeah, I can tell.' We laughed together, and he squatted down next to me. 'Mum told me everything's a circle. That it all exists at the same time. So you're still a kid. And your dad's still in the fields working.' He paused, and I let it grow. 'I don't feel alone in this country. I know it. My ancestors knew it. Even when it's just me, I know I'm not alone. Because it's all here. Plus I've got the white side of the family. They just plough ahead and never look back.'

'What do you think about my mum's idea? To bring back the bush.'

He stared out into the heat haze rising over the lake. 'The bush will come back, eventually. When we're all gone.' He looked at me and smiled. 'Be nice to see it.'

32

Simple science driving over mud: keep the engine revs up and never let the wheels stop moving. Even a moment's pause to change gear can sink the rims into that pressured suck. Then you're fucked.

'See that windmill there? On that little hill?' John pointed through the cracked windscreen. I followed his finger till I saw a spindly aluminium flower whirling slowly in the distance. 'Keep that old thing straight ahead and you'll be right.'

The land had been cleared for grain paddocks before the salt came to the surface. John gave me commentary, saying the old farmer who cultivated them had whacked a procession of long fences right through the middle. With no trees to keep the water table down, the salt came up and turned the tilled earth to muck that swallowed the palings. He fought the tide, smacking fences in till they all lay staggered together to make a duckboard road in the muck.

'When you come back you can just drive over your tracks,' John said as we approached halfway. 'Just don't stop, whatever you do.'

The tyres spun between losing their grip and biting down hard. The chassis twisted and rocked, cracking its spine like a chiropractor.

'Keep going, you piece of junk,' I said, willing the machine on. Because farm gear goes till it doesn't. Then you walk away and leave the corpse to rust. On the salt lake that wasn't much of an option. So I kept that bloody windmill truly in the centre of the bonnet, using a chip in the windscreen between the wiper blades as a crosshair and squinting in the pure light of white sky and white land till we bumped back onto a road of chipped limestone, shimmering as if it held petrol fumes.

'You ever driven across before?' I said to John, who shook his head.

'Always walked. But that was good going.' He slapped a hand on the outside of his door, like a jockey urging a horse. 'You should have asked me that before.'

Too bloody right. 'You seemed so confident,' I said, and we laughed together; boys who'd been stupid and gotten away with it. So far.

'Look out,' John said. I didn't see until it was too late. A brown snake was crossing the track, hidden till its long body thudded twice under the axles. I slowed and threw the ute in reverse to the edge of where the snake was writhing in its death throes. The body was crushed in two places, pink flesh spilling from the brown skin holding it. Alive but dead. John did the decent thing. Got out and took a shovel from the tray and smashed its head with a single blow.

'Good thing you didn't swerve,' he said when he hopped back in, and we drove the rest of the way in silence.

The vice of John's dad's handshake crushed my knuckles. 'Appreciate you giving my boy some work,' he said, hard eyes of hard miles. 'Come to the shed. I've got the kettle on.' He spoke like Australians used to, linking all the words together beneath a high-pitched twang. 'Don't mind the mess. Or the dogs. You'll get used to it.'

The property was strewn with the faded plastic of kids toys and rubbish, wild as the weeds jutting from the gap between the house stilts and the ground.

'Got three brothers and two sisters. They've all moved away,' John said, walking at my heels. 'They'll all be coming here for the wake. He's cleaned the place up pretty well.'

'Yeah, definitely,' I said, pushing dogs aside as they jumped up to sniff me. 'Do you live here? I thought you were from Mingenew.'

'Live there most of the time. But since mum died I come stay with Dad sometimes. Keep him company. My aunty used to call in too. She was mum's sister. All pretty close.'

We walked silently behind the old man – he never told me his first name, and never asked mine. He struck me as a man who'd gotten beyond that kind of thing. In the shed he gestured to a seat and handed me tea in a tin mug with no handle. I held onto its scalding sides with the tips of my fingers, while he held his cup in the flesh of his palms.

'Used to work for your dad. Back in the seventies. Lots of bad years around here. So I went on the tools. Lost touch. How's he travelling?'

John exhaled, shaking his head.

'Nah, it's okay,' I said. 'He's not doing too well. Won't be long.' Didn't go into details, and the old man nodded as if he knew anyway.

'That's the way of things.' He thought a moment. 'We didn't get on for a long time. I gave him stick about water rights. That old creek you've got near your place? It used to feed us too. He backed the council when they diverted it to the Septimus scheme. Made things here pretty tricky.'

All I could do was nod. Saying sorry wouldn't have been genuine, even if it were good form. And so the old man smiled, looking over my shoulder to a memory.

'He always got his way. Smarter than most of the blokes around here. What we used to call a true merino.' He put his mug down and blew on his fingertips. 'This place here was never much of a farm anyway. Too much salt in the soil. My woman was right about it. I should have just let it be.'

We talked about the harvest. We talked about the weather. We talked about the state of the crops and the state government. Round and round in safe topics that held no surprises. Week after week of fatigue boiled away from my body in layered sheets. Dad sleeping in a beeping bed while cancer grew inside him. Dad coughing blood. Sterlo's punch. Sparking the crop fire. Stripping and dumping. Shooting the dogs. Driving north on the highway. All that lactic acid from all those blurring moments leached all the way back to me seeing a black slick of blood shining on a Northbridge pavement beside a detective's scuffed shoes.

'This is the first time I've just sat and had a chat in weeks,' I said, appreciating the attention of my sudden, strange company. 'I haven't slept properly in two days.' The old man rose from his seat and went to a bookshelf groaning with greasy technical manuals and old magazines. There was an old leather folder slid between the weathered papers, and he brought it out to show black-and-white and sepia photographs of the land, people, men and women and cattle and crops, nameless and silent beneath clear cellophane covers.

'There's a few of your oldies in here somewhere.' He flicked to the back pages and there they were, in faded colour print, both of them young and happy and smooth, smiling in someone's kitchen as a flashbulb illuminated their youth. 'My Gladys was the photographer. Mad keen on it. Learned it from some nun on the missions. That's how we met. She went to take my picture on the stock route. Of course I said something stupid to her. "Don't you people believe that thing grabs your soul?" She told me to bugger off or she'd grab my balls.'

He turned the album to its front page, and there he was in black and white, a young man in a checked shirt and stockman's hat with his head thrown back in a perfect moment of laughter. 'Yeah she caught me alright. We had good years together.' He nodded to John. 'Not everyone understood. I never gave much of a damn what other people thought.'

I didn't ask for his life story. I made excuses to go, but he kept talking with a weary air that held me back into my seat with matchless authority.

'It's always been frowned upon. Black and white together. By the high layer of society, I mean. Not the everyday people who are just busy getting on with it. At least not most of them. There's a long history of love in this country. We ignore it because we think it's too complicated. Too risky.' He smiled at John, who smiled back, his face a smooth mirror of the old man's.

'She wasn't allowed in the pub. So I never went. She wasn't allowed in dining halls. So we ate outside. One day when she was pregnant with our first we were camped on the coast near Jurien Bay when some fishos came up to our fire and asked to join us. Course we said yes and they put a fish on the flames. We all had beers. Plenty beers. Till one of the fishers got out of hand. Asked me, "What are you doing with that black?" I told him it was none of his business. That he shouldn't speak to her that way. He said seeing as he'd given us fish and beer he could speak any way he liked to her. So Gladys stuck her fingers down her throat and brought it all up into a billycan. She said to him, "Here's your fish back." They ran like the cowards they were.'

We cracked up together while John clicked his tongue. 'That's why you won't let us eat fish.'

'Bloody right. She banned it after that. Shouldn't have been eating it anyway when pregnant. Though search me what the Japs do when they get up the duff.'

He took the album from me. 'You're lucky to see that. Maybe it'll help you understand.'

'Understand what?'

'Who gives a shit what people think.' He put a hand on my shoulder like an old mate, the splay of his fingers surprisingly strong. 'I heard what your mum's doing with the property. Bringing back the bush a bit.'

News travels fast. 'You think she's crazy?'

The old man considered that, and smiled. 'We've tried a lot of things around here. Ploughs and headers. Crop dusters. Superphosphate. There was even a mad bastard who brought a flock of ducks in, like an Asian farmer. Maybe doing nothing will work.'

He ushered me outside where the sky was darkening with clouds. He said I could stay. That it looked like rain. I just shook his hand and said, 'My condolences for your loss,' ending how I should have started.

33

The road threaded through a chicane of ice-white sand dunes, piled up by the freshening wind as relics of some ancient beach. Cockatoos coming in to roost were the only daubs of colour for miles around. I drove in a daze, given over to the vibrations of the steering wheel, the engine at two and a half thousand revs, that old photo of a young Mum and Dad a cataract in the windshield. Mum young and pretty. Dad looking dangerous. Together they'd make my world. In that faded colour print they were both still at the crossroads, though for him it was forward or nothing, and retreat was never going to happen. Mum was the only one of us who could really say she had said yes to distance, drought and debt. Would she choose it again if she had known how it would play out? Hard years on a landlocked island. Having an heir to take over the real work and a spare determined on a city job. Then my brother dies in a mine, drowned when a dam full of muck from the processing plant burst.

My foot pressed the brake and the ute pulled to the shoulder of the road. The salt lake stretched away down below. Projected in its white-on-white sheen was a cinema of memories real and imagined: photos from the mining company's report showing bodies being dug out with a bobcat, the coroner finding no fault, Dad's anger compressing like coal into an industrial diamond, spinning cancer into his cells one by one. The moon rose and fell. The crops grew while bills stacked up. He forgot his name while I stayed away, refusing to fill my brother's shoes, or help

Dad put on his own. Mum held the centre. Mum chose the life. Accepted the consequences.

'I wouldn't have helped anyway, even if she told me,' I said, switching on the CB and scanning the static for voices. 'Cancer's just another reason to stay away.'

The gearbox crunched as I aimed the bonnet away from the limestone track that led to the bitumen, which would lead to home. Down into the white, pressing hard to the steering wheel.

John had told me to drive back in the tracks we'd created on the first crossing. To stick to the submerged line of the old cockie's fence. His old man said to stay the night at his place. Don't tempt the weather. But no-one believes the weather forecast in the bush. Not till the rain is hammering on the veranda roof and the hands are scrambling to pull a tarp over the piles of wheat do we admit the bureau got it right.

And so it went that with the home shore of the salt lake almost within reach a collage of dark blue clouds shuddering with rain gusted overhead. Great falls of water carpeted down like bombs from an F-111. The drops hammered into the metal tray and knocked on the cab, sending rivers of muddy dust down the windows.

'Never on time, never enough,' I yelled, defying the sky, revving the engine to the red line. The whole back end slewed to starboard and buried the wheels hard. My brain and mouth and fists exploded.

'You piece of shit. You fucking stupid bastard piece of shit.'

The rains belted down till I couldn't hear anything except white noise. Then it stopped as suddenly as it came. The grey clouds cleaned themselves away from the sky. All around me the salt lake was a lake again, a good six inches of water soaring to the shore in perfect reflective stillness. I cracked the door and stepped out. Mud swallowed my right foot. Then the ankle and shin. It pulled like a game of tag in a swimming pool, and then played for keeps when my knee plunged below the waterline.

I grabbed onto the car frame and tried to pull myself out, crooking the left leg into a yoga stretch beside the straight right, something to push off. The mud sucked harder and the crotch of my jeans sponged up brackish water. All I could do was lean inside the driver's door and hold onto the foot pedals.

My mind raced: what would Albert do? He'd fashion a ladder from the running board of the ute, making pincers of their work-worn fingers to unscrew the bolts and rip it clear. Or he'd have had a signal rocket handy under the driver's seat, or a Swiss Army knife in the door pocket, or a foldable shovel clipped to the underside of the chassis. He would never have driven over the lake. He'd have listened to his instincts and taken the long way around. Instead of risk he would have chosen reward with a pint and parmi at the Terminus where he'd have listened to the rain rush the corrugated tin roof.

'Fuck, fuck, fuck,' I yelled, the barking echoes folding back and forth across the lake. Birds flew home to roost as twilight turned to blue night and the stars and moon emerged. My left leg cramped, my back twisted, and all I could do was plank myself down on my forearms to ease the agony of it.

'Rowan, where are you? Rowan? Come in, over.'

Mum's voice chimed from the CB speaker. The engine had conked out but the battery was still good, still keyed on. I lifted myself up as far as the mud's suction would allow and reached inside the cab. The radio was mounted to the inside roof, and the handset was way out of reach.

'Rowan, we're back at the homestead. They discharged your father like I wanted. Are you there? Look, I just had a chat to John on the phone. He said you were driving back from his place. Don't go over the lake. There's rain coming.'

'Yeah, no shit,' I said. 'Tell me something I don't know.'

She paused. 'Sterlo called me at the hospital. He's agreed to come back and finish the harvest. So you don't need to worry about leading it. Okay? Are you there?'

I smacked at the mud. Pulled at my leg. Punched the metal

door. 'Fuck, fuck, fuck.' I wanted to help. I wanted to lead the harvest. For fuck's sake, I wanted to do something for once.

'Then why didn't you go straight back?' Albert said, his memory taunting me.

'I'm on the lake,' I yelled. Useless. No point. Waste of time.

'Son, if you're there, please answer,' Mum said. Her voice was tired. Each message took longer and longer as she drew out her breathing, as if searching for the right words but couldn't find them.

'Come on, Ro. Stop being like this. I'm sick of it. I really am. Ro? Are you there? Key the handset if you can't talk.' I bashed the door twice. 'Fine. Be that way.' The radio hissed and the channel went dead.

Panic surged. I'd die of exposure. Of thirst. Break my bones trying to get free – just as those poor bloody sheep had done.

Sterlo was supposed to shoot them. He had said that he would. Maybe he'd come and put me out of my misery too.

I reached into the ute, grabbed what I could and set the items in the foot well: a book of ordinance maps for the district, an electric torch with no batteries, a few old drink cans and a pocketknife whose folding blade had rusted to the haft. Nothing of real use. Nothing of comfort. I dug my fingers into the top crust of the mud and ripped at it till my nails rasped and the flesh on my fingers went numb. The sun went low in the sky, diving for the night, and I laughed till the salt of my eyes ran into my mouth and reminded me how thirsty I was.

34

The heat of the day evaporated from the salty mud. The moon rose three quarters. The ute shielded me from its cold light, casting deep shadow. Whenever I shifted my weight to ease the burden, another joint protested, another bone bent till all over I felt like the cartilage of a bruised nose. My mind ached with the job of having to think of things to distract: girls I'd been with, places I'd been, scenes from books and movies and stories forming a constant shuffle. The creeping chill numbed my legs. Nothing could filter the boredom. Or alter the reality of being alone in the dark, lost in the wild, an idiot stuck by his own making.

Hour after hour and minute after minute and second after second and moment within moment, shuffle, shuffle, shuffle, thoughts came like incantations till I felt a blur of vertigo that made me picture myself as a tiny speck from above. I'd never get out. No-one would find me. The rain would come again and the water would rise and I'd drown like my brother.

'He finally agreed to stay,' some wiseacre would quip at the wake after my bleached bones had been buried in the family plot. 'Too soon,' someone else would correct, and they'd all get back to sinking their pints.

I shuffled again and saw John's old man proud on his starved property. Saw the bloke behind the counter at the service station on the highway, handcuffed by debts to a dusty run of days. Michael the shepherd, determined to grow his flock again. Williamson and Murphy and Sterlo following the seasons. My brother. My dad. All of those men who stayed. Despite what the years threw at them, they stayed. Then Mum, Mrs Chambers, the CWA women, the waitress in the café and the woman at the shop. They held the line, kept their posts, kicked against the pricks.

'Stop it,' I hissed. Another shuffle came. Images played in the dark. Ones I hadn't allowed for so long came to float on the salt lake's reflection.

'I'd like to thank you all for coming today,' Dad said, standing on a chair in the front bar of the Terminus. It was standing room only with all the black-clad mourners from the church silent for another respectful moment. Only Alison wore colour – the purple paisley scarf at her throat framed her stilled beauty. She looked at me from behind her father's shoulder, the tears in her eyes brimming as a sad smile came.

'It is a tragic thing to lose your son before his time. I thank you for the support you've given to our family. We've been in this district a long time. I hope we can stay a bit longer. Because if we do, we know we'll be surrounded by so many good friends.' He held his glass high and kept his voice strong. 'Here's to Albert. As good a son as you could ever hope to have.'

'To Albert,' said the crowd, and they all took a sip. Eyes watched me from over the rims of tipped-back glasses. I helped Dad down from his perch and the chatter resumed at full volume. Dad shook hands with men and accepted kisses on the cheek from women, lowering his head to acknowledge all their solemn comments. I couldn't wait to get out of there. To get back in my car and drive all the way to Scarborough where I could be alone. Where I didn't have to bounce from chat to chat with parents of kids I went to school with and friends of my parents and fixtures of the community, explaining to everyone what I was doing for work, that no, I wasn't coming back, and yeah, Dad would be needing help, but I was sure he'd manage without me.

The bar was a safe zone and I clung to its brass and wood, holding up my glass for a refill. From there I saw Mum in the far corner, sitting with friends at a booth table, all of them wiping tears from their eyes and punctuating the air with their wine glasses. Mum was holding herself straight, her back hard against the wall cushion, both hands knitted together as though she was praying.

She turned and smiled. Held a hand out and gestured me over.

I slid the drink back to the barman and went out to the car park.

Even all alone, with no-one around, shame bowed my tears. The moon shadow of the ute and the edge of the driver's seat cushion smothered the cries, but not the truth, the cold hard fact, direct language shorn of sentiment. Dad, Albert, Sterlo, Holt, my measure in their eyes – that was all bullshit. I had refused her love that day. Refused it ever since. Yet it was the only love that remained. And I was too stubborn to accept it.

My regret refracted back and forth across the salt lake till it became one scream, projected onto itself in a maddening loop that brought more memories, seen from angles I'd shut my eyes to.

'It's close to the beach and the strip. So I don't need much.' I turned the key and opened the door, standing aside to let Mum and Dad inside. The old man stumbled over the entrance step and I switched on the light to help him see inside. He whistled at the bare walls, bare floors, and bare kitchen.

'Very monastic,' he said, hands in his pockets. 'Bed and books, couch, a kettle and a tin of coffee. What more does a man need?'

'Proper furniture,' Mum tsked. Ran a finger theatrically over the benchtop. 'A woman's touch. Several I'd think, working in shifts. This place is filthy. You don't even have a sheet on your mattress.'

'It's in the wash.'

'It's disgusting.' She peeled back the blinds to the balcony and laughed at the view. 'Lets go to a café. I actually want to see the sea.'

As I locked up, I grabbed a folder from under the mattress and put it under my arm. Inside its covers was a sheaf of documents from the coronial investigation into the accident that killed Albert. I must have read it through a hundred times, flicking over witness statements, blueprints of the mine shafts, lo-res copies of photos taken by investigators. The man who led the rescue effort mailed it to me at the newsroom, saying in the cover note that he'd quit the company and hoped the information would be a comfort. To my mind it was. When I showed it to Dad, he flicked through with a satisfied air, the papers answering the outstanding questions he had.

'Your coffee's getting cold,' Mum said, sipping hers. 'Read it later.'

'It's actually very interesting,' he said, showing her a diagram amid the click and clack of cups and saucers. 'This is the main shaft here. Then there's the side access where –'

'I don't want to see it.' Mum scraped her chair back and stood. 'I'm going for a walk on the beach. Alone. Keep your paperwork to yourself.'

'I just thought it would help,' I said, hands holding up surrender. 'Get the facts straight. You know? This kind of info was held back from the public.'

'I don't need any info. My son's dead. He drowned in the middle of the fucking desert. I don't need the details.'

She took her coffee cup and strode off, shooting the waitress a look that brooked no objection to her taking the china for a walk. Dad watched her go and shrugged his shoulders. 'She'll be okay, mate. Just give her a minute.'

'What's her problem? I'm just trying to help. This is what I do for a living. It'll help her get over it.'

Dad inhaled. 'She won't get over it. Neither will I. Have you?'

The waitress took our empty cups away, a welcome

interruption. I turned in my seat and caught a glimpse of Mum crossing a car park, headed for the windbreak sand dunes and the low tide beyond.

35

High beams arced across the lake like the gaze of a lighthouse. I didn't realise they were coming for me till two figures sloshed through shallow water and started digging with their hands. 'Already tried that,' I said through sapping cold.

'I'll get the shovel then,' a man said, his voice unmistakeable.

'Sterlo.'

The woman shushed me. 'Try not to move, love.' I gripped Mum's hand and squeezed, just to make sure she wasn't a memory.

'You're stuck in here pretty good,' she said, crouching down, holding on to the ute so she didn't sink too. 'John called. Said you were coming this way. Which was pretty dumb. I've a good mind to leave you in here till you see sense.'

'I've been an idiot,' I said, tugging at my trapped leg. 'Just pull me out.'

'Wait till Sterlo gets the shovel. A few incisions and we'll have you free.' She took a hankie from her jacket and wiped my forehead, an old-fashioned gesture, something mothers are supposed to do, but she'd never done till then. 'He's been good enough to come back to work. After what you said, I wouldn't have blamed him if he never did. He's an honourable man. Always has been.'

'He's sure taking his time,' I said, chancing a joke, and Mum looked over to the ute where Sterlo was rummaging for tools, metal ringing metal.

'He's giving us a moment.'

She stood up and stretched, making the moon a halo for her hair. 'Got a call from the university. They're going to send out a team to survey the land and come up with a plan. I told them to come sooner rather than later. Maybe some of the boffins can help us load the packing boxes.'

'They'll have softer hands than I do,' I said, and sank down onto my bottom, finally letting the water win the tug of war. 'Did you tell them about this place? They'll have a job to guard our place against the salt. I didn't know it was so large.'

She leaned beyond the ute's moon shadow, her face lighting up white. 'There goes an owl. See it?' She pointed to a fast-moving wrinkle. 'There's plenty of them still around. When the bush grows back there'll be more of them. Maybe there's even hope for this land too. It sure didn't used to be like this.'

A glacier moved inside me. Sterlo would come back in a second. Perhaps I'd never get the chance again. 'You asked me in the hospital what we'd do when Dad goes. And my answer is I really don't know.'

Mum knelt back down, grimacing with the effort. 'I've told you. Buy a nice place and live the rest of my life. You get what's left over.'

'That's not what I mean. I mean us. You and me.' I took her hand again. 'When he's gone it's just you and me left.'

She touched the bruise on my cheek. 'This looks nasty.'

'It was justified.'

She nodded. 'Yes it was.' Her hands gripped under my armpits and pulled. It was just a moment's relief from the pain of holding my own weight, but enough to make me gasp, make the blood swollen in my right leg ache with the pressure of what felt like a burst pipe.

'The doctors said we could take Dad home,' Mum said. 'They asked have we made the necessary arrangements? I haven't thought that far ahead. I figure he'll cark it in bed. Beyond that I don't know.'

'That's a bit macabre,' I said.

'We talked through every detail when he was still with it. He wants to be cremated. There's a few hundred dollars set aside to put over the bar at the Terminus. He wants Bach's *Cello Suite No. 1* as the funeral dirge.'

'Thought he hated classical. Like me.'

'He knows I like it. Funerals are for the living.' She squeezed my shoulders and let go, easing me down. 'It's just a body. The spirit is the thing. His went a long time ago. We just get the echo. Soon to fade.'

She leaned over me into the driver's side, fiddled with the keys till the dashboard lit up, and pressed the cigarette lighter in. 'Want one?' She lit two from my pack on the doorjamb with the red-hot coil. 'That's been the hardest part of it. Living with a stranger. If the old him caught me having one of these he'd wring my neck.'

'He didn't mind me doing it so much.'

Mum arched her eyebrows. 'Everyone's got to have a vice. Mine was having kids.'

'What was his?'

'Farming,' she said, and stifled a yawn. 'Maybe it should come with a warning. Working on the land is bad for your health, your bank balance and your sanity. Not that that's too discouraging to men like him.'

'Takes two to tango,' I said, grimacing against the pull of the mud. 'John's dad showed me a picture of you two when you were young.'

'Oh yeah? He was pretty wild back then. Always had a harvest party at his place the night before it began.'

Our smoke twined in the air between us. Breath choked in my throat. I knew what I wanted to say. Uncloaked by metaphor or hidden behind technicalities. I hissed the cigarette into the water beside me, and allowed myself to speak.

'You were in his kitchen then. Real seventies. You had long hair. Dad had a beard. It looked like you were having a good time. The photo got me thinking about how things were before.

When Albert was alive. How I acted at his funeral. How it all changed after that. Because there was nothing for me here. Just expectations.'

Silence grew. Sterlo was still rummaging in the ute, playing for time, or delaying my rescue, I didn't care. I strained to hear Mum's voice respond, forgetting the pain in my leg, the storm in my head, pushing aside the unfamiliar fear of saying what I really felt to savour her words, listen instead of wait to speak.

'When I came out here for my teaching placement, I hated it. They warned me. Don't fall in with a farmer. They'll get you to stay. Of course that was the game, wasn't it? Sending young, single females to a place with very few of those. I knew supply and demand in economics. So I told him to convince me. Convince me to stay. So he picked me up in his ute and drove me to a ridge above the highway to Geraldton. We walked along a path through the scrub, up and up till we reached a slab of rock that was warm as a bath from a day in the sun. I could see all the way to the sea, with paddocks and valleys and low-flying clouds in the dusk. He was a looker. Strong and capable. Good family. Good prospects. I needed to know what his essence was. And it was love of the bush and the land and his place in between them. I don't know what I'd have done if he took me to the pub or shooting roos. I loved your father then and I love him now. I hate this place sometimes. I stayed because I love it too. It's where we belong.'

All my old resentments and arguments dialled in, waiting in the wings for their turn to be called onstage. I waved them away. A few incisions of a shovel and I'd be free. A few more minutes weren't going to kill me.

'How long has Dad been sick for? Not the cancer. His mind.'

Mum shook her head. Exhaled and yawned. Covered her mouth with her hand. 'Since you were twenty. It got worse the summer Albert died. He started to forget things when you got the job at the paper.'

'Albert was chipping in with his mining money,' I said, letting everything back in. 'He wasn't just going to buy out the farm. He was paying for stuff while Dad was sick.'

She nodded. 'Yeah. He was. He wanted to help. Wanted to take over. You know that. It was a decent arrangement.'

I let it go. 'Yeah. It was a good thing. I'm sorry I couldn't do it.'

Finally, Sterlo came over and cut me out, working silently, each sink of his spade wedging out a chunk of muck till my knee and shin and ankle were free. When I stood, the pain in my leg rippled to a storm.

36

I woke under white linen with all creases carefully ironed out. The curtains were tied at their waists to let in the high angle of the sun. A spray of fresh cut roses in a vase reddened the wall beside. *Let this be a dream*, I prayed, as ratchet by ratchet the pain in my leg proved it wasn't.

Hobbling and puffing, I crept through the warming house. The grandfather clock beat its restored heart in the hallway, a steady rhythm beneath the buzz of harvesters in the paddocks. Perhaps I'd slept for days. Was it the last day of the harvest? Was the house all packed and ready to leave? Maybe all I had to do was walk out to a waiting car where Dad would be sleeping in the front seat while Mum drummed the bonnet with nervous hands.

From the kitchen window I could see my charmless old Holden was the only car parked in the usual spot. The work ute was bogged in the salt lake, while Mum's station wagon was gone for the day. Like usual, there was no note in the kitchen explaining things, just a tray with tea things and a loaf of banana bread sweating under a cake stand. She must have taken Dad to the nursing post for a check-up.

With a careless step, my bad leg stamped on the lino floor. Pain burst upward. And in a lightning flash of certainty something primal asserted itself. I threw on field clobber and hobbled to my old Holden, wishing I had Dad's old ute instead. It would be too hard to pull that workhorse out of the salt lake's mud. Rust would already be eating its vitals, saline water corroding rubber and metal with equal patience. I'd work with what I had.

Turning my car's brittle little engine over, the cylinders cleared their throats for the first time in weeks with a whining belch of white smoke from the exhaust pipe. It wafted over the homestead and dispersed into an appallingly blue sky, not a cloud in sight, just white yellow sun and a faint spray of daytime stars, perfect harvest weather for the boys in the fields.

The car drove steadily and I felt like a passenger, not the driver, my hands resting on the wheel as it flicked and turned its way along the access tracks, the wheels following deep grooves cut into the surface. A great gout of dust was rising from where Williamson and Murphy were cutting through the last redoubts of ripe wheat in their headers. There was a third header at work too, a faded red unit at the far side, probably one Sterlo had borrowed to speed up the work and hit the deadline fast approaching.

As they worked I waited at the shade tree for ten o'clock smoko. As soon as the time ticked over the engines switched off and Sterlo's ute rounded each of the crew up and drove over.

'What the hell have you been doing?' he said, turning off the engine and slamming his door. 'You're supposed to be resting up. That ankle of yours will be pretty tender.'

Williamson and Murphy watched me intently as they walked over to their seats near the ashes of the campfire, scrutinising my reaction.

'I need to dig those sheep out of the waterhole,' I said to Sterlo, my voice clear and steady. 'I've been neglecting to do that.'

'No, I have,' Sterlo said. 'I'm the shepherd on this property. I said I'd do it. I'll get around to it.'

I held up my palms, both streaked with lines of mud and burst blisters. 'I'm not having a go. I'm just telling you. I need to do it. Now.'

I held Sterlo's eyes and didn't blink. I told him I was a dickhead for what I'd said to him. Said I was sorry for how I'd behaved. Asked for his help to do what needed to be done.

He looked away to Williamson and Murphy. 'Sort yourselves

out.' He looked back at me. 'You're driving,' he said, and threw me the keys to his ute.

We didn't speak till the waterhole appeared, freshened by recent rain so the mud was still slick. 'They're dead,' I said, looking at the three white shrubs planted in the mire – three ewes stuck to their bellies.

'They were always going to die,' Sterlo said. 'If I'd gotten to this sooner I'd have shot them. It would have been kinder.' He sniffed and got out of the ute, keeping his eyes hidden from mine.

I killed the engine and stepped out of the cab's air-conditioned oasis. The maddening chorus of a million locusts made the air heavy as the swale of a summer afternoon. The sun invaded my eyes. Forty degrees of heat prickled my skin, and in seconds my clothes were studded with flies searching for sweat to drink.

Sterlo seemed impervious to it, leaning on the bonnet of the ute, surveying the job and what needed to be done. There was a shovel in the tray along with a pickaxe. He took them both and walked down to the first sheep. I followed in his footsteps, waving away tendrils of shit stink that intensified the closer we got.

The first was dead. Crows has pecked out both of its eyes. Its yellowed teeth were frozen in a rictus of desperation. The second was the same. As we approached the third, I imagined signs of life: wool quivering, head moving, nostrils flaring, a low bleating 'baaa' sounding at my approach.

It was dead. They all were. Because of course they were.

'You sure you want to do this?' Sterlo asked, squinting at me in the sun.

I held a hand out for a tool, and he handed me the pickaxe. We started digging around the back legs of the nearest sheep, carving trenches into the sucking mud so we could lever the limbs out. The stench of rotting flesh and corrupting mud was overpowering. I wanted to vomit. To quit. To leave the job to

Sterlo. I kept digging. Clenching my jaw like Sterlo. Hacking at the soil like Sterlo. Giving myself to the task.

We couldn't bury them – wild dogs would just dig them up again. So we dragged the carcasses to the edge of the mud and stacked them in a heap. Sterlo broadcast a fire warning over the CB to the other work crews. Then he siphoned a measure of petrol from the ute's fuel tank and painted the mottled wool of the ewes. I tore a page from the back of the ute's owners manual, rolled it and used my cigarette lighter to turn it into a fire starter. We stood upwind as the flames consumed fur and skin and fat then died down to smoulder amongst the bones.

'Nothing else to burn around here,' Sterlo said, looking at the shorn wheat stubble all around. 'Job done.'

Tired and filthy, we drove back to the laager and found Williamson and Murphy there. They brewed a billy of tea on the coals of their cooking fire, and we sat around watching the wisp of smoke from the distant waterhole, sharing the lowering tide of the workday.

'Nasty way to go, baking in the sun,' Murphy said. 'I've never understood livestock myself.'

'What's not to understand?' I asked, pulling on the thread.

'I mean they're a lot of bother. With wheat it's just throw the seeds in and pray for rain.'

'There's a bit more to it than that,' Sterlo said. But Murphy pressed on.

'My dad ran wheat and sheep. All his troubles came from the animals. Fly strike. Worms. Getting their heads stuck in the fence. Shovelling shit and scratching yourself red from the itchy hay. I tell you, wheat is the easy option.'

'What do you think?' Williamson asked me. 'Reckon this caper is the easy option?'

I shrugged. 'All difficult to me.'

'Yeah, we noticed,' Murphy said, and he and Williamson laughed into their mugs. Sterlo didn't. He looked at me and made a slight, sudden break in his mouth, something approaching the ghost of a smile.

When we'd finished the tea we piled into Sterlo's ute and I drove them back to where the headers were parked in a far paddock, one closer to home and the finish line than where I'd left off a few days before. The old hands went to their machines while Sterlo hopped into the faded red header I'd seen from a distance. The upper case of its logo announced MASSEY FERGUSON. Dad's old header harvester.

'How did you get it going?'

'WD-40 and gaffer tape,' Sterlo laughed, climbing up to the cab. He swung the door open and beckoned me inside. 'She's pretty basic. But she works just fine. Changed the oil. Got a new serpentine belt. The rest was just cobwebs. So we had three headers going instead of two. And that made all the difference for the final push. Just a few paddocks to go now.' He flicked a few switches, turned a key and away the engine went. 'Your dad loved this thing. So take it back to him.'

He climbed down and signalled for me to drive it back to the homestead. As he followed in his ute, I took the old header for a slow crawl along the paddock sides, marvelling at the buzz cut those millions of stalks of wheat had been given over three weeks of hard yakka. At the start it always seems impossible. At the end it's just a matter of time.

Sterlo's voice squawked on the CB radio he'd taped to the inside of the Massey's open cab. 'I'll open up the shed for you. Just park her where you can.'

When we got close to the homestead, I took a side track and swung the great machine up into the home paddock, the field closest to the front garden. Farm machines go until they die. Till they get bogged in salt lakes. Driven to pieces. Hacked to bits. The old header would be the exception. I parked her in the lee of a gum tree on the fence line, left the key in the ignition and walked back to Sterlo's waiting ute.

'How much longer you staying?'

'Few more days. Help Mum finish packing.'

'What about your dad?'

'He's got cancer,' I said. His shock was instant – so at least I knew Mum hadn't told everyone else besides me. 'It's spreading. There's nothing we can do except make him comfortable.'

A magpie trilled silver somewhere. Harvesters buzzed on distant properties. Sterlo smiled wide so creases fanned his eyes.

'Your dad's a farmer, mate. He'll stick to the schedule. Just like you.'

37

Dad had shat himself on the drive back from the nursing post, so I helped Mum haul him into the bathroom where she stripped his clothes off. She wiped him down with a flannel under the shower while I watched, passing her soap and standing by to do whatever she told me. It was distressing, disgusting, confronting. For Mum it was a task. A simple series of movements.

His eyes were sheep's eyes, stupid and empty, drained of colour, rheumy whites reflecting the acid green of the shower curtain bunched in the corner. Mum stood aside, beckoned me to take the flannel and sponge his back, his arms, armpits and groin, showing me how to divide the body into hemispheres of limbs and clefts to be done in order, as though we were packing a dishwasher together.

When it was done he smiled at me. Stroked the back of my head and kissed me on the cheek. The last of the water drained down the plughole, the sound framing a long still moment. 'I'll do the rest, Mum. Go relax.' My voice thickened, straining to hold steady. 'Where are his pyjamas? I'll get him into bed.'

She put a hand on my shoulder. 'Give him his towel. He can do that part while you get his toothbrush ready.'

Little jobs. Keep busy. This was how she did it. This was how she had survived. Managing the decline as a full-time job. Yes, I could get the toothbrush ready. Of course I could pull down the bedclothes. Switch off the light. Make sure he had a glass of water by the bed. Window cracked for a bit of air.

I knew I had only made a cameo appearance in the drama. I wasn't some selfless hero swooping in to save the day.

As the last claws of daylight slid from the sky I shut the curtains and helped the old man into bed, shrugging his burden to the mattress Mum shared with him.

The beginnings of bedsores on his hips needed attention, so I pulled the medical kit from their bathroom cabinet, which held a forest of pill bottles. Painkillers and pain maskers. For nausea. For sleep. For drowsiness and infection. Each bottle and packet of prescriptions and over-the-counters swallowed down to its dregs.

'What the hell is all this stuff?' I whispered, knowing the answer. Each event in his downward spiral was a dot that I had missed joining, and the lines connecting them were spiked with doses all administered by Mum, washed down with a glass of water and a loving peck on the cheek.

'I'll go to bed too,' Mum said. 'I don't care that it's early.'

'You sure? I could cook us some dinner.'

'Thanks but no. I'd rather have hospital food.' She kissed me on the cheek. 'The nurse at the post said he's still got an infection. We can choose to keep it down or just let it go.'

'Just let it go,' I said, repeating her words, my mind still catching up. 'Just let it go.'

She ushered me out and shut the door.

I walked through the house, looking around as if inspecting a place for rent. All the rooms still had packing boxes to fill. But not the library. She hadn't touched it yet. Mum's instinct was jugular. She was dismantling a star. Leaving its heart for last. Inside the shelves and behind the closed door I still had time, basking in the surety of my father's life and the love he'd shared with me.

Taking *Pride and Prejudice* from the shelf, my version of Albert said, 'Never understood the book thing,' and a fragment of his memory fluttered the pages. 'I like the technical manuals. And the picture books. Novels are boring. Just people complaining.'

'You stick to your thing and I'll stick to mine,' I said, and sat on the couch where the typewriter was still waiting. The words I'd begun for Holt's article resumed their insistence to run on that clean sheet of foolscap and meet his deadline of Friday, two days time, a last chance to keep the leash of the subs desk from my independent neck.

```
The rudest question a visitor can ask a
farmer is 'how many paddocks do you have?'
It's the country equivalent of asking how
much money they make
```

Full stop. Capital letter. *The*. Nothing else came. I knew what to write next. That Brockman's Place had ten paddocks neatly set out in a five by five grid cleaved by tracks that allowed access for vehicles. The highway was the spine, the paddocks the ribs, and the tracks the veins. I'd set the scene of my family's last harvest in the Wheatbelt. Explain the stakes with my father's illness and introduce the people who mattered with quotes of reported speech, their colourful characters distinct against the black-and-white reportage of figures and timetables. But as though someone had cut the telephone lines and the power cables with an axe, I ripped the sheet of paper from the carriage and threw it to the floor.

I went to the kitchen and washed up the dishes. Then sprayed and wiped the benchtops. Foamed cleaner into the oven that made my lungs itch. Boiled the kettle and mopped the floor. Took out every remaining plate and cup and item of cutlery marked for packing and filed them away into the half-filled boxes cluttering the table and the floor and the hall. Whatever looked like it could be saved was saved, and whatever looked too ugly for Mum's keeping went to the disposal pile gathering high on the kitchen table.

When my cleaning frenzy faded, I heard Dad coughing, the

same rasping splutter he'd had the night he went to hospital. I itched to break the bedroom door down, fire up the station wagon and race him to care. Instead I creaked it open gently, spilling a chink of yellow light from the hallway's bulbs onto Mum's sleeping face. She looked a decade younger. Sleep smoothed out the worries of her skin. Highlighted the blonde in her hair. For the first time in a long while, I looked at my mother directly, without blurring my eyes or staring at the bridge of her nose.

'Good night,' I said, and she rolled over, hugging Dad beneath the covers.

It was solace to sit silently on the library couch and take a long while just to look at the books, travelling my gaze along the spines arranged in Dad's haphazard order; sometimes alphabetical, sometimes categorical, usually stuffed wherever they fit. The only clear divide was fiction and non-fiction – the left side of the room devoted to the totally made up and the right to the mostly. Mum's murder mysteries and old editions of Enid Blyton were given their own cabinet near the window.

Two books looked out of place, because they weren't books at all. They were folders, filed in the middle upper level of fiction in the middle of a set of *Tintin* hardbacks. Taking them out, I recognised the first immediately – the file on Albert's death I'd shown Mum and Dad years back, still streaked with mud and falling to bits.

The other was in even worse condition, the spine almost worn away from being opened and closed and moved around. Inside it were newspaper clippings. Page after page of black and white linked by my by-line. Everything from my cadet year, when I wrote from every spoke of the wheel: car crashes, a murder investigation, footy results, obituaries. Each block of text had been cut out with precise care using sharp scissors. The folder was Mum's work. Made for Dad to read.

With shaking hands I poured a measure of Dad's whisky into

a glass and knocked it back as he had done, shoving aside any objections correct habit may have raised. Pouring another, I sat back on the couch and picked up the typewriter, fed a fresh sheet of paper and used the momentum of drink to collapse through my objections.

The rudest question a visitor can ask a farmer is 'how many paddocks do you have?' It's the country equivalent of asking how much money they make. The curt answer you'll usually get is 'enough'. Especially if the harvest is as good as can be gotten in Septimus, a district in WA's northern Wheatbelt renowned for its steady delivery of bumper crops year after year.

This is my home – the place I left behind to come to Perth and write for this newspaper. I have returned to bring in the crops one last time and help my mother pack up our venerable homestead. My father is too ill to carry on, and I'm in no shape to lead a harvest. Not because I'm not capable. Because I'm not interested.

Like my father, like my mother, I love the land. But now we must leave it. It feels like defeat. Like we have cried for mercy where there is none. Yet I have come to understand that love is eternal – not life, nor land, or leaving either.

'Sentimental garbage,' I said, and ripped the sheet from the typewriter. My hands flinched to scrunch, but folded instead, and smoothed it into the folder.

38

The sound of harvesting machines cut through the walls. They were shaving down wheat in the closest paddock to the homestead, the final one. I woke feeling as though I were made from painted rust. The light was too bright. The shadows were too dark. When I made my way out to the kitchen, the state of the house matched my insides: open boxes, piles of rubbish, cupboards spilled open.

From the veranda I watched Murphy and Williamson get their headers going at a good clip while John took the grains in the chaser bin. Sterlo's white ute drove around delivering instructions like a sheep dog. I sipped a mug of instant coffee, observing the noise and colour without the urge to join it. The slow advance of the harvest's final stretch became white noise.

Mum came out to the veranda and stood beside me, blowing on her own cuppa, watching the machines do their jobs. For a moment we could be lazy on land that had never tolerated that.

'You should have woken me,' she said. 'I feel like shit. But I'm really happy that I do. It's been far too long since I slept in.' I let silence fall – the old reporter's trick. She had come out to say something more than small talk.

'Thanks for cleaning the kitchen. I was avoiding that.'

I smiled to myself. 'Couldn't figure out what to do with the ugly plates. You're right. Grandma had no taste.'

Mum snorted. 'She passed that gene to your father. You know he once got me a knife block for Christmas?'

'Not far off,' I said, doing the sums. 'I forgot about it.'

'Christ, so did I. That's the first mention of it I've had.' Her face shaded with sadness. 'No-one wants to remind a soon-to-be-widow of what's supposed to be a happy time.'

Dad's forest of pills juddered in front of me. 'Reckon he'll last? I mean, if we took him to a hospice. Got a nurse in –'

'He'll go when he's ready.' She took my empty mug. 'You don't need to know every little detail. You don't need to be in on every decision.'

We went back into the kitchen where the phone was off the hook. No way for Holt to intrude. No visitors were expected. A feeling of aloneness crept over, so the house became an island with the paddocks as a wild sea and the driveway as a jetty.

'This is no place for nostalgia,' I said, and Mum cocked her head to the side, looking at me as though I were afflicted with something. She put down the cutting knife and turned on the radio, tuning the dial to an oldies station where Smokey Robinson's 'The Tracks of My Tears' was fading out.

'What's gotten into you?'

'That's what a detective told me. Right before I came here. He was yabbering on about drugs and fights in Perth and he said "this is no place for nostalgia", probably hoping I'd quote him. But I left it out.'

Mum opened the fridge and took out two beers from a sixpack I'd bought, twisted the caps off in the web of her hand without even a wince of pain, or a flinch that it was well before midday. She seemed to understand – to be able to read between the lines I was so shabbily making.

'What use is looking back around here?' she said, and took the first sip. 'We talk about last season's crops. Rain from ten years back. It's just talk. Nothing can help us but what we do right now. We need to pack.'

We woke Dad for dinner. He called me 'matey' and refused to take his pain pills. 'Never on an empty stomach,' he said. 'They make me sick.' I crushed them up, swirled them through his water glass, and fooled him into drinking. Then slowly, step by slow step, I led him to the table and sat him at its head.

Mum served the meat and two veg with loving precision, arranging the elements neatly so each white plate was a palette of things grown, harvested and slaughtered in a twenty-kilometre radius of her chopping boards. 'This is the last of the lamb,' she announced, fussing and sweating. 'One carcass has seen us through two years. You've got to admit that's impressive.'

'Well, it was just the two of you,' I said, artlessly. 'That deep freeze is genius. That time Albert switched it off – I've never smelled anything worse.'

Mum winced. 'I still get a waft of it every now and then. No matter how much I scrub.'

Dad chewed his food slowly and grimaced. 'Will the two of you shut up? I'm trying to eat my flaming dinner.' He flopped a fist on the table. 'I've got to be up early you know? Sterlo's expecting me. Going to look over his header for him. So lights out quick smart tonight.' He raised his knife at me, the blade shaking up and down. 'That goes double for you, boy. You're coming with me.'

Mum put a gentle hand on his arm. 'Love, you don't have to go anywhere in the morning. You can relax, okay?'

He looked at me with milky eyes. Pure confusion. Then it was as though candles had been snuffed. 'I can live with that. Pass the bread, will you?'

My ears whined with dying frequencies. Though Mum seemed happy for us to eat in companionable silence, for me each click of cutlery was ten times louder. The moment Dad finished his last mouthful I excused myself to watch TV, flicking through the three channels again and again finding nothing to settle on while Mum fussed over Dad, taking him to the bathroom, getting him to brush his teeth and get ready for bed.

When the routine was done, Mum leaned over the couch and

tousled my hair. 'Let's play Scrabble. Dad's sitting up in bed. We could join him there. See if he can string a word or two together.'

She set up the board beside Dad's knees, which were covered by the doona. He placed his tiles on a holder and waited for his turn while Mum and I brought chairs to the bedside. Mum drew the lowest letter and went first, playing NEVER across for eight with a double letter score on the R to make nine, then double again to eighteen for going first.

'Always hated that rule,' Dad said, looking around the room with unfocused eyes.

'It's fair enough,' Mum said. 'Going first is a blank slate.'

'Fast game's a good game,' I said, and laid down OVAL for thirteen with a triple letter score on the L to make nine. 'You'll catch up, Dad.'

'Sure bloody will,' he said, laying tiles at the bottom of our words. His hands shook. His eyes were unfocused. Still his word was QUILLS. No bonus points, but fifteen wasn't bad.

'That's you ahead of Rowan,' Mum said. 'I knew I should have built down at the start.'

He winked at me. 'Make sure you shuffle the letters thoroughly. I don't want to get all vowels or all consonants.'

Dad's turns skipped over with nothing of the focus that he'd had for QUILLS. He breathed raggedly at times, swallowing and then breathing out so hard his tongue flicked out. Mum and I kept the game going with a mad tree branch of words ranging from the simple HEART to a showy FILAGREE and an obscure ZAX – a kind of sword. Finally Dad said, 'I can't go anywhere,' rubbing the last two tiles together between his fingers as though they were poker chips.

'Time for bed, love,' Mum said, and kissed him on the cheek. She set out his final slug of pills and handed him a glass of water. 'Take them. Or you forfeit.'

He saluted as he swallowed the handful of colours. 'It's not even late. Isn't the cricket on? I feel like staying up.'

'All over,' she said. 'I think Australia won. Or was it a draw? I can never tell the difference.'

'It was a win,' I said, not even knowing.

Mum took my hand and squeezed. 'Come on, you. You can put the kettle on.' She switched off the light and tucked him in like a child. They kissed on the lips and he stroked her hair. Instead of blushing or walking away like nothing had happened, I watched them love each other, both seeming to forget just for a quick moment that nothing was going the way anybody would wish.

'We'll finish the packing tomorrow,' Mum said to me as she shut the door. 'You know what? Whatever we don't get to, I'm just going to leave it. It's a university taking over. They'll sort it out.'

I nodded to the library door. 'I was thinking they should be left as they are. Like a gift.'

'Good idea,' she said, and yawned. 'We're running out of days.'

39

Dad died on a plain Friday at the tail end of November. Mum listened to his breathing change from a slow and steady struggle to a skipped beat. Just before a quarter to six, the start of working day, he stopped. She lay beside him till the sun rose, then woke me with the news. We didn't cry. We just went to the kitchen, boiled water for coffee and sat down to breakfast.

At the stroke of seven o'clock she phoned the hospital in Geraldton to report the death. Then she spoke to the police station in town, which sent two constables – one young and one old – to check that there was no foul play involved. The young officer seemed like he was in his first week of the job and stuffed his lines, saying, 'We're here to make sure your husband's okay,' when Mum opened the front door.

'You'll find he's beyond that,' she said, a woman of stone.

The older copper took over.

'We just need to make a few checks,' he said blandly. 'Sorry for your loss, Mrs Brockman. Bryce was a good man.'

'It was overdue,' Mum replied, and when they'd done their inspection she ushered them out and stood on the veranda to watch the squad car crawl slowly for a polite distance, then accelerate in a streak of dust to the highway.

'Go into town and get a slab of beer,' she said, coming back to the kitchen. She slid the station wagon keys across the benchtop. 'Six loaves of white bread for sandwiches. Get paper cups and plates too. I'm not doing any washing up.'

Town was quiet when I got to the main drag. The sun hovered above the gables of the street-side verandas, and pools of cooler air clung to the shadows they cast. Bore-water sprinklers chittered and chattered on the lawns of the primary school. Magpies trilled in the neat rows of municipal gum trees.

'Morning, Rowan,' a woman said, arms full of bread and milk and the weekend paper. 'Beautiful day for it.' I didn't recognise her, pretended to, and agreed that it was a good day.

The pub's drive-through opened up early and sold me a carton of beer, Swan Draught for old times' sake. I carried it back to the ute and set it down on the passenger side, a gold, white and red box too bright for the occasion. The inside of the little supermarket was lit with fluorescent tubes that stripped the colour from everything. I bought six loaves of still-warm white bread, and managed to find dusty packets of paper cups and plates in the domestic goods section. I couldn't get the notes out of my wallet to pay for them. My fingers refused to part the leather and extract the paper.

'Big night, mate?' the cashier said as I handed over the wallet. She took what was needed and handed the wallet back, looking at me with raised eyebrows.

I walked out clutching the change tight in case it shook from my grip.

By the afternoon the funeral director had arranged for Dad's body to be taken to Geraldton for storage in a freezer at the morgue and prepared for cremation. I took Mum for a walk in the dry creek bed while the first part of the journey was completed. From the veranda we watched the van crawl up the driveway, passing cars full of every farmer and his wife and their workers from across the district that'd come to fill up the kitchen and lounge room and veranda with sympathy and questions.

'How was he at the end?'

'You must be relieved, though it's a hard thing to say.'

'Your poor mother. She's been through so much.'

Mum stood in the kitchen like the captain of a ship lashed to the wheel. She boiled the kettle over and over, making cups of tea for anyone who asked, refusing all offers of help. It must have been good to have something to do. A bit of theatre to do with the hands.

I wandered through the rooms topping up drinks and saying a few words here and there, thanking people for turning up, and feeling as though I were working harder than any other day during the harvest. The men drank lukewarm stubbies of beer on the veranda in a wide circle of leaning poses, spread legs and terse expression. They talked about crop yields and grain prices and the 'idiots in Canberra' while their wives colonised the couches and chatted at the tops of their lungs, balancing cups of tea as they surreptitiously went through the boxes of packing still lying about. It was like a wake, only without the release of the burial, the benedictions and eulogies. One voice broke the monotony.

'Fancy seeing you here,' Alison said, poking me in the back. I turned and said hello to her and her mother, and kept a straight face when the boyfriend shook my hand with a grip too tight.

'Sorry for your loss, mate,' he said, his eyes meeting mine. A good-looking rooster.

'There's beer on the veranda if you like,' I said to him, and offered tea to Alison and Mrs Chambers.

'We can sort that out,' Alison said, and her mother went to see mine. She put a hand on her man's chest and kissed him. 'Go on, love. Go talk machines or whatever. I'll have a word here.' He strode outside and said hello to the men, shaking hands with the nearest to the door and quickly falling in with the patter of cracking cans and talking shop.

'He came up a few days ago. We're giving it another go.' Her smile was flat and unconvincing. 'Sometimes you just have to give things a chance.'

'I'm happy for you,' I said, meaning it.

She touched my shoulder. 'I'm sorry for your loss.'

I looked down the corridor and saw the edge of his bed through the open bedroom door, the sheets all stripped away leaving a stained mattress and swirls of dust motes.

'When are you leaving?' she said.

'The plan was tomorrow. I'm supposed to be at work on Monday. And I've already been off nearly a month.'

'So take some more time. They'll understand.'

'They won't.' I imagined Holt on the phone, agreeing to an extension with gritted teeth and consequences. 'We have to arrange the funeral. Then the movers are coming. Mum's got a place lined up on the coast. At least I think she does.'

Alison tutted. 'Don't be so stubborn. You have friends here. I'm sure Mum's talking to her right now. She can come stay with us till it's all sorted. Hang on a minute.' She went outside and got her fella to fetch her two beers. 'Here,' she handed me one. 'You'll think straighter with this.'

As we started talking again, a door opened in my guts and I felt myself disappear into the floor. I just nodded and murmured as Alison talked.

Dad was dead. All I could feel was relief, like a splinter had been removed. While everyone else went round and round, question and answer, point and counterpoint, my heart went still. I couldn't remember him. The real him. Not the light bulb without a spark that had taken his place. I excused myself from Alison and went to the kitchen where Mum was still making tea, surrounded by friends with best intentions.

'Come have a break,' I said, and pulled her out of there. No-one noticed me take the station wagon keys. I switched on the kitchen radio and tuned it to a music channel to stoke the conversations higher.

Neither Mum nor I suggested we go to the rock at the Hoths' place. It was just understood that it was where we were going. As if the noble stone was magnetised by the distant tide that had pulled the moon into place right above it, so there was dusk in the west and a glow in the dark in the east. The sunset and the moonrise bathed the dark rock in a pincer of contrasts, so it looked fresh and wet like the first dabs of a watercolour.

Mum's hand gripped my left hand so hard I had to change gears with my right and balance the steering wheel with my knees. When I pulled over with a few hundred metres still to go she gripped it tighter still, staring through the dust streaks and insect smears on the windshield at the immense granite monolith. I switched the engine off and listened to the metal tick and settle.

'Am I a horrible person?' she said. 'I just couldn't take it in there. Those women are my friends. I've been at their places when their dads died or when their kids got sick. Brought round meals like they all did. There's always tuna casserole. Did you ever notice that? I suppose it's easy. It keeps for a long time in the freezer. I think I still have some in there from when he first got sick. If I serve it up later, think they'll notice?'

I cleared my throat to say something. She squeezed my hand again.

'I hate feeling this way. That this is just so embarrassing. I know that's awful to say. But it is. I know you agree.'

I looked away. She let go of my hand.

'Christ, I nearly melted the kettle making cups of tea. As if that's medicine or something. And my house – all packed up like some travelling exhibit. How many times do I have to get asked the same question? When are you leaving? Are you sure you want to go? Who have you sold the place to? How much did you get? Think it's a good idea? What's best for the family? My husband's just died. I mean for God's sake my husband's just died. My husband's just died.'

She opened her door, snapped the seatbelt off and got out. 'Tell me you have cigarettes.' I patted my pockets. Nothing.

She nodded at the rock. 'Let's climb the thing.' She slammed the door and left me to scramble out and catch up with her just as the dusty ground became a rising littoral of stones. We climbed like toddlers do, bent down with our hands on the surface and legs held straight, crabbing up and up till we reached the flat summit.

'If your brother was here, he'd fight you for the eulogy,' Mum said. She sat and patted the space beside her. 'Not to do it. He'd just want to shit you. Make you squirm for a bit on proper form and procedure.'

I sat and leaned against her – a pose from another time, from boyhood, when my shoulders would prop against her sides. Now they met on the level, tension to tension, and warmth transferred between.

'If Albert was here he'd have never let anyone in the door today,' I said. Mum's shoulder rose and fell against mine. 'He'd have put a chain through the gates. Told everyone to fuck off.'

'Language,' Mum corrected, stifling soaring laughter with a snort. 'He would have. He's just like me. Ice in the veins. You're more your father. You can be a diplomat. When you aren't being an arsehole.'

'I did what you asked me to do.'

'You could have got some ice for the beers. You can make up for that at the proper wake.' She clasped her hands together, rings on the outside so the tiny diamond on her engagement band caught the last of the sun in its dusty prism.

'Are you still leaving on Monday?'

I went to say yes – caught the word before it passed. 'I'll ask for another week.' She frowned. 'Two then. I'm already in trouble. I missed the deadline.'

Mum arched her eyebrows and explained the plan, shunting Holt and the harvest aside. Dad was to be cremated in Geraldton at a mortuary where only Mum and I would attend. Then we'd drive his ashes back to Septimus, with a service to be held at the church of St Thomas, the stone-built bulwark of religion on the highway just outside town. The finish line would be five hundred dollars over the bar at the Terminus.

'We'd better get going,' I said. The last glow of the sun was long gone, and the moonlight replacing it was not enough to get down safely with.

'Don't be such a sook,' Mum said, leaning back as though staying forever. 'Your father and I used to stay out on the land all the time. Spent the night more than once. Just a swag and the stars.' She looked up and whistled at the necklace of the emerging Milky Way. 'That's how I'll remember him. Laying down up on the open ground and pointing up. Crapping on and on about the bloody stars.' Her finger rose high. 'That one's Canis Major. That's Andromeda. And over there is the Southern Cross. You knew that of course.'

'He showed me too.' I pointed too. 'That's the False Cross. Looks almost like the Southern.'

'But it can steer you wrong,' we both said, just like he had.

Dad came back to me. I imagined him down below, getting out of the station wagon and waving up to us from the gloom. He was just as he had been.

As night deepened over the land, Mum and I climbed down from the rock and drove back to the homestead where the lights were on and the kitchen had been made spotless by many hands. Strangely, it felt as though the rain had just fallen. Like something approaching new life had just dawned.

40

Just about the whole community of Septimus turned up for the funeral. Everyone who had a program folded and flapped it inside the stifling hot church. A black-and-white picture of Dad got front-page treatment, an image of him as a young man in the pride of his days, from the same era of photos that John's dad had shown to me in his old album. Both of them were standing at the back with Sterlo and Murphy and Williamson. Packing the pews in front there was Alison and her boyfriend with Mr and Mrs Chambers, the mayor, the Hoths and the rest of the big families, workers and tradies, old mates and old hands, all of them stupefied by the dry enunciated words flowing incessantly from the vicar's throat.

'And now a reading from the Book of Common Prayer,' the vicar said, dull as the stones of the little church.

'We therefore commit his body to the deep, to be turned into corruption, looking for the resurrection of the body, when the sea shall give up her dead, and the life of the world to come, through our Lord Jesus Christ; who at his coming shall change our vile body, that it may be like his glorious body, according to the mighty working whereby he is able to subdue all things unto himself.'

Dad had requested every reading and every detail, and Mum enforced them to the letter. The prayer for the burial of the dead at sea was probably his idea of a cheeky way to end things, to make the landlocked nautical, and give me a platform to make sense of things with the eulogy.

'Don't fuck it up,' Albert said, in my head. I rose to take the lectern in hand and looked down at the throng, meeting their eyes with focus.

'These aren't my words,' I said, and looked to Mum, who wiped her tears, holding my eyes in hers as we held focus together. We had stood in the crematorium together, watched Dad's cheap pine casket descend into the retort, felt the cold efficiency of the checklist of death: certificates, stamps, release forms, the scrape of fingernails on an unglazed urn. She smiled support as I unfolded a letter from my jacket pocket and read her handwriting, neat and strong, steady veins giving voice where I had none.

'It is hard to come to the land. Farmers are a different breed to most. They face flood, famine, pestilence, death, heat and all those bloody flies. And yet they stay. They refuse to pack up and leave. They stay. Come hell and high water. Wind and rain. Cut thumbs and lost limbs. Disease and hardship. We endure these things and carry on.' I held on to the words, their pronunciation, saying one after the other. 'That's why it is so hard for us to leave now. It feels like defeat. Like we have cried for mercy where there is none. Bryce Albert Brockman was never a quitter as many of you who have drank with him will know.'

Laughter rippled and burned out.

'Septimus and Brockman's Place were the centre of his universe, with all others swirling around. He never wanted another. Some may pity that. He was a true salt of the earth. A farmer. They say ashes to ashes and dust to dust. I beg to differ. Ashes to ashes, and then back to the soil.'

Gossip applied easy as a coat of varnish to the wake at the Terminus where the men drank beer and the women drank wine, one group in a wide circle and the other in a tighter one, husbands and wives split between the public bar and the dining room. Sterlo told raucous stories about Dad in his pomp. The time he stole a car from a shearer to impress a girl – this was long before Mum – and crashed it into a tree. 'Cost him two months wages, and a black eye,' Sterlo said, and basked in the merriment that kindled.

Five hundred dollars can buy a lot of beers. But Dad's money ran out quick when the fellas worked out they could order boilermakers and tipples from the top shelf. I drank my own beer slowly, taking small sips in the cheers and refusing top-ups from the jugs being handed around. I wanted to get pissed, to eradicate this day from my mind. I had to get Mum home.

'Shame about the farm,' someone said, just out of my eye line. 'One of the best properties going around here. Them sons should have seen it through.'

So there it was. Finally said out loud – or said within my hearing. 'Yeah, I admit it,' I said, addressing no-one in particular. 'Would have been nice to keep the place on. That's not us anymore.'

I clacked my beer glass on the bar counter and went outside where Sterlo, Hoth and Williamson were inspecting someone's car. They looked to me and opened their circle – Williamson patted me on the back and handed me the smoke he was working on.

'Cheer up, mate. It's supposed to be a wake,' he said, and my anger simmered back a touch. The man inside had only said what everyone was thinking. 'Cop a look at this thing.' He pointed at a sky-blue Holden Commodore so shiny it looked factory fresh. A gaudy racing kit plunged around its thin pressed body, making it look like something from the Bathurst 1000.

'Know whose it is?' Williamson said.

Didn't have a clue. 'Must be a blow-in's. If Dad was here, he'd think about stealing it.'

Sterlo shook his head. 'He was a Ford man, mate. He would have thought about keying it.'

We all laughed together, then all shook hands, firmly and

surely. Murphy and Williamson were following the harvest down to Esperance. John was heading to the Pilbara for stock work. Sterlo was going to help hand Brockman's Place over when the new owners arrived. Maybe they'd give him a job.

'Look me up when you come to Perth,' I told him, and he promised he would, heading back into the pub where the chatter rose to greet him. Mum passed him on the way out, looking half drunk and completely convinced of something.

'I've had enough of the reminiscing,' she said, grabbing my arm and marching me toward the car park. 'I know how we can get rid of all that horrible crockery.'

'Pull!' Mum yelled. A royal crested serving platter shattered into slivers of gun-shot china. 'Bullseye,' she shouted, her ears stuffed with toilet paper. 'Give me another. The soup tureen. No, not that one. The Peter Rabbit design. Load it.'

I placed the delicate heirloom on the target trap, pulling the hinged arm back to its furthest reach. Maybe Grandma saved the old bit of china thinking it could be useful for Albert and me. Or our own kids one day.

'Pull.' The pop of breaking bone china wrapped itself around the hollow boom of the twelve-gauge, then the click-clack of the pump action ejected the spent shell and loaded another.

'Your turn. I want to sort the order of them out.' She lowered the gun barrel to the grass and passed the long weapon over, rubbing her shooting shoulder. 'We can always switch to birdshot if you like.'

'Just make sure you load them right,' I replied. 'Perfect centre or they fly off at the wrong angle.'

Time stretched as we warmed to the work. One by one Mum lined up plates, pots, mugs, casserole dishes and serving platters and fed them onto the throwing arm. Its spring protested shrilly as she wound back to its lowest crouch, but after a few rusty goes the cobwebs cleared and it threw its ammunition high in beautiful arcs that I tracked and destroyed with squeezes of the shotgun's trigger.

There went Holt's deadline – shoot.

There went the article – shoot.

There went my police round – shoot.

When I'd emptied a box of shells she took the gun back and I loaded for her. She didn't miss once, her face scowled in concentration and determination.

'Pull,' she demanded, going faster and faster, racking the shotgun's slide till the magazine clicked empty, then expertly reloading – two shells at a time one-handed.

A final brace of plates sailed out high into the darkening sky and was exploded like the rest. The silence that followed was immense. Mum laid the shotgun on the grass to let it cool. Smoke unwound from the barrel and the breech, the wet sulphur smell of gunpowder mixing with the perfume of cool night, cut grass, summer weeds lurking.

'I hope they don't mind the mess,' Mum said, looking over the white shreds that had turned the lawn into a stormy night sea. 'I might leave a note warning to watch out for prickles.'

I grabbed her as she sank forward, holding her tight to my chest. She howled. Screamed into my flesh. Her weight went dead as we sank together to the grass. A decade of despair leached out in a crowded minute.

'Do we have anything to drink?' she gasped. I helped her down on the lawn and went to get the whisky from the library. When I returned with the bottle and a pair of glasses she took it neat from me and swigged the fiery stuff straight from the neck. 'Load the gun,' she said, taking a final swallow. I slid a single shell into the magazine. 'Don't miss.' She shifted up onto her knees, steadied herself and threw the bottle high up toward the dry creek. The barrel followed. The trigger squeezed. The bottle exploded and a gust of wind rained a fine mist of alcohol.

'Are there any beers left?' Mum said. There was an edge to her voice. Something beyond grief. Closer to anger.

'I'll see what I can get us.'

'Us? No. You're the sober one for now.' She pointed to the shotgun and the loose boxes of ammo. 'I'm getting drunk. When you're done cleaning you can join me.' She stood and hugged me tight again. 'Ashes to ashes, and then back to the soil.'

41

On the last day, Sterlo came around to say goodbye. Since he'd finished up at our place, he'd been working at the silos, organising shipments for the grain trains to the export ports. 'Shit of a job, but they pay better than you mob ever did,' he said, refusing my offer of a coffee. The kitchen still had the basics. The bedrooms had a few suitcases of clothes. The bathrooms had toiletries bags beside the sinks. All the keys to all the locks were laid out on the kitchen bench. Sterlo picked up the bit for the big shed and ran his thumb over its teeth.

'Mind if I take a last look in there?' I nodded yes, and watched him through the window as he opened the sliding door, ransacked Dad's tools and loaded as much as he could into the tray of his ute. When he was done he came to the veranda, where Mum walked out to meet him.

They talked for a long while. They laughed. Hugged a few times. Wiped away a few tears. Finally Sterlo extended his hand, shook Mum's, then bent and kissed the blade of her wrist.

'Bye for now, Rowan,' he called through the window glass, splaying his hand into a starburst goodbye. He walked to his ute and drove off.

'Maybe he'll come and visit me in Perth,' I said to Mum as she came inside. 'Maybe you could come when he does.'

'I think he's keener on visiting me,' she said. 'Perhaps you're right. This is no place for nostalgia.'

The house was empty. The fields all stripped. Brockman's

Place was no more. All we had to do was pack up the last of our things and leave.

Shorn wheat fields beside the highway west to Geraldton gave way to toast-brown yields still to be cut on the southern run to Perth. White smoke hung in sheets as farmers back-burned the long grass framing their paddocks to reduce the risk of crop fires. The further south I drove, the more harvest there was still to complete, the timetable following the slow shift of ripening sun and the tilting earth.

Just before Perth's outskirts an unseen meridian flicked the temperature down ten degrees and the metal of my car seemed to dump a month of sunlit heat into the air. Mum would soon follow my journey on her own, then go further down to the south coast where her new place was waiting, cooler again by a degree of latitude.

When I reached my flat in Scarborough I fumbled with front-door keys and spilled inside with tired annoyance. I stalked around the rooms dumping luggage, peeled my sweat-sodden shirt off and stood outside on the stubby balcony. A couple fought a few doors down. Cars drove past on the street below with stereos thumping. A siren wailed somewhere. I was back to the city and suburbs, the coast and the commute, with a view of the strata bins and a sliver of the ocean at night.

Instead of showering, I stripped off and put on a pair of boardies, slipped on my thongs and walked all the way down to the beach with a towel over my bare shoulders. The rushing churning moving of waves hissing through the shallows lured me through the lights of shops and hotels, past kids doing laps of the streets in their cars, looping round a cursive clock tower whose hands read eight o'clock – twelve hours till I was due at work.

Down on the sand, the loom of lights from a new high-rise hotel spilled onto the faces of the breakers, making them taller and wider. Inhale, dive, swim, I went through the rolling rock roar of the foam to the even water where I lay on my back and floated. Brilliant stars in the sky. A plane flew up high on its way to the east, the triangle of its navigation lights winking white, red and green.

Turning over, I screamed underwater, muffling my fury in the dark. I hadn't cried at the funeral. I felt I had no right. Not with Mum beside me, who had been through so much more. So I held the tears in, saved them up. The dark salt water would take them.

When it was done I struck out for shore and bodysurfed a wave back in, coughing and hissing from gulps of salt water burning my lungs. A teenager ran down from the shadows of the sand dunes and asked if I was okay. I strode away listening to him explain to his giggling mates, 'Just some idiot taking a swim.'

Holt's office. The door shut. Watching newsroom hacks through the soundproof glass: bashing the phones, arguing, gossiping, slacking with professional poise.

'Anyone senior in this racket has either been through the Great Depression, the Second World War or two divorces,' he said, his words too off the cuff to have not been rehearsed. 'They smoke. They swear. Them out there make no exceptions for grief. You need to get on with it.' He picked up a paperweight and slid a pile of yellow legal pads to the centre of his desk. 'Off you fuck then.'

A few of the old hands on the subs desk gave me a pat on the back and said welcome. The rest blanked me. They knew I'd been shunted aside, made roadkill in a place that valued only the next thing, and the next thing, and the thing after that. As I settled in, Holt came over and took a chair at the main desk, imposing himself on the early edition copy flowing in for the noonday deadline.

'Harris, front and centre,' he barked. A skinny reporter strode over, eyes to the floor as scores of others followed him.

'Read this aloud for me,' Holt said, passing him a sheet of typed paper.

'The state government has failed to reach agreement with the teachers union on a pay rise for WA's primary school educators.'

'Did they promise to do that? Promise specifically to reach agreement?'

Harris swallowed. No, they hadn't.

'They said they would negotiate in good faith. Which enfolds the possibility of a positive or negative outcome in its scope. Negotiations don't fail. They simply go unresolved till the next round.' Holt snatched the paper, crossed out the line with red pencil and handed it back.

'How about "stalled in its attempt"? Walk it back. We all want to hang them. But do it the right way.'

Harris strode away with blushed cheeks. Holt came over, fixed me with his good eye and spoke from the side of his mouth. 'They are worker bees. Out gathering honey.' He took a cigarette from his top pocket and lit up with a match. 'You can correct the sport today. Just remember no Oxford commas, colons, semicolons or anything fruity. Just the facts. Direct language shorn of sentiment.'

'Everything else is literature,' I said, quoting his lines back to him, and he showed tobacco-stained teeth and laugh lines. 'West, get over here.' He waved to a grizzled sports journo who shambled over, shoulders hunched, face streaked with sweat and worry.

'Who's this bloody child?' West said, not looking at me.

'New to the desk,' Holt said. 'He's going to have a look at your copy on the America's Cup. Not long now, eh?'

'Couldn't come quick enough. Bores me shitless. Sit in the sun half the bloody day for a boat that could be beaten by a bus.'

Holt rummaged an in-tray and selected a story sheet. 'Scan and find something wrong. Quickly now.'

I forced my eyes to fall from line to line, letting the meaning come in a single clot. A news story should tumble like a rock falling down a hill. Anything that kinks the movement is discarded.

'The front of a yacht is more commonly called bow, not the prow,' I said. 'Both are acceptable. Bow is vernacular. Which is our style.'

Holt silenced West's harrumph. 'Anything else?'

'Two T's in attempt. And John Bertrand won the America's Cup in 1983. Alan Bond just bankrolled it. The honour goes to the skipper.'

'Smartarse,' West said, and snatched his copy back.

Holt made a buzzing sound. 'You'll make a professional pain in the arse yet,' he said, and slid more papers over.

I drove the long way home, through the city and right out to the coast road where the sky held that purple time between the working day and free night. Out at sea, a line of freighters wallowed outside the Gage Roads channel. I could simply turn the wheel and drive over the dunes to the water and float out there with them.

After night came, a patter of rain began to fall. I took a chair to the balcony and smoked a cigarette, watching the streets, waiting for something to happen. Maybe a car would skid out of control on the bend and crash into a light pole where a drug deal was happening in the disc of illumination. I'd get the scoop. Deal myself back in the game. The rain became a torrent and the whole of Scarborough shut its doors. I shut my eyes and listened to the drainpipes glugging. This was the kind of rain we prayed for on the farm.

The phone rang inside. It was Mum, marvelling at the rain, soaking as far down the coast as Mandurah where she was settling into her new place. How was the first day back? What did I eat for dinner? How about this rain then?

'The subs desk is going to take getting used to,' I said.

She sighed. 'That's a euphemism. I know big words too.'

'Might get you a job then.'

'Stop talking in riddles. What's wrong?'

Hard to say. So I said it – plain and simple. 'Doesn't feel the same here.'

We could go back to Septimus. We'd be visitors. We could visit Brockman's Place. By appointment only. Dad's ashes had been scattered over the rock at the Hoths', and of course they said we could go there whenever we liked. Nothing was ours anymore.

'What furniture do you have?' Mum asked.

'Classic bachelor pad,' I said, bare walls and floors.

'Well, there's your problem. How about I come up on the weekend? The cheque's cleared.'

I thought on it. Then said, 'How about I come see you?'

'Drive down on Friday night and we can go shopping on the Saturday,' Mum said. 'I'll just get it delivered in a truck.' There was no stopping her.

'I'll get chesterfields then. And antiques.'

'You'll have pine and like it.'

She rang off just as the rain stopped. Birds chirped in the trees, an odd sound at night, after rain, and I went back inside and switched on the lights. She was right – the place could use some furniture. Bare walls and an old couch was hardly a home. Humouring her, I picked up the snowdrift of post that had been delivered under the door and found a catalogue for a department store. One page boasted of 'prices you wont pass up'.

'Missing an apostrophe,' I said, and threw it in the bin.

42

The highway to Mandurah was fast and mostly deserted. I made good time breaking the speed limit on back roads that went past a chain of lakes and paddocks that petered out just before the coastal city's outer suburbs. Mum's flat in a retirement village was austere and clean, with a simple kitchen right outside the bedroom and bathroom. No extras or frills. It was a space to live simply in, with the sound of the sea ever present as the ticking of the hallway clock, an ornate country touch out of place in her simple sitting room.

'No fences to mend, no crops to tend, and no meals to cook save breakfast,' she said, giving me the grand tour. She'd covered the walls with photographs of her and Dad and me and Albert, all of us together and all of us separate in black-and-white and colour, all ages and phases. Most of everything else had gone into a storage unit.

'I don't have any photos like this,' I said, lingering on a portrait of Dad in his wedding suit.

'I've boxes of them. Take your pick.' She patted the couch. 'This folds out. So you can sleep here. Just take care not to be too obvious. Visitors aren't supposed to stay overnight.'

'Even sons?'

'Especially sons.' She put hands to her throat. 'There's many a family fortune here up for grabs.'

'I'd use a pillow,' I said, and we cackled together. 'Let's get to the pub.'

'I've got other plans.'

She opened a sliding door that led to a small courtyard lush with ferns. From there she retrieved two long wooden poles with metal baskets attached to their ends. 'The blue crabs are on. It's the first day of summer tomorrow.'

Pictures came. Frozen moments of the years we came to the coast for summer holidays after the hard work of the harvest. All those days in the sun together. It was suddenly strange to be there on the same ground with so much time in between. I felt older, more solid, with a weariness I'd never considered possible before.

'I've got garlic, butter, cream, wine and chilli,' Mum said, pulling me back to the moment. 'If we catch enough I'll knock up dinner. If not, we'll get fish and chips.'

I took the poles from her and loaded them into my car. They wouldn't fit easily, so I wound down the back window and stuck their ends out. We drove to the mouth of the Murray River like a pair of sunstruck old fishermen, resting our arms on the poles set between us.

We weren't so expert at the water's edge.

'Do you dig them into the mud and stir them out?' Mum said as we both rolled up our trousers. 'Or do you wait till you spot one and scoop him up?'

I set a bucket down on a narrow strip of sand, kicked off my shoes and waded in. The water was warm on my bare legs, brown and rich. The estuary was a wide abundance of reed banks, ducks and seabirds in flight, then the lucky flash of a porpoise playing in the quickening channel dividing the fresh water from the salt, the join made murky by fishing tinnies cleaving their way to the river and the sea.

We walked together in the shallows, both of us scanning the muck at our ankles for the telltales of little crabs. My feet sank into the mud and I squirmed with fear of stepping on something sharp, or slimy, or both. Alby would have laughed. 'There's nothing down there but razor-sharp crab claws that will nip your little toe off. Stop being such a wuss.'

Dad would have joined in. 'If the crab holds on, maybe we can boil your foot up too. Make the dish go further.'

'Oh rack off,' I said to them, laughing at their jest to show I was game. Mum patted me on the back, bringing me back to water, wind and the fading afternoon.

'Where to then?'

'Over there,' I said, pointing to a patch of water shot through with seaweed. 'They'll be hiding amongst that.'

Mum scooped her pot down and flushed out a brace of crabs, catching them all once with a quick flick of her wrists. She grinned with triumph and waded back to shore, her catch held high then plopped into the bucket for safe keeping. 'Four in one blow,' she announced, bowing to the picnickers on the shore and the boaters passing by. 'Come on, Rowan. I can't do it all by myself.'

I threw my scoop into the water, churned it around and around and pulled one crab out. It looked undersized. 'How's that for a fisherman?' I said, tipping the little one out.

'Office hands,' Mum drawled. 'You've gone soft again.'

I levered the pot in again. Five crabs tumbled into the metal rose and I lifted them clear. 'More like supple,' I said, igniting a frenzy of fishing till the bucket was full to the bag limit with twenty good-size crabs. We marched out of the water as though we'd won a war. Mum put her pole down and sat on the river beach, no longer caring if her trousers got wet. I sat beside her and we watched a young family wade into the water, the mother and father leading the way with a girl and boy in their early teens sullenly following.

Gusts of wind creased the water and brought a sudden cold to the remaining sun. She moved closer to me, and pointed to the family. 'You were just like that. Had to drag you kicking and screaming to everything.'

The boy had his arms crossed and shoulders hunched. The girl was looking to the far distance, as though pretending she was somewhere else. The mother and father worked a fishing net between them, casting around the shallows, pointing and whooping as they circled round a cluster of crabs.

'How many do you think they'll get with that thing?' I asked, and Mum shrugged.

'Plenty now that their bloody kids are lending a hand.' She leaned against me. 'Thanks for coming.'

'It was no trouble. Friday's edition is all sport anyway.'

'I mean the harvest. I appreciate what you did.'

I didn't know what to say. So I said nothing. Just held her weight on my body and watched the family gather their catch.

We drove back to Mum's place, crossing an old wooden bridge whose pylons were stacked with seagulls and pelicans waiting for the fishermen to haul something out of the water. It felt good to have a feed in the bag already.

Her kitchen was miniscule. The oven at Brockman's Place had more bench space. Somehow we managed to make a go of it. She spiked the brains of each crab with a kitchen knife, then fed them into a pot of boiling water one by one, gritting her teeth through the killing job while I chopped onions, garlic and chilli for the broth.

When the last was in, she placed a tea towel on my shoulder. 'That's how your father wore it. If you're going to cook his favourite meal you have to do things the right way.'

She flicked on the radio just in time for the news. I listened hard, slowing my chopping as the newsreader told of a car crash, strikes at a steel plant and government plans to push inflation down.

'Anything interesting?' Mum twisted the dial to a music station playing something bluesy. 'It's a strange crop you harvest. Perennial as the grass. You always think you're going to miss something.'

I put my hands up in surrender. 'Old habit.'

Crabs boiled and drained, the rest of the ingredients went into the pot and I turned the gas burner low, its steady hiss holding just below the drum beats kicking from the radio speakers. Mum poured white wine into glasses and we drank slowly, watching the pot shimmer as the temperature did its work.

'Good enough for cooking,' Mum said, frowning at her wine.

'I can go to the bottle shop,' I offered, and she said no, took her glass and mine and poured them down the sink.

'Still can't stand white,' she said, taking a bottle of red from her small pantry.

While I stirred the clattering shells and claws, she set the little table in her living space for two, placing a clean pair of wine glasses in the centre.

We stood there for a long time, dinner simmering with the sound of the sea and the wind. All that had happened before was gone. We were just breath and heartbeats and memories, together in a rented home by the sea with nothing that was our own but each other.

ACKNOWLEDGEMENTS

I'm writing on the ferry from Tasmania to Melbourne, savouring one of the final days of a caravan trip around Australia with my young family. As the swell of the Bass Strait twists the ship's spine, I remember long journeys must be embraced, lest they drive us wild.

Locust Summer has been a long journey, crossing many years and borders. The book drove me half wild. But like the best of journeys, the juice was in the doing. Best was sharing it with my partner in all that's good, Carmen, the Allan to my Petale. Thank you for your support, timely kicks up the backside and all-encompassing love. You are my centre.

We've picked up a few hitchhikers along the way. Thank you to my whipsmart daughters, Ruby and Brontë, who remind me what wonder there is in being full of the joy of life.

Locust Summer was written in many places throughout Asia, at dawn under a view of Agung in Bali to the temples of Kyoto in Japan, and I am indebted to the hospitality and kindness of so many people whom I met along the way.

The final version was completed in Australia, all over, and I wish to acknowledge the Traditional Owners of country throughout Australia and recognise their continuing connection to land, waters and community. I pay my respects to them and their cultures; and to elders past, present and emerging.

To my parents, Paul and Lisa, thank you for the sacrifices you made to keep a roof over my head and a good school in my grasp, for your years of belief and love and encouragement. Thank you to my brother, Jonathan, who read early stuff and offered much-needed encouragement. And to my sister, Rebecca, who helped kindle my love of reading and never doubted.

To my parents-in-law, Keith and Vanessa, thank you for the good living, love and support, and for always opening the expensive stuff.

I'm grateful to have met so many fellow travellers who helped *Locust Summer*'s journey. Thank you to Ruth Cohen, David Cuneen, Holden Sheppard, Hayley Lawrence, Cassie Hamer, Brooke Dunnell, Emma Young and Tom de Souza for their constant support in the trenches.

My writing group in London, Chalk the Sun, set me on a windward course, especially Ardella Jones, Jo Hepplewhite, Jonathan Wolfman, Joan Lecky, Fiona Parker-Cole, Jerilyn Bence, Jim Sanderson, Matt Salts and Hafiz Younis who shared so many lively sessions at the Balham Bowls Club.

Thank you to the judges of the 2017 *Australian*/Vogel's Literary Award – Stephen Romei, Rowan Wilson and Jenny Barry – whose shortlisting of this book's early manuscript changed the game.

Thanks to Varuna, The National Writers' House, where I was fortunate to share my fellowship time with Toni Jordan, Gabrielle Carey, Linda Jaivin, Judith Rossell, Barbara McKenzie and Carol Major, powerful women who generously gave their knowledge.

Every writer needs a good editor. I'm fortunate to have had three greats.

John Rudd ablated my bad habits as a young journo and rebuilt me from the ground up to write simple declarative sentences – mostly.

Dr Laurie Steed opened the door with true friendship and expert incisions that pushed this work (and me) to the next level. You kept me pointed true North, and I'm forever indebted to the faith you showed in the book's soul.

Georgia Richter at Fremantle Press believed in this book from her first reading and has been a steadfast guide through the final ascent while marshalling the power of the press's incredible team. Can't ask for better, especially with Jane Fraser, Cate Sutherland and Claire Miller on the case.

Deep thanks to the teachers who encouraged a boy with too much on his mind: Susannah Jefferies, Mungo Alcorn and Kevin Owen.

Thank you to Robert Louis Stevenson for the celebration of elixirs quoted in this text from 'The Scotsman's Return from Abroad'. Winston Churchill's line about the years that the locust hath eaten comes from the Bible, Joel 2:25.

Above all, I want to thank the Cullen family for the love you inspired in me of the land and those who work it. A great journey began at your farm gate.